Madagascar

New & Selected Stories

Also by Steven Schwartz

MADAGASCAR

*New &
Selected
Stories*

Steven
Schwartz

Engine Books
Indianapolis

Engine Books
PO Box 44167
Indianapolis, IN 46244
enginebooks.org

Also available in eBook formats from Engine Books.

10 9 8 7 6 5 4 3 2 1

ISBN: 978-1-938126-40-6

Library of Congress Control Number: 2016934982

Contents

The Theory of Everything

MY SON IS FEARFUL. Not scared. Scared is all right. I was scared during the war, but fearful is something else. He can't get out of bed some days. He stays in his condo with the blinds closed. After his wife Cheryl left him, I went over there one morning and found him walking around in a daze without his pants on, just a T-shirt. The kids were there. This is why he can't take care of them.

Even when Cheryl was around we'd come over and the house would be a mess, dirty dishes, not even in the sink but still on the table, clothes on the stairs, the kids—Abby two, Jeremy six then—plopped in front of the TV. And always fighting, the parents, not the kids. Over money. Rex asking where it went what he gave her, and she telling him he's a lazy son of a bitch and got no right to accuse her. He's not lazy, he's got this disease, so I want to take up for him, but you should see how she lights into me. "Mind your own business!" she shouts at me. "I'm trying to do the best job I can and all I get is criticism." Then she turns to Rex. "I married you, not your whole fucking family!"

All this happens in front of the kids. "Please," I say, "the children."

"Fuck this," Cheryl says and goes into the bedroom and slams the door.

Rex stands there with his shoulders slumped, his belly bigger each time I see him. He's always struggled with his weight. Comfort food he takes to a whole new level. He's got a handsome face, his mother's green eyes, thick curly black hair, but he can't take care of himself, and always that shameful look. "I'll talk to her, Dad," he says. "She gets upset when she thinks everybody's blaming her. It's not her fault."

I look around the house. At this time, they're living in one of my rental places that I let them stay in for half the going rate. Is it too much to ask that they don't keep it like a pigsty? I go over to where Jeremy's watching cartoons. "How you doing, buddy boy?" I ask.

"Fine," he says, and keeps staring at the TV.

"You want to maybe go to the batting cages after school today?" They got a slow pitch one that he likes.

"Okay," he says.

In the high chair, Abby pokes at her Cheerios with her finger. I can smell her dirty diaper from here. "Maybe you should get some help," I say.

"We're fine, Dad. We're just under a lot of stress right now. Cheryl wants to go back to school and get her nursing degree, and she's frustrated trying to do everything." This woman wants to be a nurse? "We don't need to see anyone."

"See anyone? I'm talking about a maid. Somebody to sweep up, make a nice place for the kids—"

"Shhh," Rex says, "she'll hear you."

"She should hear me," I say. Something smashes, like glass breaking, in the bedroom. I look at Jeremy, who doesn't budge. You'd think the little boy was deaf.

"You better go," Rex tells me. "I'm in a difficult position here. She doesn't need to get any more upset."

"Fine," I say, and that's the last time I see the woman. This is more than four years ago. She walks out the door with the money that I leave for the kids' new clothes for school. Up her arm. Jeremy, he'll remember her. Abby won't know a thing. Better off she's got no memories.

Since then, Louise and I take care of the kids full time.

I stop over at one of my houses. It's near the beach on Dakota Avenue right beside San Lorenzo Park, a very nice neighborhood, a two-bedroom home that three girls share who go to the university here in Santa Cruz. I don't allow more than three in a place. These girls, I know their families. The parents gave me their home numbers and said if I should have any trouble call them right away. But so far so good. Now I understand a window is broken—somebody threw a rock through it. They want it repaired; I said I'd come over and take a look. "Did you call the police?" I asked them. They said they didn't realize it was broken until this morning, and so here I am.

Two of the girls are at home, one with blonde hair and wearing flip flops and a flashy green jogging suit, the other with the low-cut jeans and the belly exposed like they all do now and golden tan. I'm not a man immune to the charms of young women. Believe me, I still look. The cleavage, this bare midriff business, but I keep my eyes on the girls' faces when they tell me they woke up this morning and the window was broken. It's a big window that looks out on the front yard. It will cost me a pretty penny to fix it.

"So you didn't hear anything?" I ask.

"No way," says Shannon—she's the one with the shiny green jogging suit. "We came out and we're like *what happened?*"

"You were sleeping," I say.

"Yeah," Angela, the other one, says. "We had the fan on."

"So maybe we should call the police," I tell them.

I see them glance at each other. "I'm sure it's okay," Shannon says. "It was probably, you know, a one-time thing."

"You think so," I say.

"Oh, yeah," Angela says. She's got a big smile that could light up a tunnel. They're nice girls, but I know they're lying to me.

"You could be in danger," I tell them. "What if this person comes back and makes more trouble? We should let your parents know about this."

Shannon fingers her necklace. Why she's wearing a fancy pearl necklace with a jogging suit and flip flops I don't know. But I got some idea. I bet if I search in the garage I'll find a recycling bucket full of beer bottles. "I have to ask," I say, "where's the rock?"

Angela looks at Shannon, who says quickly, "We put it back."

"And you cleaned up the glass?"

They nod their heads. I look at the window. Most of the glass is on the outside of the window. I checked before I came in. "So did anyone have to go to the hospital?"

They both look at me.

"I'll tell you what," I say. "I'll make you a deal. You pay half, I pay half. I won't ask for details. You had a party maybe. It got a little wild. Maybe there was a fight. Somebody got pushed against the window or just backed up too hard. I don't know. You're lucky no one got seriously hurt. You promise me you won't have a party again, and I don't call your parents. Plus I help you out with the cost. You've been here almost a year, with no problem. We got a deal?"

Angela, the one with the bare stomach, crosses her arms over her belly, as if to hide herself, shame on both their faces. They nod, and I tell them I'll have the glass company here by the afternoon. It's too big to glaze myself. They tell me they're sorry, they were afraid if they told me the truth, I'd evict them. I'm the nicest man they've ever known, they say. Young people say such things to old people. I'm eighty-two, I should know. They think we're like children who surprise them with how smart we are sometimes. Then they fall all over themselves heaping praise on us just for having a brain that still works.

After school gets out, I take the kids to their swim lessons. We go to the municipal pool at the Simpkins Center. They've got four pools, including a big warm water pool they keep at eighty-six degrees. Abby, she took to the water right away. She raced through the different levels—seahorse, barnacle, guppy, goldfish…now she's up to a sea otter. This would be a good thing, except her brother who is four years older and eleven is at the same level. He should be at least a sea lion. All his friends, they're already barracudas. So I said, enough with the fishies, let's just learn to swim, and we got a private instructor who teaches both of them. Dana. She's a college student, full of "awesomes" and high fives.

I sit on the bench and watch where Jeremy can't see me. He stands on the edge of the pool, and Dana tries to teach him how to dive. He's got to do a standing dive to pass his test and be allowed to swim in the deep water here with friends. She shows him how to bend at the waist and point toward the water.

"Hey, Jer," Dana coaxes, "just aim and fall in."

"I can't," he tells her.

"Sure you can!"

"I can't."

"You can't or you won't?"

"Is there a difference?" he asks.

"Of course there is, sweetie," says Dana. At which Abby, sitting nearby on the edge of the pool, stands up and offers to show them. "Let's just concentrate on your brother," Dana tells her. "Maybe you want to go down the slide a few times."

"Can I?" Abby says.

"Absolutely." She goes off, happy as can be. When she's around older females it's like she's auditioning to be their daughters. It breaks my heart.

Dana says, "Should I give you a little push?"

"No!"

So he stands there, looking down at the water like a man on a cliff.

Amazingly, he does it. Okay, it's not the best dive, more a roll into the water, but still it counts. Dana high-fives him. Jeremy doesn't crack a smile, but on the way home he tells me he's glad that's over with. He won't have to do it again. "Of course you'll do it again. You did terrific!" I tell him.

"I looked ridiculous," he says, staring out his window. Abby is in back playing with a purpled-sequined wrist purse Louise bought her the other day.

"You did not," I say. "You tried, that's what counts. And you went in."

"I half did it."

"You'll do the other half next time." We stop at a light on Ocean Street. I look back at Abby. She's dangling the little purple purse on her arm and inspecting it in the light from the window.

"There's Daddy," she says. She rolls down the window. "Daddy!"

I see him now. Rex is coming out of the bank. I pull into a handicap space and wait for him to walk over.

"Hey everybody!" he says. He's got a suit and tie on, his wavy black hair nicely cut and combed, and a royal blue dress shirt with gold cufflinks. I haven't seen him wear a suit in years. When he dresses up like this he's an attractive guy. You'd stop and think here's a man who's somebody's handsome husband.

He works putting up drywall, a job he's had almost three years, a record. I don't know what he's doing here in the afternoon.

"Daddy!" Abby says and reaches through the window for him. She's a small child, and he pulls her out, grabbing her under the arms and spinning her around. If you didn't know better, you'd think he was just getting off work and thrilled to see his kids at the end of a long day.

Abby hugs his neck, and he boosts her onto his back, then he taps at Jeremy for him to roll down his window. "What's happening, pal?" he says and bumps knuckles with Jeremy, who lets his wet hair be ruffled. "Looks like you've all been hitting the surf."

"Tell your father what you did," I say.

"What'd I do?" Jeremy says.

"The dive."

He shrugs.

"He dove into the pool."

"You did?" says Rex. He acts puzzled. And why shouldn't he? He's got no idea that his son practically has a phobia. "That's great. From the high dive?"

Jeremy stares at him like he's crazy. "From the *side*. And I wouldn't even call it a dive. I *interacted* with the pool," he says. This is the way he speaks. Half the time I don't get what he means.

Abby, still on Rex's back, stretches her neck around to him and shouts in his face, "I'm a sea otter!"

"Wow," Rex says.

"Daddy, I want to go with you," says Abby. "Take me to your house."

"Hey, pumpkin, can't do it today. But soon. You want to come over and cook spaghetti with me again?"

"Yeah! Now!"

"Soon, I promise."

He puts Abby down beside the car and opens the door for her. She gets in reluctantly. By now, she knows there's no use begging.

"Dad," Rex says to me. "There's something I want to talk with you about." All smiles. "It's exciting. Really exciting."

I look at the bank. I look at Rex in his suit. I know it's got something to do with money. "I have to get the kids home," I say.

"We'll talk tomorrow then, all right? I'll call you." He puts his hand on Jeremy's shoulder. "I'm going to be at your soccer game Saturday. Okay, tiger?"

"Don't bother," Jeremy says. "I hardly do anything except stand there and let them kick the ball by me. I might as well be an obelisk."

"Great, then," says Rex. "Wow, I can't believe I ran into you guys. You're all so—" He steps back and pumps his fist in the air. "Unreal!"

Two days later I get a call from Rex, who says he needs to meet me for lunch. I tell him I've got a busy day. I have to pick up the tile for a bathroom I'm redoing in one of my places. "What's it about?"

"I'd rather tell you in person, Dad."

"I'm in person," I say. "As in person as I got time for today."

"I'm sorry."

At least once every time we talk he says he's sorry. It doesn't do any good. He doesn't change, and what am I going to do? He can't take care of himself, simple as that. You have to be in the situation to understand. I sat with him during his worst spells, I got him into the bathroom after he soiled himself, I made him take his medication, I stayed all night in a chair and watched him that he doesn't slash his wrists again. And how's he going to take care of the children when he's like this? When you got a child's welfare on the line you don't make ultimatums, because you're making them to somebody who doesn't react like a sensible person. From the outside it looks like we're hurting more than helping—we make it possible for him not to take responsibility. I've heard it all before. Coddling, spoiling, "enabling," whatever term you want to use. But throw the children in there and all the tough love goes out the window, in my opinion.

When I think of dying, this is the worst part. I don't know what I believe. If an angel shows up and says, "Mr. Halper, please step this way for your heavenly reward," fine, I'll be the first on the bus. If there's nothing afterward, I know from nothing. Either way, I don't place bets. But if you ask me what I'm ready to do now, I'll tell you. I'll make a deal with anyone, good or evil. It doesn't matter what happens to me afterward. Just let me live until the kids don't need me anymore.

"Dad, just listen. Can you hear me out?"

"I can do that," I say, and for the next ten minutes he tells me about this coffeehouse he wants to buy in Watsonville. The owner is selling. Rex says it's on a side street but business is booming. In Watsonville, the market isn't saturated like it is in Santa Cruz. And farmland there is being converted into residential property every day—upscale homes—and retirees are moving in, too. He's got all the figures on the business. It hasn't turned a profit yet but he knows he can make it happen if he takes over. The bank's willing to give him a start-up loan. Only one catch. I got to be a co-signer. The collateral? My three rental houses.

That's my income, beside my pension from the aerospace company.

But I know better than to say anything on the phone. "You get all the figures together and we'll talk."

"So you're interested?"

"I'll hear you out. That's all I can promise."

"Dad, thanks, *thanks*. We can drive out there tomorrow and see the place. When do you want to go?"

"Since when do you have all this time on your hands?" There's a big pause. My question has already been answered. "You're not working, are you?"

"It's not what you think. I didn't get fired. I'm just taking some time off. Preston told me I can come back anytime. I needed to stop for a while because my back was killing me. Last week I pulled something and I couldn't even straighten up. And I'm taking Advil like candy. That's not right. I have to find something else."

"So go back to school, study for a career."

"I'm forty-one, Dad. I don't have time to be a freshman again. Just let me show you the place. It's sweet, I'm telling you. You'll fall in love with it."

I can't give him money, and I'm not signing away my security so he can open the billionth coffeehouse in California and then go out of business. He'll scream at me that I never support him, that I've got no confidence in him, that I'm the reason he's screwed up, that I never give him the chance to help himself, that I want to keep him "infantilized" (this he got from years of therapy), that he's going to take back the kids. Can you imagine? He's going to take back the kids. That's what he threatens me with. But it's what scares me, too. "We'll talk about it tomorrow," I say, just so I can think.

In the afternoon the following day, I've got an hour before I pick the kids up from school. Jeremy has soccer practice and Abby a sewing class that she's in with her grandmother. Louise doesn't drive much anymore, so I have to take her places, to the doctor, shopping, to her hairdresser. Sometimes we call Lift Line and they come for her. The sewing class is something Abby and she are doing together, even though Louise could make a whole dress from scratch if she wanted. But she says it's an activity to do with Abby that doesn't require too much exertion, and anyway, it's a mother-daughter class, so she needs to go.

The blinds are drawn at Rex's apartment. The porch light is still on at two in the afternoon. My heart starts beating fast. I'm always afraid of what I might find.

I knock, I hear shuffling, then the door opens. He's washed and shaved, dressed and in a clean knit shirt and navy slacks. Nothing's wrong. He's not curled up on the floor with his hands tucked between his knees as I've found him other times.

"Dad?"

"I thought I'd stop over before I pick up the kids."

"Um, maybe I should…" He steps outside and closes the door behind him. "I'm a little busy right now."

I get what he means. I'm not naïve about such things. "You've got company, no problem." I apologize for not calling first and start to leave when the blind is pushed aside and I see Cheryl.

"What's she doing here?"

"Now just take it easy," he says. "Everything's fine."

"Everything's fine? How long has she been here?"

"Dad, I know what you're thinking, but we've been talking—"

"Who's been talking? You and her?"

"Things have changed. Cheryl has a job in San Jose and she's been living by herself and staying clean. She wanted to see if she could reach the one-year mark before she even contacted us again. It's her anniversary today—"

My head's exploding with questions. "Anniversary? She got remarried?"

"Her anniversary of staying clean and sober, so I made arrangements for her to come here last night."

I feel my knees go weak, and I sit down on the white plastic chair on the small balcony. "She's gone four years and she just shows up and everything's fine?"

"Listen, Dad, you're not an uninvolved party here. I know that. And I know I can never repay you for all you've done. I can't change what I did, but I *can* change. Cheryl wants to be part of that."

"My God," is all I can say. I feel my age suddenly. "Why doesn't she come out here?"

"This isn't the best time. She's doing great. Maybe a little shaken up about coming here and trying to prepare herself to see the kids. But she's taken responsibility, Dad, that's the main thing. And she did it on her own. She's not asking for anybody's forgiveness. Believe me, she'll be the last to ever forgive herself. But we want to try again."

I can't even show him my face, which is hot with fury.

"That's why I need to talk with you," Rex says. "I know we can make a go of the business."

"What business?"

"The coffeehouse. We've got a lot of it figured out. Cheryl's been working as a hostess in a restaurant, she knows about keeping the books, about how to manage a business. It's still a work in progress, but everything's falling into line. Just let me explain it all to you, okay? Not now. But tomorrow. I've got to go up to San Jose and talk to someone about a new roaster for the place. But after I come back?"

"Look," I say, and forget what I'm going to say.

"You all right?"

"I have to pick up the kids now."

"Actually, we were thinking about doing that this afternoon. A surprise."

"No!" I say. I stand up and tell him to his face. "No more surprises today. You don't just show up and introduce her to a daughter who has no memory of her! Are you nuts?"

"Calm down, all right? We weren't going to do it that way."

"I don't care how you're going to do it. Not today. I'm picking them up like always."

"What should we do?" I say to Louise that evening. Jeremy and Abby I've told nothing. Jeremy complained of a sore knee after soccer practice. He said, "This could be as serious as Osgood-Schlatter disease, which tends to primarily affect boys my age, or as minor as a sprain. I suspect the swelling will respond to a combination of ice and anti-inflammatory therapy, but the prognosis isn't good for me to play in Saturday's game." This is his way of explaining he's looking for an excuse not to play.

I tell Louise that I've heard of grandparents going to court over such matters. "We have no official custody but we could make a case, a good case."

"I'm not so sure we can," Louise says.

"You want to just hand them over to her?"

"Keep your voice down. The children." She's got a gray shawl around her shoulders and her lips are blistered from the cold she's had. The kids bring home all the stuff that's going around. "We need to speak with Marvin," she says. Marvin's our lawyer, who's helped us in the past. He's got a young associate in his office who knows the ins and outs of family law.

"And what if Marvin tells us that they're the parents and that's who gets them? Are you prepared for that? Are you willing to list in affidavits all the bad things she's done and talk about your son's problems in front of a judge?"

I can see by the way she twists her mouth she isn't. She's always felt it was her fault what problems Rex has. She was forty-two when she had him, and it wasn't so common back then to have a child that late. We tried for years with no success. He was our miracle baby. Somewhere he's still a miracle in her mind.

She pulls the shawl tighter around her shoulders.

"You should go to bed," I say.

"And you," she tells me. "You hardly touched your dinner."

"I'm fine." Inside, my stomach turns over as if I'm on the Cyclone at the Santa Cruz Boardwalk, a ride Abby makes me go on with her.

"We find out what they have in mind," Louise says. I say nothing. "When we know the facts then we can discuss it with Marvin."

"Marvin's got nothing in his pocket to help us. We should have severed her legal ties when we had the chance."

"We never had the chance."

"When she abandoned her children, we had the chance. We waited, like fools."

Louise gets up from the table and pours a little cream over sliced pears for me. "Eat," she says. "It will do your stomach good." She sits down next to me and puts her hand on my neck and rubs with her thumb and forefinger. Her fingers feel tiny back there, but they've still got strength in them. "We do this together," she says to me. "You understand that, right?"

I carve a crescent of sweetness from my pears and eat. I can promise nothing.

We talk to Marvin. He says the law is on the parents' side. "There are precedents for grandparents having custody but the case has to be clearly that a child's welfare is endangered by remaining with the parents. It's a high bar. It might be easier to have a child yourself." Louise snorts at this. "The truth is," Marvin says, "if she's clean and sober, and willing to assume her parental responsibilities at this time, it's going to carry a lot more weight than anything that's happened in the past, particularly if you haven't carefully documented it. And if they want to, they can even contest visitation rights by the grandparents. It's a question of how much to push before they push back. You can gamble, but they could win and be vindictive. I've seen it happen too many times."

I leave discouraged. Louise and I don't speak for a while in the car, then she says, "We have to accept the inevitable. He didn't divorce her. She never gave up custody. We stepped in and now we have to step aside."

"So that's it? Just like that? Since when are you so blasé?"

"I'm realistic," she says.

"I am, too. That's why it's not going to happen."

"What's not going to happen?"

"I'm prepared for a fight," I say.

"You're prepared to take the children away from their father and mother for good?"

"She comes back from God knows where, supposedly all cleaned up and motherly, and wants them back, and our son says, great, terrific, we're a family again, come home, children, and you say *we're* taking them away? What about them taking away from us!"

"You heard what Marvin told us."

"I don't care what Marvin told us. And you're always too ready to do whatever your son asks."

Louise puts her hand on my arm. We're at a stoplight on Mission Street and a boy not much older than Jeremy, a Hispanic kid, crosses in front of us with a surfboard on his head. "It will come to this eventually," Louise says in a quiet voice.

I remember a piece of a conversation I heard at the pancake house when Louise and I took the kids out for brunch one weekend. A young man was saying to a woman, maybe his wife, "I'm talking about thirty years down the road." I imagined he was speaking about their future, what his business might be, or what he pictured for their kids one day. Maybe a second home somewhere they all could meet for vacations. I thought to myself I can't even say, *I'm talking about five years down the road*. This is what Louise means in her soft voice when she talks about "eventually."

What did I expect? Maybe somebody in a nice pair of slacks, a tasteful blouse, a trim-cut blazer, and a little makeup to freshen the face, like the moms at Jeremy's soccer games. Cheryl was always a pretty girl. But this Cheryl is thin and all sharp bones, her cheeks more sunken, her eye shadow too blue, and rings on four of her fingers, including a big silver one with a black stone. She wears snug jeans with embroidered pockets and a leather vest over a tight white sweater blouse.

Cheryl bends down and extends her arms for Abby who shies away. On the way here we told the kids, "Your mother is in town and wants to see you." Jeremy nodded. Maybe he knew this day was coming. He remembers her, of course, but he never speaks about her. Abby said, "I knew she'd come back. I knew she would." She became so excited that she made us go back so she could wear her Annie Oakley costume that she got for Halloween in three weeks.

Abby, a finger twisted tightly around her hair, finally goes over to her mother.

We all stand there a minute while Cheryl makes a big scene of hugging her. Cheryl's on her knees in the sand. We decided it was best to meet at Seabright Beach and have a cookout in one of the fire rings. A neutral place.

Louise gives Jeremy a little push to go over too. I feel like he's being shoved toward a stranger, but I keep my mouth shut. Now the tears come. Cheryl is crying, hugging Abby and reaching out her other arm for Jeremy, who keeps his body sideways but lets her put an arm around his waist. She turns her face from one to the other like she's been on a long trip and planned all along to come back. I look away.

"Let's eat," Rex says. He's got his hand on Cheryl's shoulder this whole time.

"Wait a sec," says Cheryl, and she jumps up and runs over to where they put down their stuff. She comes back with a present for each of them. Abby, who's in her Annie Oakley outfit—never mind that her brother told her not to wear it because it looked stupid—gets a stuffed orangutan with a baby orangutan wrapped around its neck. Jeremy, who doesn't rip open his present like his sister but instead neatly peels off the tape, has some kind of board.

"It's a skim board," Cheryl tells him. "You throw it out along the shore and jump on for a ride."

"I know what it is," Jeremy says, staring at it. He's folding the wrapping paper back up in a perfect square.

"Oh, honey," Cheryl says. She's got a husky smoker's voice. "Do you already have one? Rex said no. Right? You said he didn't have one."

"That's what I thought," Rex says.

"Do you have one? You're not disappointed, are you?"

"It's fine," Jeremy says flatly. "I don't have one."

"But you like it right, honey?" Cheryl asks.

Jeremy looks at me.

"He's not so big on water sports," I explain.

"Oh," says Cheryl. Her face is about to collapse.

"It's fine," Jeremy says again.

"Fine?" Rex says. "It's a little more than fine, son. This is a top of the line model."

Jeremy turns it over in his hands. "I'm most appreciative," he says, "of your generosity." This is the way he talks when he doesn't want to talk anymore. He makes a little house of such language and shuts the door from the inside.

"Anybody hungry?" Louise asks.

While Rex starts a fire in the pit, Cheryl takes Abby by the hand and walks along the beach. Couples, groups of teenagers, other families come down to watch the sun set. It's already too cold to go in the water but surfers go out with their boards and kids slap their bare feet along the water's edge.

"So what do you think?" I ask Louise. Jeremy is next to his father, who's fussing with the fire. Cheryl walks with Abby down the beach, telling her something. Her arms fly out, she jumps up, she squats down and gives Abby another hug. Then Abby shows her how she can do a cartwheel and a handstand.

"I think," Louise says, "that Abby's vote is yes."

"You notice she hasn't said a word to us. She went right to work on the kids."

"She's their mother. What do you expect? She doesn't have to win our approval."

"We're fools."

Later in the evening, Abby will get on the skim board and zip along. Jeremy won't have anything to do with it. Cheryl will show Abby her blueberry-colored nails and tell her that they can get manicures. Jeremy she's going to take to the music store. She says she wants to buy him an iPod. Does he download music? What are his favorite bands? Does he play an instrument? She wants her kids to play instruments. What's his best subject in school? She hardly gives him a chance to answer, and when he does, he says, "The sun is supposed to set at 6:02. It's a minute and a half late. The tides must be disappointed." Rex chews a burnt marshmallow and says, "You kids!"

I watch the waves break on shore. My heart gets pulled out to sea like it's in a rip current.

•

The kids spend the next week at the apartment with their parents. At first, Abby, when we pick her up for the sewing class with Louise, is all smiles and glee. She tells us Cheryl takes her shopping. They go out for fudge sundaes and to the movies. They carve pumpkins and bake the seeds. They cut out pictures from American Girl magazine and put them on Abby's side of the bedroom she shares with her brother. But then, the following week, she doesn't say so much. "Tell me what you're up to, snookums," I say. I'm trying not to make judgments. I keep busy on my houses, read a biography of Eisenhower, catch up on my sleep. My arthritis lets up a bit. I'm thinking I can make the adjustment. They're trying hard to be good parents. In fact, Rex doesn't even call for my help with the kids.

"Can you get me a new leotard?" Abby asks. "Mine is ripped."

"You can get one at gymnastics," I say. They have a little store there that sells all the accessories the girls need.

"Can you buy it?" Abby asks.

"Yes," Louise says.

"Did you ask your parents?" I say.

"Cheryl says she can't afford it."

"We'll get it," Louise says.

"I thought she had all this money saved," I say, referring to Cheryl. That's what she had told us.

"Never mind," Louise says.

"You got anything else you want to tell us?"

"Shush," Louise says.

"Don't shush me," I say. "Maybe she wants to talk. Abby?"

"What?"

"You got anything else to say?"

"I'm tired," she says.

Two days later, when Jeremy comes over to the house, I find out things aren't going so well. Rex and Cheryl are fighting again. We're sitting on the hood of my Chrysler Imperial. I've had the car for eleven years and I should trade it in for one with better gas mileage, but I bought it the day Jeremy was born. He has his soccer uniform on now. I've had to pick him up from his game because Rex and Cheryl drove out to look at the coffeehouse. I went with them once and was not impressed, a rundown building with too many flies inside. Every day Rex calls and asks if I've made up my mind. I tell him no, I haven't decided, and in the meantime he should think about going back to work for Preston. Why don't I tell him the truth? That I'm never going to sign. Because he's got the kids as leverage. He could hold them hostage from us if I don't cooperate, and in the meantime I can only hope he loses interest or the place gets sold to somebody else.

Jeremy and I are sharing a package of black licorice. It's his favorite candy. I eat only one piece because of my dentures, but he chews away. Between bites he tells me about physics, that we exist in ten dimensions but can only experience four of them. He thinks we have many parallel lives that we're undergoing at the same time. "In one universe I've scored five soccer goals. In another I'm just an energy force. Another has no cause and effect and I'm able to jump off a building and land safely on my feet. That one is very dreamlike. But in this one I'm sitting on a white car believing in time."

"You don't believe in time?" I ask.

"For the moment, I do." He gives me a sly smile. I get the joke and we bump fists like the kids do nowadays. At this "moment in time" I ache over how much I love him.

"She's drinking," he says out of nowhere. He's got a long sad face. He takes my index finger and wraps his own fingers around it. "One day, grandpa, I'll be able to merge into other universes. I shall call myself The Permeator and solve TOE."

"What's this TOE?"

"The theory of everything, grandpa," he says, as if I should know. "I expect that won't be soon enough, though." Tears start down his cheeks. I know what he means: I'll be dead by then.

What I do next I'm not proud of. I call Cheryl when I know Rex isn't at home. She agrees to meet me at Lighthouse Point, and I wait for her on a bench. I can see her approaching across the grassy park behind the bluffs. It's the day before Halloween, and Abby has asked if we could take her out in our neighborhood, where she knows more people (and can get better candy, she believes).

"What's so important?" Cheryl says, getting right to the point. I've only seen her a couple of times since that first night at Seabright. She wears a baseball cap with her hair in a ponytail threaded through the back. From one shoulder to the other she keeps shifting her suede handbag.

"I wanted to talk," I say.

"So let's talk. I'm here." She's wearing open-toed white sandals and I see her nails don't have that pearly polish they did the first night. Now they're chipped and dull, and I wonder if she ever took Abby for the manicure she promised. "If you came here to give me a lecture, you can save your breath. I'm not in the best frame—"

"I don't want to lecture. I want to make an offer."

"What offer?"

I gesture toward the bench for her to sit down. It's eleven a.m. and people are coming to eat their lunch. She sits carefully, not taking her eyes off me. I see an unhappy woman, a tormented person, a scared little girl inside her, but I got to do what I think best.

I reach in my sport coat and take out money from my inside pocket and hold it in my lap, then cover my hands over top like I'm putting a damp cloth over warm dough.

"What's this?" Cheryl asks.

In the park, there's a bunch of people around my age doing Tai Chi. They've got loose white clothes on and look like ghosts. The waves crash below, seagulls above caw, and here I sit with ten thousand dollars in my lap.

"You can get a new start," I say.

"Are you trying to buy me off?"

"I'm giving you options."

"Oh, my God. You think I'm going to take this money and leave the kids? You must really think I'm scum."

"Not everybody should be a parent."

"You arrogant old man. Who the hell do you think you are?"

I expect ugly names, but she hasn't walked off yet. "You let us take care of the children. Maybe you live nearby. Maybe you live, say, in Watsonville and run a coffeehouse. I don't know. Maybe you want to go away and think about whether you're up to being a mother with full responsibility right now." I don't say maybe you shoot the money up your arm and drink it away. "Maybe we have an agreement about this, and then nobody makes a big legal scene."

Cheryl's mouth twists in an unpretty way, like she could spit on me, which would not be a surprise or undeserved.

"You've always hated me," she says.

"I don't hate anyone. I'm a practical man."

"I've never been a whore. No matter what happened I've never gotten that low. You want to know something? This is *lower* than that."

I look at my fingers. They got dirt wedged in them from crawling around under one of my houses to fix a pipe.

"Rex would think you're despicable. You'd be lucky if he ever speaks to you again. You'll be lucky if I ever do. Shit, you think you can hustle me!"

"I'm making you an offer. What you do with it is your decision."

"I should tell you to shove that money up your ass."

When I hear this word, this simple word "should," because everything when you think about it comes down to the difference between should and did, I know what will happen. I stand up and leave the money on the bench. I count to myself, one, two, three seconds, and I know if I make it to ten, she won't run after me and throw the money in my face. When I get to nine, I keep walking. I'm afraid to turn around, just like in the Bible because I've done a terrible thing that could turn me into a pillar of salt. But I don't look behind me. I don't look ahead. I just keep going.

Lives of the Fathers

MY FATHER IS TELLING me about Victoria again. I smile, nod, remind him I am a journalist and that I cannot just sit down and write a book about Victoria because he is sure it will make a bestseller, full of romance, intrigue, and heartbreak.

"It's rags to riches to rags again!" my father says, not listening. "A story you won't be able to put down!"

"You've told me."

"What happened to her would be no big deal today but back then, who did such things? She was a bohemian! And beautiful, everyone says so. It's a tragedy! And don't forget the love story here, Adam. The composer. At that time he was nobody. That anybody should know he would become Mr. Hollywood, least of all Victoria! The two of them were bohemians! In Atlantic City they'd take a room together at the Shelburne—torn down years ago—and go to the shows and the dances and the burlesque houses, and the liquor they drank...all without care what people thought! They believed in free love. Okay, so maybe it's not front-page news now—"

"Please, Dad," I say. "Can we get on with this?"

I am helping my father move into an apartment outside Philadelphia, a few miles from the house he has lived in for thirty-seven years. My mother died last year and although he didn't want to move, the place has become much too big for him. "I forget things. I'll come home from shopping and leave the groceries in the car and then I'll look out the window later and see the trunk open and remember that's where the groceries are and I haven't finished taking them in." He told me this over the phone, long distance to Tucson, where I work for *The Arizona Daily Star*. "Maybe if I had a smaller place I could keep track of things better." It was the opening I'd been waiting for. "I'll help you move," I said. After our mother died, my sister and I had begged him to find a place he could manage; he wouldn't consider it at the time. "Where will you find a view like this?" he said, pointing to the park across the street.

But in thirty-seven years—the house is as old as I am, my parents moving in two weeks before I was born—the area has deteriorated. Next door, on what used to be the spacious front yard of an older home, three small bungalows have been squeezed together, only eight feet apart, the minimum allowed by code. And the park, neglected over the years, has litter clinging to the backstop of the baseball diamond where I once charged around the bases and dove head first into home, winding up in the hospital with a broken collarbone. (I was safe.) The once stately oak trees at the park's entrance stand like weary, bent petitioners at a gate, too many unpruned branches broken and dead from storms, swinging loose in the wind like discarded canes. On weekends and holidays teenagers wash and wax their cars on the grass, letting the soapy water run into our driveway. My father sees none of this, just his preserved view of many years ago: my sister and I on skis about to descend the mild incline of the park's snowy hill toward a stream that now has soft-drink cups and rusty hubcaps in it.

"A beautiful woman once, even your mother admitted as much. Gorgeous red hair and a figure that made history. Like a goddess she walked around. Yet innocent. She knew nothing. A schoolteacher she wanted to be when I met her. No wonder he fell for her."

"Who?" I say. My father has a habit of referring to everyone as "he" or "she," a problem worsened by age.

"The composer," he says, looking at me surprised. "He was nobody back then, a few minor songs he wrote. Victoria showed them to me. My own were better."

Today the composer is a famous man, an Oscar-winner for his movie themes. This is the "love interest" my father wants me to include. My father sees it all, the innocent girl from Philadelphia, the New York composer (unknown and struggling) falling in love on the boardwalk, Victoria's subsequent initiation into decadent Manhattan society, their torrid ten-year affair, the terrible fights, his jilting her after she is hooked on drugs, her acting career ending in nude photos for girlie magazines, the simultaneous meteoric rise of the composer ("True to life," my father says, "the S.O.B. gets what he's after!"), the eventual end of Victoria in an institution, where she leads a reclusive life for the next twenty years.

"I'm telling you," my father says. "It's what the public wants to read. You can't take an hour a day to work on an idea that will bring you millions?"

I wrap the wine glasses in newspaper and put them in the box. My father is holding up a decanter that I remember us using only once—the night my parents had an engagement dinner for my sister and her husband, who live in Seattle now. Before my mother died, my parents bickered constantly. Whatever anger was buried during our childhood surfaced in those later years after my sister and I moved away from home. My father, insisting my mother not work (she'd been an office manager in a Manhattan bookkeeping firm), had taken her away from her five sisters in New York to Philadelphia, where he wanted to settle after the war. Her lifelong struggle with agoraphobia grew worse and frustrated them both. Near the end she was afraid to leave the house at all for fear of…well, anything from crime to not having a bathroom nearby for her bladder, which was always acting up from her diabetes and the drugs she took for high blood pressure. My father retired to take care of her (he wouldn't put her in a nursing home), helping her to the bathroom, getting her meals, doing all the shopping, making the beds, keeping the house clean. My mother didn't want a maid. The house had been her whole life. One minute she would yell at my father for overworking himself, the next she would complain he didn't do things right, the way she'd done them when she'd been able to get around. Nearly blind and barely able to walk, she nevertheless followed after him, criticizing him for the way he loaded the dishwasher, wiped down a table, threw in the laundry without sorting it first, left the butter out, put away silverware…"Who ever heard of keeping silverware in a second drawer?" she'd say. Or, "You bought that lousy Tyson's chicken again." Or "Why didn't you get that Tyson's chicken we always eat?" My sister and I pleaded with my father to just bring someone in; what was Mom going to do? Stop the person from cleaning? He wasn't young himself, seventy-two. But he wouldn't hear of it. "She'll pull out of this," he'd say, blind to my mother's condition, desperate to deny anything was really wrong. "She's just venting," he'd say. "It doesn't bother me. She puts up with my craziness and I put up with hers. We've been doing it for forty years. That's what love is." And he'd go back to buying the wrong kind of mayonnaise or running the dryer on high or ironing a blouse that she hated to wear, a thousand little stubbornnesses they assaulted each other with every day. I think it would have gone on like this forever had she not suffered a stroke and been helpless to protest, paralyzed, unable to raise even a finger to scold him. He brought in a housekeeper then, a victory for neither of them.

Now, my first time home since the funeral, my father and I haven't spoken once about my mother's death, how frightening and horrible it was to watch her decline. Instead, he talks only about Victoria. "I never touched her, Adam. She would call and say, 'Newman, I'm lonely. Why don't you ever come see me? I'm by myself here tonight.'"

"So why didn't you go?"

"Go? To see her? I was a married man by then!"

"But before that, when she was the bohemian on the boardwalk or whatever—didn't you even date her?" I can't believe I've gotten suckered into this discussion.

"Of course I dated her—but I never touched her! 'What a gentleman you are, Newman,' she would tell me. 'I've never met such a nice man,' she'd say. I gave her music lessons, every Thursday at four. I taught her the piano, boogie-woogie. She wanted to be a jazz singer for a while. I brought her home to meet my mother and father and brothers! Did they like her?"

I shrug. "Did they?"

"Of course they liked her! Everyone did! She was a beauty! Hair down to there." My father motions somewhere with his hand, the basement—or hell. I don't know. I'm losing track of the day and the conversation. In a week I have to be back at work, and Claire, my wife, is seven months pregnant with our first child. It's not a time I particularly want to leave her alone.

"Dad, can we talk about Victoria tomorrow? We should concentrate on packing. You just let me know what you want to keep here."

"I'm telling you, this is an idea you can count on a hundred percent. You make a little outline and send it off. I guarantee you'll get fifty offers."

"It doesn't work like that. So let's forget about the book—"

"A blockbuster! We're talking wide audience appeal. The younger people will understand the bohemian side, the rebellion. Him—"

"Who?"

"Her father. He was a stiffened Prussian who could spit cold water on you, icicles. You see what I'm talking about here? She rebelled against him. He was this main influence on her life and she ran away from her family to be with him—"

"*Who?*"

"The composer! That's the part the kids can relate to. I've got notes to show you."

"No, please. I don't need to see them. I can imagine it if I ever want to write about this."

"So you'll do it?"

"Let me sleep on it, Dad," I say, just to calm him down.

"He saw her naked."

"What are you talking about?"

"Fred Rose. The photographer. He took pictures of her for her portfolio. She wanted to be an art model then. I saw them one day on his desk when he was out to lunch, the big envelope with her name. I couldn't look."

"That's considerate of you," I say.

"Did I tell you she'd have hold of my arm as we walked down the aisle of the Robin Hood Dell to our concert seats? I don't exaggerate, thirty heads would turn."

"Why didn't you marry her?"

"Him," he says.

I throw up my hands. "*Who*, Dad? Can't you use names?"

"I'm sorry. The composer. She fell in love with him while we were going out. One day I went over there to take her out to Fairmount Park and there was a note on the door: she had to see me that day—urgent. I called her all day, all evening, late into the night. I couldn't close my eyes without being frightened what had happened to her. The next day I call and she tells me she thinks we shouldn't see each other anymore. She's going to marry this young songwriter."

"The composer."

"Right. But at the time, I'm also writing songs, so I feel doubly bad. Not only has she thrown me over for another guy, but he's a songwriter too."

"So then you met Mom."

"Many years later. I was a different man then. In my thirties."

"You carried a torch for Victoria all that time?"

"Sure, what's ten years when you know someone like her?"

I shrug.

"Tomorrow we'll go see her. I haven't spoken to her in twenty-five years but I think I'm ready now. You'll go with me and take pen and paper, right? It's all settled."

"No, Dad," I say. "Ab-so-lute-ly not."

•

Victoria, Bohemian of the Boardwalk.

This is the title my father wants me to use for the novel about Victoria's life. We are driving down Route 95, on our way to Wilmington, Delaware, where Victoria lives in a nursing home.

"Dad, you don't just drop in on someone you haven't seen for twenty-five years."

"Why not?" he says. "Won't she be surprised."

Victoria's brother, who owns an appliance store in South Philadelphia, has given us the address. Early this morning my father called him and said we wanted to visit Victoria. I was writing a book about Victoria's life. I heard all this as I was coming down the stairs, with sleep in my eyes, my mouth dry, aware that we'd hardly accomplished anything together yesterday. All night I'd been up packing while my father slept on the couch. "Just going to take a little five-minute snooze," he said, and he was out for the rest of the evening.

We pull up in front of the Golden Meadows Care Center. In the lobby several people in wheelchairs and bathrobes are watching television. There is a chalkboard with a list of such activities as Senior Aerobics, Health Awareness Check, and Creative Cake Decorating.

Someone calls to my father. "Mr. Holzman, how you doing?"

It is Moses Rudolf. I haven't seen him in over fifteen years.

"Moses," my father says, "I had no idea you were here." Moses is in a wheelchair, one of his legs gone. He sees us staring down.

"Blood clots," he says. "Been quite a while now. How you all doing?" He extends his palm flat out for us to shake hands. I look down at his hand with the same amazement I did as a child. Moses had worked for my father in the jewelry store in Philadelphia. When my father would go out to lunch, I'd stay behind with Moses and watch the store. Look here, he'd say, and show me how all his fingers could bend back at the knuckles. His elbow reversed too, so he could stroke the long skull of his head with his fingers as if it were another person's hand. It was both exciting and repelling, especially since he'd put opal rings from the showcase on his fingers to do it.

I take Moses' hand in mine and shake it. His hand is warm and I can almost feel the opal rings pressing into my palm. His hair, which used to be tight black curls, lending him a sinuous invincibility, now is thin and white, and I can see the pinkish brown skin underneath. It occurs to me that he is at least ten years younger than my father, who, with his blue knit golf shirt and arms tan from working in the garden, looks like a picture of youth next to Moses.

"So what you all doing here?" Moses says. "I guess you all didn't come by just to see me—or my better half." We laugh nervously. "It been a while," Moses says. "I'm used to it." I try to picture Moses—the double-jointed arms and elbows of his one-legged torso—bent back and stroking his head preciously. It is a frightening yet enthralling image of roving, serpentine arms, like a Hindu god, and has the same power to make me stare dumbly at him as I did years ago.

"You retired youself, am I right?" Moses says to my father.

"Ten years now," my father says. "I was ready to leave." He spreads his hands out, as if to contemplate a globe while he speaks. "Comes a stage when you have to consider making changes. Life's too short to spend so much time in one place."

"Here today, gone today," Moses says. "How's the wife doing?"

"She's dead, a year now."

"Sorry to hear that. I didn't know nothing about it."

"To be honest, it was a blessing for her. Very sick. Great pain for her."

Nobody says anything for a few moments. Then Moses asks, "How about you, Adam? What you doing now?"

"He's doing terrific," my father says before I can answer. "A big reporter out in Arizona." My father bends over and taps Moses on the shoulder with a stiff finger, speaking in a stage whisper. "He broke that Mafia story on the Nicosi family in Tucson. You read about it, right?"

Moses shakes his head. "I just keep up with the sports."

"We're going to have a baby," I say, trying to add something I care about. The Nicosi family turned out to be nothing in the end, dismissed at the grand jury level for lack of evidence. My father forgets to add this, as he does anything that might diminish my greatness in others' eyes. When I was in law school he liked to tell everyone I had a judicial internship lined up at the Supreme Court. "I only inquired about one," I told him the summer after I dropped out.

"Well, congratulations to you, Adam. You gonna make a fine daddy."

"Yes?" I say, and wonder about this, why his casual compliment strikes me with such force, and then I realize it's because my father has never said anything so simple and easy to me. "Thanks," I say softly.

"He's writing a terrific book about her."

I wince. Moses looks puzzled.

"We're here for someone named Victoria," I explain.

"Schmidt," my father adds. "You know her, Moses?"

Moses shakes his head. "Can't say I do." A bell rings. "Lunch time. You all want to join me?"

"We should find her, Dad," I say. "Ask at the desk about her."

"Moses," my father says, "I know where you are now."

"You know where I am," Moses says. "Don't be no stranger."

"You can see the woman she used to be, right? I mean, for the book you could use your imagination, now that you met her."

I don't say anything. I'm driving back. It was obvious once we left the nursing home, with his shortness of breath and hands trembling as he searched himself for his keys, that he'd been too shaken by the experience to drive. Near the Pennsylvania state line, we have traveled almost twenty miles from the Golden Meadows Care Center in uncomfortable silence. But the farther we drive from the nursing home, from the real Victoria, the more I can feel my father regaining his confidence.

"You should hear her laugh. She wasn't up to it today. Delightful. Like a little arpeggio." My father raises an imaginary flute to his mouth and plays fanciful, silly tones that sound as if he's inhaled helium. "I used to live for that laugh. Once—"

"Stop it, Dad."

I pull off at a rest stop.

"You have to go? Go ahead. Do your business. I'll wait here."

"Listen to me," I say. I turn off the engine. He squirms in his seat.

"All right, maybe it wasn't such a good idea. I warned you she might not be in such good shape."

"Good shape? She was pitiful."

"Tragic, I told you, it's a tragedy what happened—"

"It's not a tragedy, it's just pitiful. Did you look at her? Did you?"

My father doesn't answer. I think of Victoria, sitting on a plastic chair in a corner of the recreation room, her mouth and throat scarred by cancer, her hands clutched at her stomach as if to hold a warm stone there, her complete lack of response to my father's pleading *It's Newman, Victoria, it's*

Newman, his hand on her bony shoulder, the dull green fabric of her robe with its smiley face button that an attendant had pinned to a worn lapel.

"We'll go visit her again while you're here. She may need time to feel comfortable with seeing me again."

I shake my head. "Who exactly are we talking about? Victoria?"

"Sure, Victoria."

"And you can't see how hopeless she is? She didn't even know you were there!"

My father gets out of the car. He goes over to a picnic table and sits down with his hands on his knees. There's a row of newly planted spruce trees behind him, staked down with wires. On a blanket in front of the trees a family sits eating lunch. A toddler industriously picks up paper cups and drops them in a cooler, takes them out and drops them in again. I feel a pang of loneliness for Claire, for our unborn child, my own family. It seems months since I've been gone.

"I've always been an optimist," my father says.

"Listen to me. You can't just throw this fantasy into the pot and make everyone come out happy."

He doesn't respond.

A truck pulls into the parking space in front of us, the whoosh of air brakes being released.

"Mother's dead. You never mention it. You never admit it. I can't get around that. I can't even help you move out until you acknowledge that in your heart—grieve over it for God's sake! It's got you completely stuck, and me too, now."

We are sitting beside one another like two old men on a park bench, with all the time in the world. Not a word from him.

"You don't face things," I say, driven now to force a reaction. "You won't even visit her grave with me."

He remains mute. When I turn I see that his eyes are moist and my heart seizes. He pats my knee. "We won't talk about her anymore," he says, leaving the pronoun eternally ambiguous.

That night my mother sits with me in a sewing room on the third floor, a floor that doesn't exist in my parents' house. A plaid blanket lies over her paralyzed legs, the same blanket my father covers himself with, summer or winter, when he sleeps on the couch.

Why won't you come down? I ask her. She has been up here a long time.

How is the baby? she says. There's no strain in her voice, none of the tension I remember as a child when she would tell my sister and me to go to our rooms and play because she was sick and needed to lie down.

I let her know the baby is fine, Claire too. Will you come down now? Please?

She pulls my father's blanket tighter around her waist.

We need you. *He* needs you.

My mother lowers her head and parts her hair with her fingers, exposing the white roots. I look closely and discover a tiny gem, like a bindi, the bright red dot Hindu women put on their foreheads, only this jewel is deep blue. I wonder how long it has been there, how it is embedded in the skin.

Does it hurt? I ask.

My mother smiles at me. I will be disappointed when I wake up, because she hasn't looked at me with such pleasure and curiosity in a long time. No, she says, it doesn't hurt.

Does Dad know about this?

She laughs. All the fathers know, she says.

A week passes. I'm still in Philadelphia trying to get my father moved.

"He's impossible," I complain to Claire during one of our late-night phone calls. My father is asleep on the couch as usual. It is where he used to sleep when my mother was sick. He has never dropped the habit.

He has been to see Victoria every day since our first trip. His visits grow longer, stretching out to three, four, and five hours. He tells me he is "making progress," though I have no idea what this means because I refuse to go with him, staying behind instead to pack, angry at him for leaving me with this task. My editor has reluctantly given me another week's extension, and Claire has become impatient, listening in cool silence.

"Maybe you're part of the problem," Claire says now.

"How do you mean?"

"He can rely on you to take care of everything while he goes off and lives out this fantasy."

"What can I do? I have to get him out of here. The realtor is calling every day asking whether we'll be out by the closing."

"Will you?"

"I don't know. We'd better. It's three hundred dollars a day if we don't."

Silence.

"What's wrong?" I say.

"I just miss you, Adam. This was supposed to be our last vacation before the baby."

"If I could just get him away from Victoria."

"It wouldn't matter. He'll find some other way to keep you there. He's afraid. He doesn't want to be alone."

"How are you doing?" I say, wanting to change the subject. "Still being dropkicked?"

"Every night right at ten, just as I fall asleep. Apparently baby doesn't want to be alone, either."

"All right," I say, "I get the message. I'll try to wrap things up here in a day or two."

But the next afternoon my father returns from the nursing home and informs me that he's bringing Victoria to dinner tomorrow evening. He'd like my help in preparing the meal. I'm stunned.

"In the car," he says, explaining how he'll transport her here. Shouldn't it be obvious?

"Dad, are you actually talking with her now?"

"Of course I talk with her."

"Does she talk back?"

My father looks at me as if I'm crazy. "What do you think—I go around talking to myself?"

"I can't believe it. I just can't believe this!" I've been staring at the dining room table pads for the past half-hour, wondering which of my three piles they belong in: the apartment pile, the storage pile, the trash pile. Unable to decide, I put the pads in an "undecided" pile, which grows exponentially as we near our deadline. We have three days left before the new owners take possession. I called my sister in Seattle to ask for help, but her vacation starts tomorrow and the whole family is leaving for Hawaii. "Why didn't you call earlier?" she asked.

I thought I could do it myself. I wanted to. She had spent so much time here when our mother had a stroke; I felt this was my contribution. "Have a moving company do it," my sister said last night. "They'll put everything in boxes and get it on the truck." But it's too late for that now and I would feel even more ashamed of my failure. Also I've gotten sidetracked by mulling over my own past, high school yearbooks, honor roll certificates, desperate letters to adolescent girlfriends whose faces in memory blur into a composite not unlike the youthful, fiery Victoria laughing in the salted sea air of the boardwalk.

"You need to help me pack, Dad. I'm sorry, but you're going to have to postpone the dinner."

"I can't," he says. "It's our anniversary."

"Your anniversary? Of *what?*"

"When we first became engaged."

"You were engaged now!"

"For a day. Then she called it off. She'd gone back to her home in Darby, run away from the composer. She called me, crying. She said he was all wrong for her—no respect, no security, no future. Later I learned he'd taken up with somebody else and that's what she was so upset about, but at the time all I heard was she wanted to marry me. She begged me. I had all the stability the composer couldn't give her, a pretty good business over on Samson Street. It was right after the war and I was selling diamonds like postage stamps. I couldn't keep enough in stock—"

"Wait a second. After the war—you were already with Mom, weren't you?"

My father stands at the refrigerator, eating what's left of the rice pudding. He keeps his back to me. "We were engaged, too."

"Too! You were engaged to Mom and Victoria at the same time?"

"Yes. That same day Victoria called me I gave her a ring."

"Mother knew about this?"

My father nods. He puts the lid back on the rice pudding and pushes it far back onto the shelf filled with the leftover takeout food we've been eating every night. He refuses to look at me, won't move from behind the refrigerator door.

"In other words, you broke off the engagement with Mom."

"It was a bad thing. Very serious."

"I'll say."

"She shouldn't have taken me back."

"Mom?"

"She shouldn't have taken me back. Or she should have forgiven me. To be married all those years and never forgiven. She's also to blame." He closes the refrigerator. Rice pudding has stuck to his chin. I reflexively touch my own face, so much the image of his, reversed only in that it shows shock, where his shows resignation. "You look back and you say, I should have done things differently. But you look back hard enough and you know you wouldn't." He shakes his head. "You wouldn't. It's a whole new life you need. I'm going to nap."

"Dad—"

His eyes close on the couch. In seconds, he's asleep.

"More wine?" my father says to Victoria.

We are sitting at the dining room table, surrounded by boxes stacked up to the ceiling.

Victoria raises one finger. My father smiles and fills her glass to the rim with the wine, a white Bordeaux.

She wears a blue dress with a silver satin collar, a small white bow fastened with a cloth button the size of a kitten's nose to each short sleeve, the elastic of which fails to grip her upper arm. A hairdresser who visits the nursing home every Thursday has coifed Victoria's white hair, swept back and folded behind her head with what seems a generous amount of hair spray. At her throat rests a pearl choker—my father's gift to her for their "anniversary." We have gone through appetizers (bruschetta with prosciutto, ricotta, and arugula from Mateo's), and veal (from the Chalet), and now on to dessert, a Black Forest cake (from Engleton's). My father spent the entire day gathering food from the best restaurants in town. He unpacked a set of dishes and some silverware from one of the boxes I had sealed. He pretended to be making all the food himself in the kitchen. As far as I know, Victoria believed him.

"Adam, would you do the honors?"

My father sets the cake in front of me with a knife. "Excuse me," he says. Victoria leans over to say something to him. She cannot raise her voice above a whisper, the throat cancer. "Victoria says none for her." She whispers again. "She wants to know why you didn't eat your veal."

"It's inhumane," I say.

"I slaved for hours," he says.

I smile weakly at him, then glance at Victoria, her eyes glassy from the wine, her thoughts only half here as she stares off toward the ceiling while my father takes her hand and helps her up from the table. She has moved in and out of being with us during dinner, speaking only twice, with great pain, once to say the food was excellent, the other time to inform us that at eleven she would be picked up by her mother (who died twenty years ago). The staff at the nursing home made a big production about her going out. "She had four attendants dressing her!" my father announced over dinner, his arm paw-like, hanging like a large gourd over her tiny shoulder, squeezing wide-eyed looks from her as she sat mute and dazed in all her aged smallness. "It could have been her first dance! You should have seen everybody standing on the steps waving goodbye. Do you know she hasn't left the grounds there for fifteen years? It's a miracle she's here."

Earlier we had stood in the kitchen "preparing" the meal, a hush-hush operation while Victoria sat in another room waiting for the end of an imaginary toast, her arm extended for the few minutes we'd been gone, a courteous if strained smile on her face. Meanwhile my father and I had had a tug of war over the dinner plates, with him insisting he would wash and repack them and me demanding he use paper ones.

Now my father sits with Victoria in the living room while I clean up. I hear him talking to her although I cannot make out what he is saying. It sounds as if they are having an actual conversation, punctuated by laughter and teasing. I dump all the Styrofoam containers and paper cups into the trash, then wash the silverware and repack it. The movers will be here tomorrow and I am finally ready for them, having marked every box with the appropriate apartment room. The sense of accomplishment I feel from all this is ridiculously great.

When I enter the living room, I see my father sitting at the feet of Victoria, who, between the wings of a floral chair, has only her legs visible to me in their navy hose. I picture Victoria's face, imagine her pale yellow eyes staring vacantly at my father, a dimly lit warmth retrieved from near hopeless depths.

"Victoria will be staying for breakfast," he says.

She leans forward. Her expression conveys shyness and mild flirtation. The bows on her sleeves dance with mischief, her pearl choker a high marble wall to be surmounted for the pleasure of her throat, her exhausted body all things to all men. I do not see the hollow flesh, the dead cells, the bones so fragile they break like tiny glass tubes, the laying her out sacrificially on my mother's bed.

I run upstairs and lock myself in his bedroom. I call Claire.

"*He wants to sleep with her,*" I hiss into the phone.

"Adam? Is that you? Where are you?"

I cannot believe how my heart has begun palpitating. "I can't allow this."

"Victoria and your father?"

"Yes," I say. "Yes. *It's* crazy. He's crazy. He wants me to witness all this, make me an accomplice, prove to the world he's finally captured her. This ultimate expression of his megalomania!" I motion downstairs, as if Claire can see me. "He can't do this. It's against the law."

"He's forcing her?"

"Against the law of *nature*."

"Where are you now?"

"Upstairs. I've locked the bedroom door." From below I hear my father calling me.

"Adam, you can't stop them."

"Claire, this is my father we're talking about. He's about to defile this poor woman. For God's sake, she's been in a nursing home for twenty years! She doesn't even know what's happening to her! She can't take care of herself. It's cruelty."

"Does he love her?"

"What's that have to do with it?"

"Does he?"

"Claire, the question is utterly inappropriate here."

"Is it?"

Neither of us speaks for a while. I play with the switch at the base of the nightstand lamp, an antique, the one item I've left unpacked because I want to take it back with me. I consider knocking the whole thing over, the delirious sound the brass shade will make. Claire says, "All right then, are you coming home tomorrow like you promised?"

"Do you realize the situation that's developed here tonight? I can't just let him destroy her like this. He has no compunction, no awareness of what he's doing. It will *kill* her."

"Adam…"

"What?"

"I want you back."

I put the phone against my shoulder. Downstairs I hear music. The piano. A snappy tune marches up the stairs, twirls and descends.

"I want to know something," Claire says. A high C pings over and over, like a knife tapping crystal. A music lesson? "Are you going to be the same kind of father?"

"I don't understand."

"Never around. Never here for your child."

"Of course not," I say, but a shiver goes through my body.

"Because if you are..." Claire starts to cry. "Because if you are, I want to know about it now. I *have* to know."

I think about Claire's parents, divorced after thirty years, her mother saying to us on a visit from California, "I was Sleeping Beauty—in reverse. He kissed me and I fell asleep for thirty years."

"We're going to be fine," I say.

"Don't tell me that. It's not true. And you can't promise me anyway. You're not even here now."

"I didn't have a choice, Claire."

"Why did you wait until I was too pregnant to fly before you went? Were you trying to get away from us? Is it that you're scared of being a father?"

"Claire, look," I say, but I'm not sure what I want her to see. That I've pleased no one by coming here? That my father married the wrong woman? That my mother died trying to find love in this house? That my father, demonic in his obsession, is about to fuck the lights out of the dead, rotting past?

"I'll be home tomorrow. I promise."

"But do you *want* to come home?"

"Are you kidding?"

"I want to hear you say it, Adam."

"I want to come home. I want to see you. I love you."

"You love our baby?"

"I'm crazy about our baby."

"How do I *know*? Can't you tell me something that will make me believe you?"

I'm lost.

"Adam?"

"I'm yours," I say, simple enough. "That's what love is." I shake my head, unable to believe I'm quoting my father. "I'm yours."

I sit for a moment after I get off the phone. Under the green felt bottom of the brass lamp I've placed a photograph for safekeeping. I pick up the picture and study it: my mother kneeling beside me, her arms wrapped around me. Her eyes are dark brown—clear of illness. The side of her face is crushed against mine; she hangs on with a passion to have me unfairly in her arms forever. I am six years old and missing my front teeth, toothlessly ecstatic to be in her embrace, so that now, looking at the child pulled toward her in desperate love, I feel the lock on my heart break, and silently I cry out for her.

When I go downstairs I see my father at the piano playing a song I know from childhood, the words about a young man who pulls the moon along on a string so the tide will rush out and he can dance at the bottom of the sea with his lover. On the couch, with her arms at her sides, is Victoria, and for a moment I think she is dead. My father gets up from the bench and goes over to her. His lips touch her ravaged cheek, caress the back of her neck, move up to the bony protrusion at the base of her skull. I see the brainstem quiver with life under their warmth. He strokes her hair, then looks up at me and tells me with his eyes to mourn us all.

Summer of Love

THE RADIO STATIONS WERE calling 1967 the Summer of Love, but my father informed me it was to be a summer of work, and made arrangements for me to be a waiter at my Aunt Letty's hotel in the Catskills. The lodge was near Liberty, New York, between the more famous resorts of Grossinger's and Brown's. After I flew from Ohio, where we lived and where I would be starting college in the fall, I took the bus from the Port Authority up to Liberty and then a cab from there to Aunt Letty's place, Hy-Sa-Na Lodge.

The hotel's driveway was a mile-long gravel road overhung with trees. The cab bumped along the single lane that narrowed with tall weeds brushing the windows and doors, until we came to a three-story lodge. Patio tables, their blue and white umbrellas folded, lined a veranda that ran along three sides of the hotel. The hotel, my father told me, warning me not to expect too much, had been a fashionable resort in its heyday, the forties and fifties, with "Broadway Entertainment" and dancing, but over time, and with Letty's husband, my Uncle Bumin, dying years ago, the place had deteriorated.

I paid for my cab and went up the steps. The screen door had holes in it, and I saw that the paint on the walls was peeling. Fat pigeons cooed and dropped their feathers into crooked gutters. Aunt Letty stood behind the front desk, her hand shaking as she wrote. She had Parkinson's disease. I had not seen her since I was five, when she came out for my mother's funeral. She had kept me company, helped me color pictures of dinosaurs and whales and played quiet games with me while mourners came to our house to sit shivah. I was told my mother would be "in heaven missing me." Sadness collected in empty spaces I never knew existed in our house— places that I came to understand are always reserved for such grief.

"Ivan!" Aunt Letty said, looking up. "You're here!"

We hugged each other and Aunt Letty asked me did I want something to eat, a glass of milk, some tea? No, I said, I was fine. It was just nice to be here.

"I hope you won't be too lonely up here, Ivan."

"Are there any other waiters?" I had come a week early; the season officially opened on Memorial Day.

"Two," Aunt Letty said. "They'll come soon. One is from Massachusetts, and the other is a young man from Long Island. Both seem such nice gentlemen. The young man from Long Island wrote me a long letter about his military background and training. He sounded very responsible."

It didn't sound good to me. I'd gone on a chartered bus to Washington to march against the war, and I'd turned down a scholarship to Purdue University because R.O.T.C. was required.

"What military school is he from?"

"West Point, I believe."

"West Point!" Even I could be impressed by West Point.

"Ivan, I don't know if your father told you, but many of our guests are older here. I hope this won't bother you."

"Of course not."

"Some are very old."

"I like being around older people, Aunt Letty."

"Good. You'll let me know if there's anything you need. I want you to be happy up here. I so loved your mother. She was my favorite cousin when we were children."

"Yes," I said. "She thought a lot of you, too," although I didn't know this for sure. I was used to making up a personality for my mother since she had died when I was so young.

Aunt Letty smiled. Her teeth were square, conspicuously false.

"I try to keep up the place, Ivan, but it's so hard by myself. And we just don't have the funds that we used to." Her voice rose nervously when she said *funds*. "I don't think we can go on for too long the way things are now. We have our regulars but less and less come back every summer. And now, the young people, with their new ways, the long hair and all this trouble about the war and the riots in the cities, who understands any of this?" I sat and listened politely and then Aunt Letty said, "I'm rambling, Ivan. Please don't let me do that. Come, I'll show you where you will sleep, darling."

•

A hundred yards up a dirt path, the old recreation hall once showcased the big bands and comedians who played the borscht belt. Now the building housed only bats and mice and an occasional opossum. Aunt Letty had offered me a private room in the main lodge, but I didn't want special treatment, so I chose a room in the back of the recreation hall, one where other waiters in years past had carved their moment in history on the lodge's walls: Lewis Goldberg ZBT, 1962; Mike Michaelson, Hofstra University, 1950; Miss Lucy Fishman and Mr. Barry Weinstein slept here, 1947. I moved the rickety card tables out of the room, swept the floor, covered the missing pane in the window with cardboard so the mosquitoes wouldn't eat me alive, and set a clock up on a conga drum that I'd found behind the stage.

During the day, dust would swirl in the light that streamed through the splintered rafters of the ballroom and cobwebs would glisten silver, but I could imagine the dances and shows and gala parties that had once taken place here, the orchestra on stage, the drummer swishing his brushes, the droll bassman, and then—a sudden change in tempo—the band leader puts aside his trumpet and beats a tattoo on this conga drum, while my mother and father and their friends do a steamy rhumba. I missed my own music now. The small radio I'd brought up got poor reception in the mountains and the two Beatles records I had gingerly transported had nowhere to be played. At night, I'd lie awake for a long time and listen to the bats in the ballroom, their wings flapping. I'd imagine their furry bodies and crinkled faces and red eyes and razor teeth—their sonar pinging off my head. Once, when I couldn't stand it anymore and turned on the light to see, a group of ten or so swooped like a single large and reptilian wing from one end of the ballroom to the other—then shot back into the rafters. After that, I always left the light on and pulled the covers over my head to sleep. In the morning, with the bright sunshine, all would be quiet, the bats back in their holes, the mountains green and smelling of wild lilac and mint, the air cold and the grass dewy, the smoke rolling up from the kitchen's chimney as I walked down the dirt path to eat breakfast.

I was alone for a week, and during that time I helped Aunt Letty set up the dining room. I polished the silver, inventoried the dishes (meat and dairy plates—I had to learn about kosher service), separated the worn linens, filled salt and pepper shakers, and shampooed the carpet in the dining room. At the end of the week, Lester Malmar arrived. He threw his duffle bag down on the bed in the recreation hall's long front room. He opened the bag, took out white cadet gloves, and placed them carefully on the room's dresser. He was tall, with black curly hair, but I thought a little overweight for a West Point cadet. His legs were especially flabby, his skin pale under the hair. His sandals were held together with electrical tape.

"Where you going to college?" he asked me.

"Ohio University," I said.

"Major?"

"Psychology."

"In Russia you'd be insane."

I realized, with a sinking feeling, that I'd have to go through the whole summer with Lester Malmar.

"That's what they call people over there who don't believe in Marx's little red book."

"Mao's," I corrected.

Lester laid an attaché case on the bed, popped open the snaps and lifted the lid. Inside was a pistol.

"Don't worry, it's not loaded. I keep the bullets separate. That's one thing they teach us in weapons class—firearm safety. You want to do some target practice sometime? I'll show you how to shoot."

"No thanks."

"There's plenty of places around here."

"I hate guns."

"Suit yourself." Then Lester flopped on the bed and laid the gun tenderly on his stomach. He lit a cigar, something else I detested.

What saved me from Lester was Jeff showing up the next day. Jeff brought his stereo with him and a terrific collection of records. He wore rose-tinted granny glasses, a rope belt of bells, silver studs along the seams of his jeans, and baggy white shirts from Mexico with bright embroidery. His hair, wavy brown and parted in the middle, came over his ears, and with his dark lashes, brown eyes, and wide mouth he looked like a cross between George Harrison and Paul McCartney. It didn't hurt the resemblance that he played guitar and sang in a band, and that his voice, deep and rich, could fill the entire recreation hall. The weekend after he moved in, he brought back a date from town and set a chair for the girl in the middle of the dance floor. On stage, he entertained her, a cappella, with Elvis, Roy Orbison, Jerry Lee Lewis. His encore, to the wild applause of us all, had been Gerry and the Pacemakers' "Don't Let the Sun Catch You Crying," and he had crooned the song in such dulcet, plaintive, and heart-seizing notes that his date, a first date, leaped up at the end and shouted, "Marry me!"

I hoped I would meet someone, too, that summer. But there were no girls at the hotel. Aunt Letty had been right: all the guests were old, and canes were prominent. I had to remember to speak up when waiting on my people, and to make sure I saved a serving of pickled lox for Mrs. Shoenbaum, and that even if Mr. Edleman wanted a Danish not to give it to him (his fifty-year-old daughter had warned me) because he was a diabetic, and to always bring Mrs. Fine "a little hot water with lemon, please—hot, please, bubeleh, hot," and to remember that Mr. Wallach had a "reaction" to the kosher dairy substitute for cream and so I was to empty out the kosher substitute and put in plain milk, though never to tell Mr. Wallach because he would die of a heart attack if he knew, and to Mr. Rosen give no salad because the roughage "makes my ulcer grab like a python."

At the end of the week, they would each call me over, on the porch or outside where they'd be walking slowly up and down the driveway, with their large sun hats, their white summer shoes, dark socks and plaid shorts. A five-dollar bill would be crushed into my hand. "So good you are," they'd say, or "So you should go to college and be as good a doctor as a waiter," or "Please, next time, a little hotter the water, hot, bubeleh."

One day in early July, Jeff and I walked down the road to the Brown's Hotel. Brown's was famous for Jerry Lewis—they'd named their nightclub after him—who had once worked at the resort as a busboy. Jeff had said, "Let's go in the lounge for a drink." I agreed, although it made me nervous. I had turned eighteen in April and only drank 3.2 beer in Ohio, which I knew was not sold around here. So I ordered what Jeff did, which was a shot of tequila. Although I remained perfectly composed on the outside, a flame like a gas derrick's shot through my stomach.

I turned in my chair to watch Jeff, who had gone over to the large windows that bordered the pool. He tapped on the glass at two girls outside in bikinis, motioning them to come inside. I panicked. I couldn't believe he was doing this to me.

They told him to come outside instead.

Jeff walked back to where I was sitting. "Let's go talk to them," he said.

"Do you know them?"

"No. Should I?"

His voice had already dropped into that chocolatey, deep register he used for singing and talking to girls.

"I can't, Jeff."

"Why not?"

He looked at me as if it would never occur to him that such a thing as shyness existed in the world. With his good looks, his bedroom eyes, his easy words, his light curls—what would he know about a choked voice, sweaty hands, a heartbeat loud as a cowbell? The girls weren't going to be interested in me, serious, analytical, preoccupied with the war, not to mention skinny legs and the rash on them from some weeds we had tromped through on our way.

"I can't go out there." I just couldn't imagine how. The girls in their bikinis: the light catching the necklace in the taller girl's cleavage, their slick, wet hair and golden shoulders, their eager hand signals to Jeff, their fingernails pink and sharp against the glass…how experienced they looked through the window. The tequila, rather than relaxing me, raced through my system and melted connective tissue, my will oozing out like sloppy airplane glue.

"I'll help you," Jeff said. "I won't leave you hanging." He put his hand on my shoulder. Here was a leader, I thought, here was somebody who could get men up a hill into battle.

"You talk with them by yourself. Really, it's okay. I'm just not in the mood," I lied.

Jeff sat down next to me at the bar. He studied me for a minute, then said, "No big deal. There will be lots of other chances. You ready to go back?"

"Yes," I said, immensely grateful that he hadn't taken my suggestion and left me.

Although I'd had a girlfriend in Ohio, we had broken up before I left for Aunt Letty's hotel. Elise thought making the separation official would be a good idea since we were going to different colleges anyway and she wanted to be free. We had slept together twice, near the end of the school year, but there was something too quiet and mechanical about it, as though we were taking turns touching each other rather than making love, all mixed up and wild. She'd held me in such a peculiar way, more as if to contain me than embrace me. I had been glad to be going away for the summer.

After a while Jeff stopped asking me to visit other hotels with him and instead took Lester. They would come back late at night, loud and drunk, pounding my bed, wanting me to wake up and share the rest of the wine or vodka or tequila or beer. Once, they both returned with girls. I pulled the covers over my head and waited. Then it started: the rustling of clothes, the sound of zippers, the dropping of change, the giggling, the squeaking of bedsprings, the moaning.

I stayed awake long after everyone became quiet.

Aunt Letty asked me to watch the desk while she went to talk with the chef. A cab stopped outside and instead of a shaky foot and orthopedic shoe touching the ground, out jumped a young girl wearing jeans and a blue workshirt with her hair in a long brown braid.

I opened the screen door for her and asked if I could help. She looked me up and down, at my red vest and black butterfly bow tie and the ruffled white shirts we wore to serve dinner, then at my polished shoes, and said, "You're Ivan, I bet."

"How did you know?"

"I'm Maida, Letty's granddaughter."

"Oh," I said. "Nice to meet you." We shook hands and her fingers curled around mine, kindly, with affection. Her face was open and friendly and I immediately relaxed. I was even able to joke about her suitcase, tied together with twine and taped in the corners. "Did you drag that behind the cab?"

Maida laughed and said she liked it because it had belonged to her father, who had taken it everywhere with him. He had loved to travel.

The logical question would have been, Do you like to travel, too? But for some reason I asked about her father.

"Is your father dead?" I said. I don't know why. Maybe I'd heard it from my father. My mother had been Maida's father's second cousin, which (and I was calculating quickly) made Maida and me distant relations, but close enough to be curious about each other.

What happened, however, in that first moment was one of those glitches of conversation when the unexpected remark or question becomes the truest one and a clumsy bump turns the world right side up. "Yes, he's dead," Maida said. "He killed himself." I nodded and took her hand again. I remembered now I knew this. Then I picked up her father's battered suitcase and we went to find Letty.

Maida and I began spending all our free time together. We'd swim or take long walks between my serving meals and then, at night, we'd sit on the porch and talk until late. When it was my evening to work the card room, she helped me serve tea and coffee. All the guests fussed over her and said, "Come, Maida, sit with us, darling." She would kiss the men's cards for good luck or pretend to know which ones they should throw down. Thursday evening was music night. Nathan the Piano Man, who toured the smaller resorts, would appear promptly at eight. With a dreamy smile, the suggestion of misunderstood genius about his eyes, the faint proudness of a man who could not endanger his hands by changing a tire or touching a hot plate, he would play ancient, moody melodies. Maida would stand with her arm through Letty's and they would sing "Rosie" together, as Letty used to do with Uncle Bumin.

I wanted to learn everything about Maida, and about her side of the family, which I didn't know well, my mother's family. I told Maida about my mother, what a shadowy figure she had been for me and how I didn't remember her too clearly even though I was already five when she died.

"Maybe it's too hard to remember," she said.

We were sitting on the porch steps of the recreation hall and I was picking at the rotten wood. I had a hard time talking about my mother, knowing what to say or what people expected me to say.

"Why didn't your father remarry?" Maida asked.

"I don't know why. He was pretty busy with his law firm. He tried with me. We'd go on camping trips in the summer and he'd come home from work to check on me when I got back from school in the afternoon. But I always felt he was as lonely as I was. I was aware we were different from other families, flying on one wing, so to speak." I paused, then said, "I thought that if I'd had a brother or a sister things would have been easier."

"Well, you have a cousin," Maida said.

She put her hand on my knee. I leaned over and kissed her. I felt her mouth open wide and the blood rush to my fingertips touching her cheek.

Elise had never kissed me with her mouth open or pushed her tongue inside. I pulled away. "Is this all right?" I asked.

"Of course, silly."

"I mean about us being cousins. I think we're third cousins."

"Who's counting," Maida said and cupped my neck, pulling my face back into hers.

Maida would come up behind me in the dining room and put her arms around me, whisper to meet her upstairs (in her room) the minute I finished serving. She'd be waiting for me. But if I showed up unexpectedly, she'd be agitated, upset, as if she didn't want me there, pacing around the room or telling me she had to finish writing a letter or reading a novel. Any display of passion I initiated was gently but clearly rebuffed. I'd rack my brain as to what I'd done wrong. Finally, one day, I just came out and asked her why she never let me surprise her. We had taken out the sole canoe to the middle of the lake and were drifting slowly back toward the shore, a stem of fat grapes between us that we'd grabbed over the screaming protest of the hotel's pantry man.

"I don't know," Maida said, pulling away from me. She'd been lying against my shoulder. She sat now in the middle of the boat, facing me. Wearing one of my shirts over her bathing suit, so her shoulders wouldn't burn, she had tied the tails in a bow across her stomach. The down on her arms had turned almost white from the sun. "I just like my privacy."

"But you come to my room all the time," I said.

"You told me I could. You said you *liked* to be surprised."

"It's more than that," I said. "You always have to be in charge, don't you?"

"What makes you say that?" Maida smiled and pushed a finger against my chest, leaving a white spot in the center. "Can't we just stop talking about this? It's so boring, Ivan."

"You're not bored with anything else we talk about. Why this?"

"Maybe you should be a lawyer instead of a psychologist."

"Maybe you should be an evasive witness."

Maida sighed with great, heaving annoyance. "Okay, so I don't like surprises. Is that any big deal?"

A fish jumped in the water. The lake was overflowing with rainbow trout but there was no one to fish. Only eighty-six-year-old Mr. Wallach,

Hy-Sa-Na Lodge's oldest guest, came up here occasionally in his chest waders.

Maida scraped her sneaker back and forth against the bottom of the canoe. "Ivan…"

"What?"

"Come over here. I want to tell you something." I slid over to where Maida was sitting. "Come closer. It's a secret." She wrapped her arms around my neck and pulled me into the water. We floated around down there while she held tight to my neck, and for a moment I thought her secret was going to be that we would drown together.

Jeff was a regular topic of conversation between Maida and me. Maida didn't share my admiration for him, nor find him nearly as charming as I did.

"Oh, look at him, will you, Ivan? He can't even talk to women without coming on to them."

"Which women?"

"Me! He's constantly fluttering his eyelashes—he might as well have a motor behind them. And buzzing in that bee voice of his."

"I love his voice!"

"It reminds me of runny marmalade."

"Why do you dislike him so much? What's he ever done to you?"

"Nothing. He just bothers me. That car he bought." Jeff had spent his money from the summer so far on a '63 Triumph, while I carefully deposited mine at a bank in Liberty.

"It's his choice," I said. "Why should he have to be practical if he doesn't want?"

"It's his attitude, that he's so clever and cute. What's he going to do next year? Is his sporty little car going to save him? I tried to talk to him about going to college, just for a year to buy himself some time. No, he wouldn't think of it. He's not going to hide behind some pompous professor's robes, he told me. I mean, come on, it's one thing to make a point on principle, but that's not his reason. He's just acting out some juvenile rebellion against his father."

"His father! How do you know this?" Jeff had never mentioned anything to me about his father.

"His dad is a big corporate executive who wants Jeff to follow in his footsteps, go to Stanford like he did."

"I'm amazed he told you all this."

"That's what I mean. He tells me all these things because he thinks I'm just naturally interested in his life—wouldn't any girl be? It's his tone. He was actually explaining, in boring detail, how to do the backstroke in the pool."

"Well, he was on his school's swim team."

"So was *I*."

"I think you're too hard on him, Maida."

"And I think he's the brother you always wanted. He can't do much wrong in your eyes."

"Maybe," I said, feeling suddenly caught.

Still, Jeff had the only car and it forced the three of us together. Lester was left out, mostly, we told ourselves, because we took the Triumph and there wasn't room for him. It became embarrassing to sneak away, for that's what it felt like, a quick goodbye and then we'd hurry down the steps, leaving Lester on the porch squeezing a handgrip and looking after us with a stern military grimace. One evening we came home late and found Lester wearing his cadet uniform, with white-gloved hands behind his back, standing in front of a map of the world he'd mounted on his wall. Besides listening to military marches and famous narrations of great battles, he plotted troop movements, his troops, in the Vietnam war. Tonight the allies (the blue pins) had invaded every communist country except, as far as I could see, Russia. Jeff went straight to bed. Lester and I remained side by side facing his map. "It was a hell of a war," he said.

"Was?"

He nodded at the map. His face had broken out in hives the last few days but only the left side; the smooth right side was cleanly shaved. The doctor had told him not to shave the other side until the rash cleared up. The smooth profile was toward me. I tried to follow his gaze. "What are you nodding at?"

He pointed at Russia.

"Yes," I said. "No blue pins. Why?"

Lester turned his full face toward me now—the rashy, hairy, left side and the clean-shaven right. "It doesn't exist. I've eliminated the problem."

"I'm going to bed," I said.

"You can run but you can't hide."

"Figure it all out, Lester, and let me know in the morning what happens to the world."

"I feel sorry for you, Ivan Ivanovitch! I had such hope for you when I first came here. You seemed intelligent, if misguided."

"Give me a break."

"Give yourself a break and wake up, man!"

"Shut up!" Jeff shouted from his room.

"And him, they'll break him in two minutes. The bamboo shoots under his fingernails, the leeches on his testicles, the grains of rice soaked in urine and ground into the razor cuts on the bottoms of his feet. He'll be begging for the bullet through his head."

"Where do you think of this stuff, Lester?"

"Read Tom Dooley, my friend. Tortures beyond our minds."

I started to walk away. Lester called after me. "Wait a second, I want to tell you something."

"What?"

"I've conquered sleep."

"Mazel tov."

"Fatigue," Lester said. "Fatigue is the enemy." He smiled at me. "Why don't you join me—if you think you can take it. Unless you want to crawl into your bed, a wasted hophead like your fellow traveler in there."

"Hophead?"

"Go ahead. Smoke yourself into oblivion. Wake up with a bayonet in your soft white gut!"

Jeff appeared in the doorway. He was scratching his crotch and squinting through sleep at us. "Look, man, can you please keep it down? Go outside and talk at least."

Lester pulled his heels together, thrust out his chest. "Request denied! Recruit Jeffrey Jeffvanovitch will not cross the demarcated line of Captain Malmar's quarters!"

"You are such a retread," Jeff said and turned around, shuffling back to his room.

The next day I told Maida.

"He sounds sick. He really gives me the creeps."

"Should we tell Letty?" I asked.

"I don't know. He hasn't done anything wrong. He's just acting so weird."

Maida didn't like to be around Lester and would avoid the recreation hall if she knew he was there. He called her "Ma'am," as he addressed

Letty and anyone in a position of authority; he assumed Maida to be a superior because she was Letty's granddaughter.

"I catch him staring at me sometimes. But it's not as though he turns away when I meet his eyes. He keeps looking, Ivan." I rested my head in Maida's lap and kissed her smooth belly, her salty skin warm on my mouth. We'd come up to her room after lunch. "He's really not sleeping anymore?"

"That's what he says. Maybe he takes naps. How else can he stay awake?"

"Is he serving his guests all right?"

"Seems to be. He's always there—on both feet. He takes their orders, brings their food, then stands at attention by his coffee service, his chin up, until the last guest has left. He cleans up and goes back to the recreation hall."

"Maybe he sleeps then."

"No, that's when he polishes his shoes and cleans his gun."

"Gun! What do you mean, gun!"

"He has a pistol. Issued to him at West Point."

"They don't give out *handguns!*"

"How do you know?"

"They just don't." Maida got off the bed and went over to her dormer window. She put on a T-shirt and hugged herself. I came over to the window and held her. Her whole body was trembling.

"Are you okay?"

"No, I'm not okay. Do I look okay?"

"Well, don't get mad at me. I didn't bring him here."

Maida looked at me strangely, as if she didn't know who I was or couldn't trust me anymore. Later, I learned she had seen her father shoot himself.

I should say I was stoned during much of the summer. But whereas I would want to lie on my back and enjoy the effects of my circumlocution—stringing long words together and watching them spin off protoplasmically toward the stars, Maida wanted to fuck. Sex was what interested her most about grass. My brain's busy catwalks, which Maida was willing to traverse when we were straight, annoyed and scared her when we were stoned. "Don't talk like that, Ivan," she might say, or "Everything's getting too complicated and chopped up in my head." She didn't like me to tease her either, or talk in funny voices or do scary things like hold the flashlight under my chin and roll my eyes back. I reminded her too much of her father when I was stoned.

He'd been diagnosed as manic-depressive. In his manic phase he would stay up all night making phone calls to radio talk shows or friends if they would listen or, when there was no one else, all-night grocery stores to ask if they had a certain cereal or brand of tuna that he thought they should be carrying. In the morning, he'd be waiting at the bottom of the steps for Maida, telling her how to dress for school, which part to try out for in the class play, what to eat for lunch to keep her figure, leaping from one subject to another. He'd have gone over all her homework and commented on the teacher's comments. In high school, she had taken a course in shorthand; it wasn't unusual for him suddenly to clap his hands while they were watching TV (he would watch TV standing up) and command, "Maida, take a letter! To William Lensenk, Director, Royal Shakespeare Company. Dear Bill, Recently saw your production of *Richard III* on PBS and was ferociously disappointed. In Act I, Scene 3, Richard is *not* downstage. How can this be? To hide Richard at such a vital moment as this!"

Her father had been an actor and then a director of a reputable theater in New York before the war, where he had met Maida's mother. But he never achieved the recognition he thought he deserved, and he spent his life working as a salesman for a theater supply store in Manhattan. When he was depressed he couldn't work and once, refusing to eat or take care of himself in the most basic ways, he had been hospitalized. In the early Sixties he had been put on lithium and this helped him function normally enough to work. But as time passed and he showed no extreme swings of behavior, he claimed he was completely cured and no longer needed the medication. One night he was working at his desk, writing a play, his first attempt in years. Maida, sixteen and talking with a girlfriend in the living room, always with an ear out for her father's sudden shifts in mood, heard the typing stop, the only time his relentless pecking had ceased all night. She listened to him pull a page from the carriage, heard his sharp laugh and then went to see how he was doing. He pulled the trigger as she walked in the door. No one even knew he had a gun.

One would think (yes, one would think, I have said to myself many times looking back on that summer), knowing all this about Maida I wouldn't have pressured her into taking LSD. "Aren't you even curious?" I asked her.

"I'm scared. And, yes, of course I'm curious. You know I'm not a timid person. I just know it's bad for me."

This sounded perfectly reasonable, but still I persisted. "My first time I want you to be with me. We could take it Sunday, right after lunch." We didn't have to work Sunday evenings.

"I don't know. Let me think about it, Ivan." Jeff would get us the LSD and guide us through the trip; he had taken acid several times already and swore by its powers.

"What's it like?" I had asked him.

"It has to be experienced," he said. "You can't explain an acid trip in words."

Which didn't sit well with me, since words had become an obsessive pursuit and I'd already filled four steno pads full of new vocabulary. The longer the better. If it had five syllables, a Latin derivation, and could be dragged from one's mouth like a wall of computers, I would work it into a conversation with Maida. "Your father longed to be a symposiarch," or "What tremendous vox angelica!" (about the final note on *Sgt. Pepper's*). I suppose Maida tolerated this as best she could. I thought I was speaking with clarity and precision and that my words would bring forth substance and color from an otherwise dull mind—my secret fear about myself then.

"Why can't you talk in simple language and let your ideas stand on their own?" Maida would ask.

"Form is ideation. And language is the form overarching all other modes of human perception—mathematics, art, prayer. If there's no experimentation with language, there's no evolution in our awareness and the culture of ideas ceases to grow. And besides that, it's just fun."

"It's not very much fun for me. I have to keep a dictionary in my hand if I want to understand you."

"No need," I retorted. "I shall promulge a translation at your request."

(Where does arrogance like this come from? And how does anyone get away with it?)

Maida agreed to take LSD with me near the end of the summer. I had finally said to her (in the most simple language possible), "It would mean everything to me if you did," implying that what "it" would mean is that if she truly loved me she would agree to do this, despite her fears. "It" had become something else, not the usual male plea for sex, but a new pressure. Maida's inner life. If I had this, I'd never lose her.

•

I asked Lester if he wanted to join us. And once I had extended the invitation, we were stuck with his acceptance.

Maida was speechless.

"I never expected him to say yes," I said.

"Why did you ask him then?"

I shrugged. I had an answer but I was embarrassed to tell her. We'd stopped halfway up the path to the recreation hall. Jeff was back there setting up, whatever that meant. "I thought he might feel more included."

"In *this*? Of all things, Ivan. Couldn't we just have gone to a movie with him if you were feeling guilty? Did you have to invite him on an acid trip with us?"

"I thought it would make him more...open."

"To what?"

"Maida, I'm trying to explain. You're not giving me a chance."

"You could have asked me first."

"I thought you would agree with me."

"About what?"

"That it might help him. Soften him up some." I turned away, embarrassed at what I wanted to say. "Help him love."

Maida sniffed my clothes. "God, Ivan, you reek of pot."

"I don't believe we can be at peace in the world until we find our enemy in here." I tapped my heart. "And until we stop hating one another. It seemed a good opportunity to practice that philosophy in my own backyard—with Lester."

"I'm getting sick."

"Look, you don't have to agree with me to respect an opinion."

"No, I'm really getting sick." Maida stepped to the side of the path and bent over. I held her hand while she took some deep breaths and recovered. With the handkerchief from my waiter's jacket I wiped the sweat from her face. "I feel better," she said. "It's going to be so crazy anyway, what's it matter? I'm really nervous about this, Ivan. Just don't leave me."

Wearing a blue satin robe, sandals, and a leather choker, Jeff greeted us at the door. "Peace and welcome," he said. He led us into his bedroom. There, in a corner, with sandals also, sat Lester. He saluted us.

"Hi," I said. "Getting comfortable?"

Lester nodded. "Just going along for the ride. I don't expect anything can happen to me. Not if I don't let it. It's good training to resist brainwashing, in case I ever get shot down."

Jeff handed me sandals. "Passengers will please remove their shoes." I could see he was making an effort to ignore Lester. Only after I'd convinced him that Lester would be less trouble if he was with us instead of marching up and down in his room playing John Philip Sousa marches or threatening to call the cops did he agree to get an extra pill for him.

"Sit down," Jeff said. He'd brought all the pillows in from the other rooms and spread them around the floor. On a foot-high shelf was a bowl of marbles and a prism. "To look at later," Jeff said. The stereo speakers stood at either end of the shelf and on the speakers incense burned in brass holders.

Maida said, "Can't I just take off my sneakers? Do I have to put sandals on?"

"Please," said Jeff. "We must be wearing the same materials on our feet for our energy to connect."

"Those are flipflops," Maida said. "They're from Woolworth's."

"They are holy launching pads. Just put the goddamn things on." Jeff smiled, politely. He'd been planning our trip for a week now and didn't like his script being ruined. He gave us each a stick of incense to hold. Lester sniffed his. Jeff coaxed us into a circle in the middle of the floor and told us to join hands. Lester reluctantly put his hand in mine but squeezed it extra hard once he did, so he wouldn't be accused of having a limp grip, I guess. I could barely restrain a yell. Jeff said, "Brothers and sisters, let freedom ring." Then he went over to his dresser, opened a drawer, and took out a plate covered with a linen napkin. It was a plate from the kitchen. He carried it over to us carefully, as though it were filled with water. When he set it down in front of us, there were four of the tiniest blue pills I'd ever seen.

"I don't want to go first," Maida said.

"I will," Lester volunteered. Jeff brought the plate over to him and he picked up the little pill—it looked harmless, almost cute—between his big thumb and forefinger, sniffed this, too, then, placing it on the tip of his tongue so we all could see, rolled it down his throat. He held his hands out. See? Nothing to it.

"It takes about an hour to get off," Jeff said.

"Sure, tell me when we get there." Lester leaned back against the wall, closed his eyes, and snored. I avoided looking at Maida.

"Next?" Jeff said.

"Could I have a glass of water? I can't take a pill without water." I couldn't. Even the smallest tablet could make me choke.

Maida said she'd get me one, then came back with a cup of water from the bathroom and sat down next to me. She put her hand on my leg. "I want to take mine with Ivan."

So we did, swallowed them together, then kissed. Lester yawned audibly, followed by a snort. He was reading a car magazine.

I tapped Maida's shoulder, pointed out the window. "Isn't that Mrs. Fischel?"

"Where!"

"Coming toward us—in the hoop skirt and Living Bra."

Maida punched me.

"And there's Mr. Rifkin. I can read his lips. *Acid Schmacid.*"

"Don't you dare do this once we're off, Ivan. I'm not kidding."

"I promise. It's going to be fun."

Lester had his size twelve feet up on the wall and was turning pages as though he were ripping them out. Jeff danced around the room waving sticks of strawberry incense. He'd wrapped an Indian sari over his shoulders and was making wa-wa noises. I checked my watch: 2:00 exactly. I felt great.

2:10: Maida gets up to use the bathroom. Jeff comes over to sit beside me. He sings in my ear, "You've got to admit it's getting better, it's getting better all the time…"

2:25: Lester is really sleeping. Or pretending so hard that he's convinced us all. He's curled in the fetal position, snoring, his big body beached in the corner with his hands pressed between his knees. The hair on his chest sprouts from the collar of a green Army T-shirt. I feel chilly and ask Jeff if this is a sign of getting off. He says not necessarily, but brings me a blanket from his bed. Maida asks me if I want some grape juice.

"Sure," I say. "Do we have any?"

She looks at me, confused by her own remark. "No. Why did I think we did?" she says, and we both break up laughing.

2:36: I have to go to the bathroom. Ordinarily I'd just get up and go, but I feel stuck. I'm suddenly worried I can't move and that this is the wrong thing to be doing. Maida is searching through her big straw bag for a pen. I've asked her for a better pen than the one I have, which is leaking all over my hand, stubby black ink dots. I have to continue making notes. She's taking all the things out of her bag and lining them up in neat soldier rows in front of her: keys, sunglasses, comb, brush, tampons, eye drops, nail clippers, chapstick, postcards, matches, checkbook, photo booth pictures of us...

"I'll be right back," I say.

Maida looks up from her bag, her hand buried deep in the bottom. "What?"

"I said I'm just going to the bathroom for a minute."

"'kay," she says in a little girl's voice and goes back to rooting through her bag.

2:50: When I come back Maida is sitting crosslegged on the floor and the articles have multiplied into four rows.

"Did you find one?" I ask.

"One what?"

"A pen."

Maida rocks forward until her head touches the floor. She turns her cheek and looks up at me, smiling. "I*van*."

"What?"

"I*van*, come down here."

I sit down. Maida's rear is in the air and she's kneeling on the floor, her face in her hands. Her cheeks are red and her eyes are pushed back so she looks Chinese, or maybe Japanese. Or Austrian. Who knows. Jeff and Lester (who has "woken up") have gone to the hotel kitchen to get some food in case we get hungry later. I estimate and make a note that they have left "in tandem at 2:48."

Maida tugs on my arm while I write. "Stop, Ivan. Come down here and play."

"I have to write, Maida."

"Write what?"

"Everything. I need to keep a log. For instance, if you were to look directly overhead"—Maida drops her head back—"and could see through the roof of this building, you'd notice that the sun is directly above us and forms an exact perpendicular angle with the plane of your legs. This is called the angle of incidence. If we are on a hillside now…imagine that we are on a sand dune in the Sahara—"

"We're eating guava fruit."

"Right. And as we sit on this dune, its angle very slowly increases in steepness, growing more precipitous, until the moment we begin to slide down—that's the angle of repose."

"Angle of repose," Maida repeats, her eyes still closed. "I see lazy people with fat stomachs. They've wrapped themselves in cool white sheets and are stuffing guava fruit in their mouths. What is guava fruit, anyway?"

"I don't know."

"It tastes delicious, though," Maida says.

"What's it taste like?"

"Green."

"Sounds slimy."

"Not that kind of green, Ivan. The color of twilight. You stopped writing."

"Yes." I was turning my hand over, looking at the back and front, watching the veins.

"Want to make love?"

"Jeff and Lester will be back soon. Where?"

"In your room. We can lock the door."

"I'd feel funny with them out here."

Maida pulls at her T-shirt. "God, I really want to take off my clothes. Do you want to go swimming in the lake?"

I pick up my pen. The fact that it's leaked all over my hand no longer bothers me; it interests me. "I don't think that would be a good idea, under the circumstances."

"I just feel so hyper. I want to do something physical. Is this what's supposed to happen? All this antsiness?"

"I don't know. Maybe we should ask Jeff."

Who had walked through the door at the moment. Lester and he were carrying cheese, bread, fruit. I had no appetite.

Jeff brought a bottle of Welch's grape juice over to Maida.

"Is this what you wanted?"

"Where'd you get it!"

"Never you mind, my princess." With a courtly bow he took a wine glass from his back pocket, unscrewed the bottle's top, poured a little grape juice in the glass and handed it to Maida. She sipped the juice, smacked her lips prettily.

"Does it meet with your approval?"

"Exquisite."

"And you?"

"What about me?" I said.

"Are you going to sit there until the cement dries around your butt?"

"I'm very comfortable." I picked up my notepad.

"He's keeping a log," Maida said.

"I see."

"Aren't you hot?" Maida said to Jeff.

"Yes."

"Want to swim?"

"Sounds great," Jeff said. He came over to me, walked around. I was sitting on my knees, my spine straight. Now that I was in this position even the slightest movement seemed extravagant. I was more interested in thinking about moving than actually moving. The body was an antiquated organism, primitive and unevolved. While thoughts could travel instantaneously, bodily parts followed behind like slow beetles.

Jeff lit a cigarette. He waved it in front of me. "See anything?"

"Your cigarette," I said. "What should I see?"

He made a wand of the burning ash and created loops, figure eights, fancy bows and spinning corkscrews.

"Wow," Maida said.

I restrained myself. I, too, saw the orange plumes from this tiny comet, but why should I cooperate? My thoughts were what interested me. Not these jokes for the eyes.

"I don't think we should leave this guy," Jeff said. "We can swim later. What do people want to listen to? Lester, how about you?"

Lester stepped out of the doorway and let his arms fly up. "Whooosh!"

"Do you want to hear anything?"

"Supremes," Lester said. He went back to the doorway and pressed his hands against the frame, Samson at the pillars. Maida was suddenly next to me. She had put her arms around my neck and was hugging me, whispering my name. I felt annoyed by the disturbance. I'd just had another thought and lost it when she interrupted.

She rubbed her hand over the back of my shirt. It was my white shirt—I hadn't changed from work—and I wondered what sustained the whiteness, how did the particles of energy hold their whiteness in place? Or was it my mind that thought it white, and the color white was actually a prolonged thought of whiteness?

"Ivan, talk to me, please."

"Why?" I said. My voice sounded far away to me, as though I were speaking through a pipe or into a coffee urn.

"You're so distant."

"I'll be okay," I said.

"I'm not okay. I need you to be more with me."

Jeff came over wearing lipstick and a turban, or maybe his lips just looked red from eating strawberries. But he had wrapped a towel around his head and taken off his shirt. He'd drawn dark circles around his nipples with my leaky pen. I remembered now he'd opened my hand and taken the pen from me, and I'd watched my fingers spread out like the speeded-up film of a rose blooming. I looked at my watch. Both hands had stuck together over the two—but that was impossible. We'd already gone past 2:10, unless my watch had stopped, but how could it go backward and stop?

"Sure," Maida said and stood up to dance with Jeff. I'd have to make a note of that: Maida stood up to dance with Jeff *as if he'd asked her*…She put her head on his shoulder. Stop, I thought, and shook my watch. Stop. Stop. Stop. But I meant the opposite. The opposite of that opposite.

Then the room flattened out and I was above it looking down and watching Maida and Jeff kiss. I heard a sound like *Moragggh*, as if the record player had suddenly been unplugged in the middle of a song. But the record was still spinning and Jeff was rubbing Maida's sides, her breasts, and she was squeezing her eyes shut and holding his hips against her, and then I saw myself sitting there watching them and I plunged.

Maida and Jeff were next to me. "What's wrong?"

"What do you mean?"

"You screamed."

"I went up," I said. "I saw you from up there." I pointed to the corner. "I was above you."

Maida rubbed my hands. Jeff put his arm around me. "It's all right," he said. "Take it easy. Think grounded thoughts. Hold onto this." He gave me his toothbrush.

"I don't want to hold your toothbrush! I was up there. Don't you believe me?"

"Ivan," Maida said. "Don't freak out."

"I'm not freaking out." Jeff had gone somewhere. I turned my head and he was gone. "My mind unplugged—my senses, that is. It sounded like the record stopping." I made the sound—*Moragggh*. "But it was my other body slipping out of my physical body. I was up there watching you."

Jeff came back with a glass of water. "Drink this slowly," he said. I dipped my finger in the water and stirred. The water's molecules jumped away from my finger. I held the glass up for Maida. "Do you see that?"

"He's really freaking out," Maida said.

They were talking about me in the third person now, so I did too.

"He wants to know something," I said.

"Don't do this, Ivan. You're scaring me."

"Do you love each other? He wants to know."

Maida looked pained.

I pointed to their eyes. "Do your two you's love your one another's?" The room was starting to spin again, like before, flatten out and be sucked onto the record disc. I could feel a tear, a rip starting in my vision. "I'm going up," I said.

"Let's go outside, all right, buddy?" Jeff said.

"Can he see her breasts?"

"Just take it easy."

"If he can see her breasts he won't go up."

I lifted Maida's shirt. She started to cry, but I had to touch her nipples. They felt warm, thoughtless, safe, pink, quiet, and down. The tear closed up.

I had a thought: Lester. Then a gun fired. The thought and the sound happened at the same moment and they were indistinguishable. Only when I saw Jeff run into Lester's room did I know something was wrong.

Lester was lying on his bed, his big body spread across the mattress, his arm over the side, the gun hanging from his finger with the barrel touching the floor. His eyes were wide open, a dead stare up at the ceiling.

"No!" Jeff shouted and began touching Lester all over, looking for the wound.

"Don't do that!" Lester said, giggling. "I'm so ticklish. It drives me crazy!"

I stared at Lester. Jeff backed away from him, then shouted, "You stupid schmuck! This isn't funny!"

Lester sat up on the bed. "I wanted to experience my death."

Jeff sunk to the floor, shaking his head back and forth. "No, no, no, no, *no*, this is all wrong!"

"It was just a blank," Lester said. He emptied the gun and showed us. "I didn't want to hurt anyone." The skin over his face tightened—as though someone were turning a handle on the side of his head. I could see the outline of his skull, what it was going to look like.

I checked behind me. Maida hadn't come into the room. I went back to where she had been sitting and she wasn't there. "Maida?" My voice echoed through the rooms—like the rooms of houses in dreams.

"Ivan, help me," Maida said, and I followed her voice into the bathroom. She was standing at the sink washing her face.

"What's wrong?"

"I can't see. I keep washing my eyes but I can't see anything."

The chef rushed Maida to the hospital. He had come up to the recreation hall because of the noise. Jeff and I went along, while Lester stayed behind. The chef kept asking me what happened, how did she suddenly go blind? I held Maida's head against my chest and told him I didn't know. Not until we got to the hospital did I admit to the doctor that we had taken acid.

He immediately gave Maida a shot and she fell asleep. He said he was almost positive she would have her sight back in the morning when she woke, but what had happened? How much LSD had we taken? How long ago? And, finally, he asked, Why? That's when I began crying. I had blinded her as surely as if I'd taken a red-hot poker to her eyes. I'd made her do this to prove she loved me. The doctor gave me a Thorazine capsule to bring me down. He said I could stay in Maida's room with her overnight.

The Thorazine helped, but I couldn't fall asleep. I thought I had to make sure Maida was all right, and that by staying awake and watching over her I'd protect her. The chef had gone back to the hotel. I had asked him to wait until morning to tell Letty what had happened. I would call Letty then and take a cab back with Maida. Jeff slept on the couch in the waiting room, half talking to me when I wandered back and forth from there to Maida's room, watching her sleep—her still body, her unseeing eyes, her quiet breathing. I apologized over and over to her. I said I loved her. I bent down to kiss her, but Jeff's face superimposed itself over mine as I did, and I withdrew my lips.

Aunt Letty asked us all to leave the hotel after the incident. I remember the shame I felt in facing her, her few but deliberate words: "I think you should go home, Ivan." She would call an agency and find replacements for us. Lester had already gone by the time I returned that next evening. He had left Maida a letter explaining he didn't realize the prank would scare her so much. He also admitted that he wasn't in West Point. He wasn't even in college, or the army. He'd been rejected from the service for a history of arrhythmia. The uniform belonged to his brother, who was at West Point. He'd signed his letter to Maida, *Sorry*, and enclosed a card for a free pizza if she was ever in Long Island.

Maida didn't get out of the hospital that next day, or the next, or the next. It was six weeks before she got her sight back. She had to work with a psychiatrist, who said the incident had been a flashback to her father's death and that her mind had shut down at the sound of the gun. I thought it was true: parts of the mind are so fragile they are thrown into a self-protective darkness at such times, the self hiding from the self.

It was three years before I saw Maida again. The episode had deeply disturbed our family, and it was generally agreed that it would be a good idea if I didn't contact her. One day she called me at college in Ohio and said that Letty had died.

I sat in the back of the funeral home while the rabbi talked privately, one by one, with each immediate family member in the front row. I could see Maida's head moving as the rabbi spoke softly to her. She was wearing a simple black dress and her hair was full and long on her back, not in a braid as she had worn it most of that summer. I felt my heart jump when I saw her and I was aware how much I had missed her.

After the funeral we gathered at her mother's house. In all the grief, no one noticed me at first. Then Maida's older sister welcomed me and said how nice it was I could come. Letty had cared a great deal for me, she said. I was thrilled at her words, this forgiveness implied not just from Letty but from her. I had carried around the blame for Maida's blindness for so long

I never thought I'd be released from it. "I'm sorry about everything," I said, and Maida's sister squeezed my hand and went over to sit with her mother.

I was standing at the table putting some cheese on a cracker, not because I was hungry but because I felt I should eat. I'd been too nervous on the plane, and now that I was here the excitement had persisted. Maida came up beside me. She took my arm and said to come with her a moment. She was wearing heels and perfume and seemed older than me, as though more time had passed for her.

We went outside to the patio and sat on a glider that creaked. Maida held her hands in her lap, formally. There was a distance between us, an affectionate distance, but still a distance. We were cousins now.

"Thanks for calling me," I said.

"I'm glad you came, Ivan."

Her sister shouted from the house. One of Maida's elderly aunts wanted to see her inside.

"In a minute," Maida said.

"Is this hard for you?"

"Yes. Although it's different than his was."

Her father's death was never far from her thoughts.

"That was more tense," she said. "Here, people are sad in an accepting way."

"What do you think was behind the tenseness exactly?"

"Bitterness," Maida said. "And I guess this is finally the sweet side of that bitterness. About time. Everybody loved Letty. You always asked me such good questions, Ivan. I really miss you."

I nodded. I was afraid to say much more.

"Are you still going to be a psychologist?"

"Trying," I said.

"I need to tell you something, Ivan. It's about Jeff. We saw each other a few times when he came down to the city."

"I know," I said. "He told me. It was one of the last letters I got from him before he went over."

"I just thought I had to tell you, in case you didn't know. I liked the honesty we had, that's rare I've been finding out. Have you heard from Jeff recently?"

"No."

"I haven't either. It didn't work out, by the way—no surprise, I guess. I think I was attracted to his flamboyance."

"Your father," I said.

Maida smiled at me. "You're such a psychologist."

Maida's elderly aunt came to the door. "Maida, darling! Maida, come here, sweetheart."

"I've got to go, that's Aunt Cissy. She wants to rave about my beautiful hair for a while. It's what she does every time she comes to visit. You'll be okay?"

"Sure," I said. Maida stood up. She took my hand and then kissed me on the cheek. Her hand rested on the back of my neck for a few seconds. I watched her walk over to her aunt and heard the old woman say, "Oh, my goodness, who has such hair!"

That afternoon I took the train into Manhattan. The sun was bright and the New Yorkers friendly, if I said hello first. I bought a pretzel and got lost on the subway. A man with a Russian accent who sat down next to me wanted to sell me a watch; I said no. He followed me up the steps asking if I needed a toaster, a radio, or a TV. I walked to Central Park and watched a troupe of mimes performing an antiwar skit; "Nixon" stood on his hands and talked the whole time with his feet. It was 1970, and Cambodia had just been invaded. In a month I would hear that Jeff was killed in Vietnam when his jeep rode over a land mine. It seemed that for being so young I'd loved a lot of people who had died.

I didn't know what to do with myself for the rest of the day. I'd told Maida I had some friends to see in New York, but I'd actually come only to attend the funeral and to see her. There was nowhere else to go now but home.

Absolute Zero

EVERY MORNING BEFORE SCHOOL, Connor ran four miles in the desert with the Marines. They did push-ups and bear crawls on the lawn in front of the recruiting center and shouted *Oorah!* at the top of their lungs. He'd shaved his head, his scalp as smooth as his mother's, only she was going in one direction and he…well, he didn't know where he was going. Since he was only seventeen, a year younger than most of his graduating high school classmates because he'd skipped eighth grade, he'd have to have his mother's consent to join up. So far she'd been lucid enough when it came to this particular matter to shake her head no and vigorously refuse. "Over my dead body," she said, not without irony. "I will stay alive as long as it takes to see that you don't throw away your life."

She wanted him to go to college at Arizona State and live with his Aunt Lyla and Uncle Sebert in Scottsdale. His sister, meanwhile, pregnant and single, would inherit the house until Connor turned twenty-eight, when he would receive his part of a trust fund. Connor figured by that time he might be dead himself. He was philosophical about it. When Sergeant Kenner, the Marine recruiter, tried to reassure him that he wouldn't automatically be sent to a war zone like Iraq or Afghanistan— after all, Marines were stationed across the globe—Connor said he would volunteer. Sergeant Kenner studied him for a long moment. "You, my friend, are exactly the kind of person that makes a leader." He further explained that the Marines didn't go after people like the Army. "Proud men come to us," he said. "They want to be Marines, and we're here to help them meet that challenge."

Connor had to admit no one had ever called him a leader, and he was flattered, manipulated he knew, but nevertheless enamored. He started showing up at the recruiting station and hanging out with the other potential recruits, called poolees, and the occasional soldier home from active duty. These were infantry grunts who had come back from Iraq and would soon be heading out again to Afghanistan. They made room for Connor at the card table—penny ante—in the rec area with its chin-up bar and free weights. They nicknamed him "Con," such an obvious diminutive yet no one had ever called him this. They included him in their touch football games, more like touch with hockey checking, and swarmed him when he caught a stretched-out, fingertip touchdown pass. They even pimped his ride, the Geo, sort of: buying him a chrome license plate holder with a placard that said THE CON. He put it on the front of the Geo and felt ridiculously proud of it and their acceptance.

Eventually, when they took his presence for granted—he was spending more and more time here—they told stories about Iraq, of dead bodies rotting in the sun and bursting apart before it was safe enough to clear them; of children missing limbs and spitting at them when they tried to help; of attacks by hajis—what they called all Arabs—dressed in military uniforms only to blow your head off in the span of a handshake; of Iraqi houses with trip wires in their front yards that wiped out whole patrols; and the comparatively mundane complaints: three weeks in the field without a shower, blistering sandstorms, scorpions and sand fleas. Did that mean they hated what they did? No, they hated those people who didn't support them, the anti-war scum. It didn't matter if the protestors said they were on their side but against the war. They were traitors.

Connor's mother, meanwhile, was one of these traitors. She'd made sure his name was taken off the list of eligible high school students so military recruiters wouldn't call. She had regularly covered the back of the Geo with anti-war bumper stickers—OLD HIPPIES FOR PEACE, WAR IS NOT PRO-LIFE—before Connor scraped them off. And until she became too weak to do so, she'd gone every Wednesday to Patriot Park at the corner of Central Avenue and Washington Street and joined a peace vigil. If there was one thing that drove her crazy, it was his wish to become a Marine.

"It's your father, isn't it?" she asked him. "Is that what this is all about? You're looking for acceptance from other men because you never got it from him. I'm right, aren't I?" She rarely spoke about Connor's father, who had left the family when Connor was five. He hardly remembered. He'd last heard from his father when he wrote from Florida on Connor's eighth birthday, some big land deal he was working on there—he'd bring Connor down soon and they'd go deep sea fishing. Connor sent him back his first poem: *Moo moo goes the sad cow. Neigh neigh goes the pretty horse. Heh heh goes the zoo daddy.*

His intention to become a soldier was the only subject that got his mother revved up and focused. Whereas she might ask him to go to the store and get her more…and here she'd brush her finger against her front teeth, finally coming up with the word, or so she believed—*cleanser!*—her brain cells worked with furious intact precision at trying to stop him from enlisting. "You have to promise me," she told him. "You have to promise right now that you won't do this to me."

"I can't promise," he said. "You know I can't."

"Why not? I'm your mother. Doesn't a condemned person get a last wish?"

"Jesus, Mom. Stop already."

"Just do it," his fat and pregnant sister said. "You owe it to Mom." They were all sitting in the living room. His mother's wig, this one a reddish copper color, was askew at a rakish angle.

"Stay out of this," Connor had warned. "You can't talk." That is, talk about making mistakes. His sister's one-night stand in a club had resulted in a child she insisted on keeping. He was going to be an uncle, his mother was dying, his sister was unmarried, and all he wanted was to make his mother sign the papers on the coffee table in front of her.

The seer had not been in school for weeks, and Connor wondered if he had died. Even in school, you didn't so much see him as sight him, drifting from the music room like a gossamer silver thread to another part of the building. He never carried books and was rumored to read by passing his hand over a page. He usually sat inconspicuously in the back of the class. One girl had claimed she'd literally seen him fade into the wall.

Wingard thought the seer had potential. "Maybe he's just sick again. Let's visit him after school."

"You know where he lives?" Connor asked.

"I'll find out," Wingard said.

Connor slammed his locker closed. His last class of the day was senior English, and he had to sit next to Heather Ward. She was always asking him how-do-you-feel-do-you-want-to-talk-is-there-anything-I-can-do-for-you? "I'm fine," Connor would say. His little secret. He couldn't be mean to people. Inside, however, he was un-nice, hateful, murderous, hacking bodies in the hallway, a bloody ax held high through a wild strangulated scream of carnage. "Thanks for asking, Heather." Like a choir boy or a priest or a sage. The seer. Let him figure this out. Everyone said he could read the future as fast as a comic strip.

Wingard was waiting for him in the parking lot with an address he'd wheedled out of a friendly student aide in the office. They drove two miles to the east side of town and pulled up to a cheery looking bungalow on a quiet street. The seer's mom was delighted they'd come by. She'd never met them, but that didn't seem to matter. "It's so wonderful of you to visit! Sandy will be so thrilled." Mrs. Seer—they didn't know the seer's last name; in fact they hadn't even known his name was the androgynous "Sandy"—led them down a narrow hallway with pictures of the family on vacations. "Sandy, you have two friends here to see you." She turned and spoke to them. "He hasn't been feeling much like talking the last couple days, so you'll have to keep the visit short. But I know it will cheer him up to have you here."

She left.

There in the bed, with railings on the side, hooked up to a war room of beeping monitors and wearing an oxygen mask, lay the seer. His eyes shifted to them, then returned to the ceiling. A scruff of his dirty blond hair fanned out in back from the strap of the oxygen mask. Connor could hear him taking deep gurgly breaths. Sometimes his mother breathed like this too, but without such desperate rattling. This was the sound of a single hoof tapping out time on a dark cobblestone street. Connor was speechless in its presence.

Wingard elbowed him. *Say something. Tell him why you're here.*

The seer couldn't have weighed more than seventy-five pounds, and that was being generous. He wore plaid pajamas with thick wool socks. He looked cold, but this was Phoenix, the desert, the happy sunshine state of Arizona, where Connor's mother was dying too and this person in front of him had wasted away, his pajama sleeve rolled up to display a pale veined arm no wider at the bicep than the wrist.

The seer's mother appeared again. She was carrying a tray of sodas and cookies. "I thought you two might be hungry," she said. "We have milk also, but I'm guessing you want the good stuff." She smiled. She was the least sad person in the room, Connor was sure of it. She put the tray of cookies and soda cans—choice of Mountain Dew, Dr. Pepper, Sierra

Mist—on a small wooden desk, and then left.

A voice delicate as a straw wrapper floating to earth came from behind Connor. "I'm sorry, but do I know you?" The oxygen mask was off. The seer's lips had sores with shiny ointment spread over them. Wingard took a step toward the door, his horror showing.

Connor cleared his throat. "Not really."

Wingard whispered, "Let's vacate."

"And you're here because?" The seer's voice had changed, the featheriness replaced by a sweetened irony, a fluted whimsy. "Help me sit up." He motioned for Connor to come closer. When he put out his hand for Connor to help him, Wingard said, "Posthaste," and fled the room.

Connor stood there. The white translucent hand hung in the air, until Connor finally took it, surprisingly warm for what he'd expected would be cold marble. Connor carefully leaned him back against his headboard. The sodas sweated under the overhead light.

"Ahh, repose," said the seer. His thin eyebrows were burned albino white by sun or illness.

"I heard you can see the future," Connor said.

The oxygen mask went back on. After a few stringy, wet breaths, the seer took it off and said, "Tomorrow is Friday. The sun will set in the west. The Heteropterus morpheus lives thirty-one days. Does that help?"

"I knew it was a hoax." He wanted to hurt somebody. Could you hurt the wind? Could you damage the absence of flesh? "I thought you could tell me something about what I should do after I graduate."

"Channel seven, please," the seer said, and motioned for Connor to turn on the television high up on a metal bracket in the corner of the room, just like in a hospital.

Connor got the remote from the desk with the sodas and turned on Channel 7. It was Oprah. "I love the Angel Network," the seer said. He watched Oprah walk down the aisle to the cheers of her adoring fans. Connor put his hand on the doorknob.

"Watch this part," the seer said. Oprah called people up onstage and told them they were getting free cars. It was the Pontiac giveaway show. Hadn't that happened years ago?

"Is this a repeat?" Connor asked.

"It's all a repeat," the seer said. The audience was opening their gift bags and finding car keys, too. They were going nuts, their faces lit up with monstrous joy, a frenzy of stupid happiness. "I never noticed you in school.

You have very little presence," the seer informed Connor.

"My mother's dying," Connor told the seer, looking into his watery blue eyes that had lost their focus on the television.

The seer waved for the TV to be shut off. "Listen," he said. His voice suddenly had strength, heft, *basso profundo*, as if coming through speakers on the wall. "You should know better than to come here."

"I thought you could help me."

"Are you listening?" The voice was becoming weak and fluttery again.

"I'm listening."

The seer patted the bed for Connor to come sit next to him. Connor did so, gingerly, lowering the safety bar and putting his weight on the edge of the spongy mattress. The seer, light as a ghost, slanted toward him, as if he might roll down a hill and be lost.

Wingard called through the door that he needed to leave. Time passed. Minutes? An hour? Mrs. Seer tapped musically on the door, came in, smiled at Connor and pursed her lips with thoughtful satisfaction at her slumbering son. She took away the silver tray with the untouched sweating sodas and the lemon-iced cookies, as if this happened all the time—her doomed boy sleeping beside a visitor who couldn't seem to leave.

The room darkened, the air circulated, the seer's breathing became so soft that Connor wondered if he'd slipped into unconsciousness. He put his ear to the feathery boy's chest. He heard a slow swishing, as if someone were moving a broom back and forth in an inch of water.

Outside, Connor slung his backpack over his shoulder and kicked the door of his car, his mother's really, since she didn't drive anymore. The Geo had a dent from getting T-boned and had never been fixed. You had to bash it with your foot to open it and then slam it like a vault door to get it closed.

He gave the Geo, purple with metallic bruises, another kick.

"What'd he say?" Wingard asked.

"Get in." Connor was giving Wingard, who had been waiting impatiently, a ride home.

"You were in there for like forever. What happened?"

"Nothing happened." In truth everything had happened, but nothing he could explain.

"So why'd you stay?"

"I felt sorry for him. Why'd you leave?"

"I couldn't take it. He was like a mummy or something. I thought he was going to put a spell on me."

Frankly, Wingard exasperated him. Fueled by a daily intake of six bowls of Reese's Puffs, he constantly networked with other World of Warcraft bangers. He slept by his computer and talked about people named Orgrim Doomhammer and Jaina Proudmoore as if they were blood relations. He'd been trying to get Connor interested in the brain-sucking game since they'd been sophomores.

"He's just a sick kid," Connor said about the seer. "I felt okay there with him."

"You were in there for an *hour*. I was in the kitchen with the old lady. You think that was fun? She was talking my ear off about her church and Sandy's faith and how we should really go watch him play guitar with the choir. 'He's a miracle, Salvatore,' she told me. *Nobody* calls me Salvatore."

"Why'd you tell her your name then?"

"I didn't. All right, somehow she got it out of me. The whole family's a bunch of aliens! So were you, what, holding his hand or something?"

How did you know? He had taken the weightless boy's hand after a while, unbidden, listening to the soft hissing of the aluminum tank filling the seer's lungs with a hundred percent pure oxygen; he had pictured the seer's red blood cells slurping up the fuel, growing darker and richer with every breath. It had been a long time since he'd felt so peaceful, and if it hadn't been for Sandy's mother knocking on the door, he might have stayed there all night.

They pulled up in front of Wingard's condo, where he lived with his mother and stepfather. "You coming in?" Wingard asked. The condos were older ones with tar-pebbled roofs that baked in the sun. A skein of yellow citrus tree leaves floated on the surface of the unused pool. Wingard, with his pale freckled skin (not unlike the seer's when Connor thought about it), had proudly declared he'd never stepped foot in it.

"I've got to go," Connor said. "I'm having dinner at Sergeant Kenner's."

"*Again?*"

Connor shrugged, made a vague gesture that he knew Wingard would detect as insincere.

"You're *crazy*, man. Why do you want to hang out with those guys?"

"You're one to talk. You sit in front of your stupid computer communing with trolls and gnomes all day."

"You hate violence. You can't even watch horror movies. You want to die in some country where they hate our guts? Hey," Wingard said, suddenly looking proud of himself. "I get it. You have a *death wish*."

For once, it seemed, Wingard's brain had not, in fact, completely liquefied from playing Warcraft twenty-four seven.

It was not the first time Sergeant Kenner had invited him to his home, a wistful, low-slung ranch house in the foothills on a couple acres of parched land studded with prickly pear cacti and bleached-out yucca that poked up like feather dusters. He'd been here three times before, mostly, he suspected, at the urging of Mrs. Kenner, who felt sorry for Connor because his mother was dying and always complimented him on his "bravery" and good manners, in the same breath. He *was* exceedingly polite—the good Connor who wanted to kill someone but would undoubtedly say, "Excuse me," before he did.

The Kenners had a seventeen-year-old daughter named Jody. She was Korean. Well, she was American, actually. They'd adopted her at birth, and she spoke contemptuously to her parents, mostly about how much she hated school, how little interest she had in what she called "world affairs," how much weight she had gained (although she was, Connor thought, if anything too thin, and he suspected an eating disorder), and how much they, the Kenners, her adoptive parents, annoyed her. Tonight she wore torn black jeans, a low-cut black knit top with crisscrossing spaghetti straps, and plum-colored, ankle-strap sandals with stacked wedges. Her bottom lip was pierced with silver, her nose studded with gold, and she laughed crudely at the table whenever her parents tried to ask her a simple question such as what had happened to the fifty-dollar check she'd (somehow) cashed that was meant for her school choir retreat.

In the three times Connor had been over to the Kenners' house, Giigee, as she called herself, had finished exactly one meal with them, barely. The other two had resulted in her being sent to her room, not to be seen for the rest of the evening, while Connor and the Kenners watched TV on the sofa together. The third time, she had made it to the end but then threw a butter knife across the table in the direction of her mother. "That's it," Sergeant Kenner had said, and walked around to (Connor hoped) rip Giigee up from the table and kick her out the door or to social services or boarding school or a psychiatric facility or junior boot camp. But, no, Sergeant Kenner pointed to her room, stocked, Connor knew, with iPhone, iPod, iPad, and Netflix, and told her not to come down until she thought long and hard about her behavior.

My God, Connor had thought, the sergeant was a pussycat—or a pussy, as the word got thrown around so frequently at the recruiting station about wannabes who had "fagged out," after "almost" signing up, unofficial talk, of course, which Connor was privy to and took as a warning that he'd better not do the same. But here, in this house, Sergeant Kenner appeared to have no backbone, as emasculated as any man in America. Why would he let Connor see him like this?

Now they were attempting dinner again. Would Giigee give her father the finger as she had last time? Would she spit in the bowl of caramelized carrots as she did when her mother asked her to go easy on her pungent perfume that wafted with deadly astringent force like some biological weapon through the dining room? Would Connor just sit there and watch this as if he'd been a member of the family since birth?

"And what did you do today, honey?" Mrs. Kenner asked him now. She had lit some tall lavender tapers in polished copper candleholders and placed linen napkins in matching copper rings on fleur-de-lis gold-banded dinner plates. A basket of warm and sweet Hawaiian dinner rolls waited in front of Connor. Fish was on the menu tonight, some kind of snapper, imported to this landlocked state. Last time they'd had meatloaf and peas, a dish he thought only existed in fifties sitcoms. Before that Mrs. Kenner had made a Mexican casserole, which Giigee had disliked and nudged away with the glittery red talon of her pinky.

"I went to see someone," Connor answered. Why not? What did he have to lose? "He's a kid who's ill. I think he's going to die." At this, the table went a notch quieter, some perceptible noise cancellation that vacuumed out any false cheer. "They call him the seer because he can read the future. I think he has a respiratory disease of some kind."

"Is it cystic fibrosis?" Mrs. Kenner asked, a bit too brightly for the subject.

"I'm not sure. Anyway, I sat with him for quite a while. It was very...I don't know...serene."

"You're a very good friend to go see him," Mrs. Kenner remarked.

"Connor's a good man," Sergeant Kenner added. He ate close to his plate, more as if he were shoveling in rice than taking bites. "He's going to make one helluva Marine. I'm proud of you, son."

"But I didn't go see him because I was his friend. I've never spoken to him before."

Giigee made some sort of hissing sound, a tire deflating, though Connor wasn't sure it was directed at him or just her general exasperation. He was used to her sounds by now, hisses, tragic sighs, impertinent burps, bellicose snorts, and tried to ignore them. "I thought he could help me. I was going to ask him about my mother. I did tell him my mother was dying. But I didn't ask him what I wanted to."

"You poor dear," Mrs. Kenner said, and reached out to pat Connor's hand. "More salad, anyone?"

"What I really wanted to ask him," Connor went on, realizing that he hadn't quite prepared himself well enough for the question and that the seer couldn't have helped him anyway, "is whether I'm a murderer."

Giigee spit out her food. "Oh. My. God."

"Whether I'm killing her," Connor tried to clarify. "My mother, that is."

Mrs. Kenner laughed nervously. "I can't imagine how I would feel in your situation, but I know all sorts of thoughts must cross your mind. And there's nothing wrong with expressing them either. I think we all know that grief makes us have irrational ideas, don't we, Nelson?"

"I don't know," answered Sergeant Kenner, shoveling food faster into his mouth. "You're the psychology grad. But it sounds right to me. I wouldn't worry about it, son. We know you don't mean it."

"I do mean it," Connor said. "I'm killing her before she dies."

Sergeant Kenner picked up his head. "Con, it can't be easy. But there's no need to be inappropriate. I'm sure you love your mother a whole lot more than you can say."

"I don't see the contradiction," Connor said. Giigee was watching him intently.

"Exactly," Mrs. Kenner said, "and that's what you're expressing with your feelings—"

"But I don't know if I'd call what I'm doing an act of love. It's more like an act of God. God behaving badly in me."

Mrs. Kenner exchanged a glance with her husband. Connor knew what that glance meant. The boy was sicker than they thought, not just sad, but disturbed—yes, that was the word, and he would just barely qualify for the service, though not if he went on like this in public. He would have liked to explain that he had deprived his mother of his company these final days of her life, and that he was causing her heartache by not assuring her he had a future other than one as a soldier in some murderous foreign land

and that he wasn't allowing her to die peacefully with the illusion of her house in order, and that he had no kindness he could fake on her behalf, and that, in this way, he was the agent of her death. It was unpretty all right, and he wished he wasn't responsible for such distress and that he wasn't killing her spiritually as well as physically. He would have liked—or tried—to make this clear if he thought for a moment Sergeant Kenner and his wife would have understood. He knew, though, they wouldn't, and he was not surprised, given all they'd been through with Giigee, when Mrs. Kenner cheerfully observed, "Well, time for dessert, kiddos."

He *was* surprised, however, when he and Sergeant Kenner were having their customary pool game after dinner in the converted garage and Giigee slunk in barefoot and announced she wanted to play. She had never done this before, always disappearing during or shortly after dinner.

She had changed into a more modest outfit, a ruffled skirt sprinkled with wildflowers and a light pink blouse, opened a respectful two buttons at her smooth tan throat and just above her snug pointed breasts. She looked composed, young and womanly, someone whose hand you might ask for in marriage from her father.

"Why don't you kids play," Sergeant Kenner said. "I'm going to hit the sack." He started for his daughter, as if to give her a kiss goodnight, then thought better of it and turned and left.

"Eight ball," Giigee said right away. "You break."

Connor did, but failed to knock in a single ball.

"Five ball in the side pocket," Giigee declared. It was a difficult bank shot requiring passage through a tight channel of balls. He couldn't see why she didn't go for the easy fifteen ball teetering on the edge of the corner pocket.

Then he understood. She ran the table. Connor stood with his pool cue in hand, shifting it from right to left, chalking the tip, murmuring sounds of approval. He hardly knew what to say. She shot with such aggressive confidence that he blinked at the explosive fission of the cue ball smacking the others. Whether with her legs spread like a gunslinger, or with the cue behind her arched back, or with the nonchalance of someone dropping letters in a mailbox, she called and sank every shot. For the game winner—corner right pocket—she stretched across the table. Her blouse slid up her lower back, and the single eye of a tattooed turquoise octopus peeked out at him.

A scratch.

"I've never seen anyone play pool like that," Connor said, dumbfounded at the display.

"But, you see, I lost. I scratched." With her fingernail, she flicked the eight ball against the felt bank. "I always blow it." She appeared sad at this confession.

"You lost on purpose. I saw you shoot the cue ball straight in."

"On purpose? You think there is such a thing?"

"I don't know," Connor said, finding her suddenly fascinating. "Why are you so mean to your parents? They're good people."

She shuffled over to him in her bare feet and ran her hand across his smooth scalp. "You should grow your hair out and dye it strawberry. It would look cool."

"You didn't answer me about your parents."

"What does the word 'good' taste like?"

"Pardon?"

Giigee backed him up against the rack of pool cues on the wall. "Open your mouth. I'll show you what 'bad' tastes like and you can make it all good."

They lay down on a couch, his pants around his knees, her ruffled skirt pushed up to her waist, her bra, which he fumbled to get undone, hanging from her neck like a sling. She grinded against him, but his erection, which had proved so ready at the prospect of sex, now wilted at the act. After a while she stopped moving. "You think I'm ugly." It wasn't a question. "Don't you like my body?"

"Your body is fabulous!" he said, sounding, he knew, like a talk show host praising a guest's new movie.

"So what's wrong then?"

"I don't know...I guess I'm nervous."

"Relax then," she commanded, pushing his face against her tits, but after sucking and licking and stroking and imitating the slew of porno examples on the web to the best of his ability, he sat up.

It was late. He had to get home. "My mother, she's not well..." A mishmash of excuses came pouring out of him. Giigee, unlike what sympathetic girls do in books and movies, didn't reassure him or tell him not to worry about it; she instead stood up, got dressed, and went through the side door without another word, leaving him sitting there with his pants literally around his ankles.

He drove home, after giving the Geo an extra hard kick, cursing its miserable black exhaust.

His mother was half asleep on the couch and trying to speak through a haze of medications. She had lost more weight and her nightgown had slipped off her right shoulder. "Is Suzie here?" he asked her.

"Suz, yes, she's outstanding," his mother said. He guessed this meant she was upstairs. Her parts of speech were decaying as fast as her organs, leaving holes in her sentences, spots in her vision: words disappeared from the page like snatched coins. She lost track of her meds and became confused about the hospice people who visited, making flapping gestures of apology in the air.

He slid the sleeve of her nightgown back up on her shoulder. "I have to get up early," Connor told her. His mother shook her head, laughed and squinted in pain, a sign that the morphine was wearing off. He'd have to give her another pill. Her cancer had spread to her brain, outwitting the latest round of chemo. The doctor had said she had only a one to four percent chance of surviving, calling it a "smart cancer."

She pointed to her heart and the puckered scarred skin around it. "You love me."

"Of course, Mom."

"I want you being happiness." This happened too, especially late at night—her words no longer stayed in orbit with one another and became free planets.

She started to cry; she always did whenever he sat with her long enough. Sometimes he just stroked her back because she seemed to like this. Her emotions came jumpily to the surface, and she would cry and laugh out of any sensible order. Earlier, when Giigee was fruitlessly trying to arouse and suck him into compliance, he had decided that the seer was the only other person he knew who truly comprehended that the coldest ice-blue temperature on earth, the absolute zero of loneliness, could be found in the gap between living and dying flesh.

Her hand was cooler than the seer's and sought the heat of his own.

He saw the papers authorizing him to enlist on the coffee table where he'd left them for the last few days. He saw, too, that his mother had scratched her signature on them. *I want you being happiness.* Spittle dribbled out of her mouth, for she had fallen asleep holding his hand, and though her body had shut down and she would lapse in and out of fitful dreams, her fingers, as if unwilling to cooperate, clamped onto his without surrender.

In the morning, he drove to the recruiting station and waited for Sergeant Kenner and others to show up. Usually, there were about five of them, counting himself and the other poolees who did their calisthenics in the parking lot out front, and then headed off in the van to the dirt trails that snaked through the desert, where they tromped past barrel cacti, mesquite trees, and cholla, hoping a rattlesnake, out for a morning sauna on the rocks, wouldn't slither across their paths.

But neither Sergeant Kenner nor Staff Sergeant Hernandez showed up. He stood around with two other poolees, until Wingard called and said he needed a ride to school.

Connor was relieved. He hadn't looked forward to facing Sergeant Kenner after his abysmal experience with Giigee. For all he knew she was telling her father right now, out of some vindictive rage, that he'd raped her. At school, he tried to get her out of his mind and was glad to have the distraction of working with Wingard—who mercifully didn't bring up the seer—on theater sets for the senior class's production of *Othello*. Afterwards, he quickly left, before Wingard could catch him, and drove back to the recruiting station. He had the signed papers with him and while he still had the nerve he wanted to give them personally to Sergeant Kenner.

A note on the metal front door said the office was closed and would reopen tomorrow. It was handwritten and there was no other explanation.

Connor looked around. Trucks roared past in the undulating heat on their way toward the interstate. His dented Geo parked at the curb looked as if it had been the victim of a can-stomping melee. A woman and her toddler walked by on the sidewalk and glanced at him, the little boy continuing to turn his head and watch Connor until his mother yanked him ahead, as if not wanting her child to stare at the solitary young man waiting under the green-lettered sign that said Marine Corps Recruitment. She pitied him perhaps, or feared for her own child going off to war, or was afraid of Connor or just impatient. He didn't know. He felt he had to deliver these papers to Sergeant Kenner, and if he didn't he'd never do another decent thing with his life or anything that involved sacrifice. It wouldn't have made any sense at all to her, but he was doing this for his mother.

He drove to the Kenners' house. He'd simply run up to the door and hand Sergeant Kenner the papers. If Mrs. Kenner answered, he'd give her the envelope to give to Sergeant Kenner. If Giigee answered...he didn't know exactly what he'd do. He'd deal with that scenario when it happened.

But as he turned up the dirt road between the two saguaro cacti marking the entrance to the Kenners' land, he saw smoke, and then he saw the astonishing sight of the Kenners' home in smoldering rubble. A single fire truck stood by hosing down what had just last night been the converted garage where he had attempted to make love to Giigee. No part of the structure remained standing except the brick chimney.

A cop stopped him before he could drive any closer. Connor opened his window. "What's your business up here?" he asked.

"What happened?"

"You can pretty much see what happened, my friend. Maybe you should turn around now. We're not letting anyone up here."

"Was anyone hurt?"

"Everybody got out all right." The cop, whose radio crackled with urgency, studied Connor's battered car. "You have some ID on you?"

Connor gave him his license, and the cop went to his cruiser to check it out. When he returned, he asked, "What's your connection to these folks?" Connor realized the cop thought he might be involved. This is what arsonists did, right, or at least some of them—returned to the scene of their crime so they could admire the magnitude of their destruction.

"I know Sergeant Kenner. I've got some papers for him." He was about to say he'd been here the previous night, but he suspected this would only cause more alarm. "They're enlistment forms." The cop seemed to soften at this.

"Well, you don't want to bother him now. You better see about giving them to him later."

Then Connor saw Sergeant Kenner himself, a forlorn, hunched-over figure at the back of what had been the master bedroom, poking through the charred ruins of his house with a metal rod. "Can I please just speak to him for a moment?"

The cop, who looked like he wanted to be anywhere but here reeking of smoke, glanced at the pad where he'd written down Connor's name.

"You got a phone number where you can be reached?"

Connor gave it to him. Again, he thought to say something else—that his mother was sick and they shouldn't call because it might really upset her if they identified themselves as the police, but this would cause even more suspicion than admitting he was here last night. His brain was reeling though, and he knew he couldn't hold out much longer without spitting out something that would get him in trouble. "Can I please just give Sergeant Kenner these papers?"

"I'll hand them to him."

"I want to give him my sympathies too." And he did: he liked Sergeant Kenner and felt sad for him. He'd been good to Connor in a straightforward sort of way that uncomplicated his life. And unlike Mrs. Kenner and just about everyone else, Sergeant Kenner never treated him as an object of pity.

The cop relented. "Just don't touch anything," he said and waved Connor past. He could see the cop in his rearview mirror keeping an eye on his car.

He parked the lurching Geo at the end of the wide gravel semicircle and walked around the perimeter of the foundation to where Sergeant Kenner was examining the ground like a man in search of a contact lens. He didn't hear Connor approach, and finally Connor cleared his throat and said, "Sergeant Kenner?" The sergeant glanced up in bewilderment, as if trying to place Connor, then gave him a small, tired wave and went back to searching the ground. "Sergeant Kenner, I'm very sorry about what happened." Connor cleared his throat again. "I really hate to disturb you at this time, but I have my consent papers for you. They're finally signed."

"That's good, Connor."

"Do you want me to bring them by tomorrow? I was hoping to hand them over to you today. I know it's a bad—"

"We have Jody in a safe place," said Sergeant Kenner, his voice weak with exhaustion. "She's going to get the help she needs."

"Sir?"

"She's under watch now. We should have done something before this."

It dawned on him that Sergeant Kenner was telling him Giigee had started this fire, his crazy daughter who not fifteen feet away from where Connor was presently standing had moaned, with more fury than passion, *Fuck me, fuck me.* He pictured Giigee dousing Mrs. Kenner's homemade peach curtains and pleated valences with arcs of gasoline and sloshing the very sofa with its highly flammable hunter green slipcover where she'd squirmed in frustration underneath Connor.

"Mrs. Kenner is fine. She's shaken up, of course, but she's fine. She's staying at a hotel downtown near Jody." Sergeant Kenner leaned a moment on the metal pole. He had been in Vietnam and the first Gulf War and had lost part of his shoulder in Iraq, all of which Connor learned from the other Marines who said the sergeant never laid shit on anybody. "You better bring the papers by tomorrow. Sergeant Hernandez will be there then, I'm sure."

"Yes, sir." Connor started to back away.

"Con…"

"Sir?"

"Did anything happen last night that I should know about?"

"I…I—"

"Was there anything Jody said or mentioned at all that might have led to this? We want to help her. We're on her side. I'm sure you can see that. But she won't talk right now. She won't say a word. They have her on some medication that's keeping her quiet, because, well, she was just screaming her head off and biting people. But I'm looking for a key. You understand that, Con, right? I'm talking to you as a father now. I'm talking to you man to man. I'm asking you as someone who doesn't have a goddamn clue. Is there anything you can tell me about why she's destroyed our lives like this?"

As he was about to answer, hoping to speak with a strength and wisdom beyond his years, he knew his mother had died. He felt it as a touch of her lips. Thrumming with blood, sweet with pleasure, and trembling with wonder—she brushed by.

. .

To Leningrad in Winter

PETER BLUM SAT DOWN at his desk in Financial Aid and looked over the appointments that ran through his lunch hour. The receptionist walked into his office.

"A Herbert Cohen is here to see you. He says he doesn't have an appointment."

Peter felt his head drop the first notch of the day. The receptionist, an impatient work-study student, tapped a pencil against her leg.

"Let me get some coffee before you send him back," he told her.

He couldn't deal with the man this early. Cohen had been pursuing him ever since they happened to sit down at the same cafeteria table four months ago. Cohen had introduced himself, then found out Peter's name. He asked in a hushed voice filled with anticipation: "Would you mind please spelling the last name?"

Apparently, Cohen was able to deduce that this was indeed the "Jewish spelling" of the name, because within five minutes he had invited Peter to join a study group at the temple. "Last week we talked about the Jewish brain. Being a professor you would be interested."

"I'm not a professor. I work in financial aid."

Cohen shrugged as if there were no measurable difference. He wore a green Tyrolean hat that sat up high on his bald head, while he slurped at his lentil soup, his lips a neat inch over the bowl's edge. "It was a very emotional discussion," said Cohen, not letting the subject of the Jewish brain drop. "I know you would have enjoyed it. Some people believe that Jews do better on IQ tests because they are born smarter—genes. Myself, I think it all has to do with the upbringing." He wiped the corners of his mouth. "What is your opinion, Mr. Blum?"

"I have none on that subject," Peter said, excusing himself and getting up. He avoided the cafeteria whenever possible after that. He wasn't interested in joining groups, especially ones that speculated on a superior Jewish brain. If he had any opinion, it was that the world's difficulties had arisen from just such conceits. But one rainy day shortly afterward, Cohen had appeared at the office. "I would like very much for you to have supper with me," he said. The felt on his Tyrolean hat was soaked dark green, despite the equally wet umbrella he dragged behind him. Even his cuffs were dripping. "I've just come from services. I was hoping to see you there."

Peter looked at his calendar—it was Yom Kippur. Cohen had evidently become soggy by walking to the office rather than riding on the holiday. "Mr. Cohen, I am not a religious man by anybody's definition. I don't wish to get involved with the temple here or anywhere else." He had been about to deny that he was Jewish but hated to degrade himself by lying.

Cohen's smile was unflagging. "You would appreciate our discussion groups. I can tell you have a good," he bowed as if to pardon the expression, "Jewish mind."

"Not interested."

"There are so few of us here in town."

"So few of *you*, Mr. Cohen."

"Would you come to dinner—once? Please. After sundown. Here, I have written out the address for you." And he was gone before Peter could refuse again, walking back across campus in the blowing rain.

Later in the evening, finding nothing on TV, not able to play racquetball with his wife, Gail, who had come down with the flu, and mentally incapable of calculating anymore aid applications, Peter—who disapproved of standing anyone up—had driven over to Cohen's, afraid the man would starve himself by not breaking his holiday fast unless Peter arrived.

Cohen's house was a small brick one with a blanket of unraked leaves frozen in bas-relief on the ground and a mezuzah nailed to the doorpost. A boy opened the door and then walked away, leaving Peter stranded in the hall. Cohen came out from the kitchen, beaming over a silver tray piled high with hot, doughy food. "Terrific of you to come," he grinned, and seemed genuinely touched by the visit.

He lived alone with his son, Stuart, a heavy-browed boy of twelve with braces on his teeth, who would shovel food fiercely into his mouth for a brief but intense period and then abruptly stop, letting his jaws lazily masticate the contents, while he squinted at Peter without speaking. The three of them ate together in considerable silence, Cohen giving explanations of the food and instructing Peter to add more salt, if he wanted, to the vegetable tzimmes. When Cohen went into the kitchen to put tea on for dessert, the boy turned on Peter. "What's the story? You with us or against us?"

"What are you talking about?" Peter said, taken aback by the stinging hostility in the boy's voice. It was the first time the sullen child had spoken a word all evening.

"Are you going to fight back or just let them murder us again?"

"Who? *Who?*" Peter cried, his throat itching from the high-pitched excitement of his own voice.

Fortunately, Cohen reentered the room, mildly reproving his son for not letting their guest finish his food in peace. Afterward, Cohen said, there would be plenty of time to talk coconuts.

Peter was unable to take another bite of his strudel. "What talk? What coconuts?" He was becoming alarmed. "I told you I'm not a joiner. I'm only here because it's rude to refuse a dinner invitation. Manners, good conduct, *these* I believe in—"

Stuart stabbed his pastry with a fork.

Cohen, always gracious, smiled and said, "Have you noticed the window decorations around town?" There had been a rash of anti-Semitic vandalism, defacement of property, Jewish property. No one knew why. The small college town hardly had any Jews to speak of. "We are planning to have a race, Mr. Blum. Perhaps you will join us. It's to express our concern for a group of refuseniks who will be running at the same time in Russia. Of course, our other purpose is to show we are not frightened and we will not be driven from our neighborhood."

Stuart stretched back his lips, baring his braces. "It's not as easy as sitting in your office. But, then again, they could find out about you, too, Professor."

"I'm not a professor!"

The boy took out a rumpled pad from his pocket and began making hasty notes, glancing up at Peter as he wrote.

"What are you writing there?"

"Just something so I can remember what you looked like. We might be asked to identify the body."

"Oh, for heaven's sake!" Peter burst out. "You're completely overreacting—talking about being attacked!"

"They write filthy things!" Stuart said with sudden desperation. "I've seen it on the bathroom walls at school: 'Jews eat yellow snow'!"

Cohen nodded solemnly at his son's words.

"That's it?" Peter laughed. "That's what you're so worked up over? A few punks scribbling dirty notes? Think how bad it would have been if they'd really been vile: Jews *sell* yellow snow. Wouldn't that have been vicious!"

Stuart seemed on the verge of tears. "You think it's funny, don't you?"

He did think it was funny, and laughed to himself again, pleased to know that his suspicions about the situation were correct, that their fear was largely self-serving, a chance to affirm their status as members of a persecuted group. So long as the faintest trace of anti-Semitism existed, the Cohens of the world could be counted on to seek it out and make it bold.

"Let's not emphasize our differences," said Cohen, trying to end the meal on a harmonious note. Peter couldn't have agreed more. He wanted no other opportunities to discover how much they differed and tried to make this clear to Cohen by curtly thanking him for the evening, without offering to reciprocate.

Not long afterward, however, he received an invitation from Cohen to attend Stuart's bar mitzvah. At the bottom a note was added: "At the exact moment my son is being bar mitzvahed in America, a Jewish boy in Russia will be having his ceremony over there. It has been arranged. I hope you can come. This is solidarity, Mr. Blum." Peter hated to be ill-mannered, but enough was enough. He threw the card in the trash without another glance. A few weeks later, when he was frantically searching the trash can for an important form he had misplaced, he came up with the invitation instead. It had stuck to the gummy bottom. This time he noticed Cohen had also written something on the back: *To Leningrad in winter— December 2.*

Peter dropped the card as if bitten, then picked it up and stared hard to make sure the words were really there. To Leningrad in winter. The expression was one his grandfather had always used. The old man said it whenever misfortune struck the family. Peter vaguely understood its intention to be inspirational: a Jewish "I have not yet begun to fight!" or "Give me liberty or give me death!"—except not that insistent. The difference was the emphasis on winter. Being Jews, they would do things the difficult way—hope to win, pray for freedom, but not so fast. In winter, that's when they would all enter the city to live in peace, winter, the eternal season for the long-suffering Jews. Sometime in winter they would finally succeed.

His grandfather had whispered the phrase when Peter came home from school one day with his face streaked in blood and a permanent tooth gone from the bottom row. He'd fought a boy on the bus, after turning around to the oversized eighth grader and offering him a stick of gum. "Drop dead, Jew," the kid had responded. Peter turned back around, thought about it for a moment, and felt the shame quicken and burn his neck purple as an eggplant. During a momentary lapse of concern for self-preservation, he exploded in a frenzied assault on the larger boy, standing on his seat and slugging down for a violent minute, then picking up his heavy geography book and batting the kid's ear. When they got off the bus, Peter took his beating. His brother, Rudy, wheezing and cheering him on, using an inhaler for his asthma, stood firmly on Peter's side, the only person. On the way home, he held up Peter's chin, letting him bleed on his sleeve, assuring Peter he wouldn't get punished for losing the tooth. It was later that night, after Peter came back from an emergency visit to the dentist and was lying in bed with a wad of cotton in his mouth, listening to Rudy heap praise on him for his courage, that their grandfather tiptoed into the dark room to offer his sympathy: "To Leningrad in winter," he whispered warmly in Peter's ear, stroking the boy's arm with his fingers that worked invisible threads all day long. Then he crept out again, as if not expecting the brothers to notice him.

Peter always thought he detected some mockery in his grandfather's voice, aside from the old man's regular screwiness. Perhaps he had just interpreted it that way when Rudy died from pneumonia and his grandfather mixed the phrase in with the rest of the prayers for the dead. There seemed little wisdom in continuing to believe the long trip was worth it then. The old man's saying pointed less to a superior truth than to a covenant embarrassing in its one-sidedness. Only one promise ever went unbroken. Death would want you as a Christian, as a Jew, from families with or without blood or mezuzahs on their doors—why make the journey any more painful than necessary? Who was there to fool that it would ever be any other place than Leningrad in winter?

•

Peter pushed his coffee cup aside and watched as Cohen stepped into the office now, polite but determined. What more could the man ask of him? He'd flatly refused to consider the study group; he'd eaten Cohen's food with haughty ingratitude; he'd ignored Stuart's bar mitzvah. How much rejection could even Cohen stand?

"Mr. Blum, I have stopped in to remind you of the race this Sunday." Cohen laid a flier on the desk. On December 2, a group of refuseniks would be running ten kilometers in Leningrad to protest the harsh emigration policies. Jews in America could show support by running an equal distance at the same time. "Leningrad is very cold in the winter, but we will be warm running together. Will you join us, Mr. Blum?"

"Not at all." The plaintive note in Cohen's voice angered Peter. "Have you thought about the forces you're dealing with here? Can you actually believe that the Soviet Union, with an arsenal of nuclear weapons that can destroy the world twenty times over, will do anything but yawn and roll over at this feeble protest?"

Cohen tucked in his chin. His eyes, for the first time, seemed tired. "Mr. Blum. In the middle of the night a man is taken from his home. For three hours his kidneys are punched. When he must come back for a second visit, what is put in his mouth is worse than dirt. When he continues asking permission to go to Israel, he is sent instead to Siberia. For five, for ten years hard labor. The muscles in his back bulge out like grapefruit. At night the cold eats him up alive. All this happens for just asking. Mr. Blum. I ask you. What is our alternative?"

"I have no alternative, Mr. Cohen. I admit that without shame." He wasn't being blunt enough, that was the problem. He had to make Cohen understand he had the wrong man: that he had absolutely no right to expect this of him. "I also confess to not pretending that I have a solution—or caring if I do." He waited for these last words to get through. Cohen continued standing respectfully, meeting Peter's eyes with unnatural hope, his back rigid with patience. "You'll excuse me now, please. I'm very busy today." He picked up his appointment log.

Cohen replaced his hat and apologized. Without another word, he left. Peter resisted the urge to call him back. He wouldn't get trapped by Cohen's abject humility, not today. Today he was too busy to chase butterflies to Leningrad.

At six o'clock, he was finally able to go home. He took the flier from his shirt pocket, glancing at it as he drove. The Russian runners were sketched with awesome physiques: comic book characters with shoulders cut from the same tread as tractor tires—the women with each breast a boxing glove! The sinews in their legs could have squeezed a tugboat to death. Then he noticed the signature at the bottom of the illustration. Cohen's son, Stuart, had done the drawing, making the refuseniks as heroic in their musculature as his little mind could imagine. Peter tried to picture his grandfather as a muscle-bound refusenik jogging into Leningrad. He could smell the old man's sweet breath (he ate Passover jellies all year long). His grandfather would rub his slack, rough cheek against Peter's smooth one. Suddenly the tears would start and the crazy muttering and he'd clutch the boy fearfully, not daring to let him go. Peter would squirm out from his grip, leaving the old man trembling and weeping softly, and he'd run outside to play.

He brushed the wetness from his face, already making up an excuse to Gail that his eyes were red because of working without his glasses again. When he drove up, she was setting the table. It was a big maple table they'd bought at an auction seven years ago, much too big for the two of them, although neither of them had ever wanted to mention this. After they had married, they'd tried to have children. When a year went by without success, they went in for tests—first Gail, then Peter. The doctor assured them they were both fertile. He gave Gail some pills to help her along. Nothing happened. They visited other doctors, and all agreed that conception was not only possible but likely; they were a young, eager, healthy couple in their twenties, with no congenital or developmental impairments, with good hearts and lungs, with determined genes and capable organs. Nature had prepared them ideally. "The situation," one doctor said, giving them a phrase they could use comfortably, "looks most promising."

Then the visits started: to an herbalist; to a naturopath; to a hypnotist; and even to a psychic. "Maybe we should stop trying so hard," Gail suggested. "We're getting in our own way," and they had tried hard not to try.

One night, years later, while they were watching television (in the commercial a man was shouting at them to buy a suit), an unmistakable glance had been exchanged. The next day Peter came home from work and said they should withdraw their applications from the adoption agencies. Gail agreed. She, too, could no longer take the accusatory looks—the irrational blame each felt from the other. They could stop punishing themselves if they wanted. They could agree to stop. They could live with the decision. Perhaps they had even wanted this all along. They would never know. What they did know is that they were finished if they continued. It would have to end.

When the phone woke them early Sunday morning, Peter thought it was an alarm being sounded by charging troops. He'd been riding over the snow in a carriage, with hundreds of cheering men behind who kept following him and wouldn't leave him alone. And there was someone else, a pathetic figure in an overcoat, with his feet wrapped in rags and ice dripping from his gray beard.

"Mr. Blum. It is a fine winter morning."

Cohen, it had been Cohen. Even in dreams he got through.

"Once," said Peter. "Just this once. That's all."

"Don't go anywhere," Cohen said breathlessly. "I'll pick you up."

He had hugged the Cohen figure in his dream, a sudden burst of concern and pity for the man—Cohen half frozen, with a tattered band of fur for a hat—wetting each of Cohen's cheeks with his tears. His pillow had still been damp this morning when the phone rang.

Gail came back into the room, wrapped in a blanket. "Who was that?"

"Cohen," said Peter, embarrassed at having to bring up the man's name so often. "I told him I'd run."

Her shoulders sagged beneath the blanket. "I thought we were going to lunch and a movie this afternoon?"

"Nyet," Peter said. "Race today. Must get samovar boiling." He folded his robe around him like a heavy fur coat and marched into the bathroom.

A half-hour later, Cohen pulled into the driveway. One side of his long Plymouth was painted with a thick, black swastika.

Gail screamed from the upstairs window. Peter, running in place outside, leaped back into the doorway.

"You see," said Cohen, "how bad it is getting."

The robustness Peter had been feeling drained from his legs. Cohen unlocked the door from inside and pushed it open, slicing the giant swastika in half. From the back of the car, the muffler thumped, and when Cohen revved the engine, the pungent exhaust fumes stung Peter's eyes. Gail tapped at the window, concern on her face. Peter raised his hand not to worry and slowly got into the car.

"Keep alert," was all Cohen said to him on the way over. Peter felt calmer once he was inside the chugging vehicle, the heater generous with its warmth, set permanently on high as a result of missing all its knobs. He closed his eyes to relax but suddenly jerked forward when something groaned in the back seat. It was Stuart. The boy had been curled under his coat asleep. He awoke now, rubbing his eyes. As soon as he noticed Peter, he glared savagely at him. Peter turned back around, taking a deep breath and wondering how Cohen had ever snuck into his dreams as a trusted comrade.

Four men were huddled together at the park where the race was to start. They broke from their circle and came puffing over in single file, all of them looking older than Cohen, who seemed sixty himself.

"They got you," said one of them. He wore a small yarmulke and clutched a knit stocking cap. "Maybe one of us should stay behind with the cars."

"I, myself, can live with the damage," said Cohen. "I think it is more important that we all participate." The men nodded. "Are we ready?" Cohen asked.

Peter looked around. This was it? Seven people? No one else was coming?

"We begin at nine o'clock on the dot," said Cohen, unfolding a map of the route. "At least one of us must finish the race by ten o'clock—the same time the refuseniks will stop on the steps of the emigration ministry in Leningrad. Is this understood?"

"Why's the time matter?" Peter said, and then realized by the sharp looks that he had asked the wrong question. He added quickly, "Shouldn't we stick together in case there's trouble?"

Cohen paused to study each of their faces. It struck Peter that Cohen must be the town's rabbi. Everything in his manner presumed a congregation in front of him. "We are here to race together," he began, "to run alongside one another, to support each other when we tire, to go on even when we think we can't. Together our feet will pound. Together our hearts will beat. Together Jews will be running all over the globe. If none of us here finishes the race, no one will know—no one in Moscow, no one in Leningrad, no one in Jerusalem. No one. Except us." Cohen stopped dramatically and walked over to his car, patting the swastika tenderly. "And them." He checked his watch. "It is time, my friends. Let us jog."

They lined up where the path began, the man with the yarmulke looking around, then all of them glancing over their shoulders, up at the cold sky and the bare trees, back at their cars, down at the stiff soles of their sneakers. "Let's go already!" Stuart snapped. He was on his mark next to Peter.

"To Leningrad!" Cohen shouted, and they were off, huffing and grunting, asking each other if they'd gone a mile yet. A white-haired man in an electric-blue jogging suit, with the sales tag still on the sleeve and the whole uniform sparkling with zippers, shuffled along beside Peter. "So let me tell you, young man," he said, "I'm glad it's not the *real* winter what's doing in Russia." Then he suddenly fell to one knee, grabbed his side, and screamed out as if being chewed by all his zippers, "The bacon! The bacon!"

Cohen ran up and put a hand on the man's shoulder. "You got a stitch, Morris?" The man nodded guiltily, confessing that he had eaten seven strips of bacon for breakfast, fearing that he would need the extra protein.

"I'll run behind with him," the man in the yarmulke offered. Cohen waved his hand and the rest of them moved forward again.

Peter ran out in front with Stuart, gradually lengthening the distance between himself and the other men. When he glanced back a while later, the three were taking tiny steps, slowing to a halt. One of them indicated he needed to pee and stepped into the bushes; another sat down on a log, his head between his knees. After a mile more, Cohen dropped out, dragging one foot lamely behind the other in an exhausted gait. "Go!" he cried, shooing Peter and Stuart away with his hat. "I'll be all right…GO!"

Peter hurried ahead, not looking back, as if fleeing a burning city. Stuart kept a few competitive steps in front of him, speeding up whenever Peter got too close. They passed underneath a winding canopy of apple trees, the branches frozen sharp and heavy without blossom. "Take it easy," Peter called. "We're supposed to be running together. You're going to wear yourself out."

"Eat my dust!" Stuart spit back, his bony arms slashing the air at his sides. What a mouth. And a rabbi's son, yet. The kid would be hiding around the bend, waiting to bite his ankles if he didn't watch out. And where was his mother? Was Cohen a widower or abandoned? Maybe that was the source of the child's hostility.

Peter circled the pond, slowing down a little. He'd have to be careful not to stretch his muscles too fast in the cold. The air bit into his lungs, and even when he exhaled on his hands, the breath chilled before it could bounce back to warm his face. Along the path, he began seeing the first evidence of trouble: a swastika painted over the slats of a bench. And farther down, carved deep into the soft bark of a birch, were the letters *KKK*, with an arrow pointing around the scarred trunk. The initials translated into a column with a three word message:

KILL
KIKE
KIDS

What kind of a sick mind would think of such things? It began to anger him, make his toes curl—make him wish they would dare show their faces. He would spring up as he had years ago on the bus and smash the sneering faces back into their holes. Like diseased rats. Like nothing fit to live. Carbuncles. Slop. He stretched out his legs.

His mouth pulled back at the corners. He lunged forward across the frozen ground—past bales of barbed wire; past men in trench coats, hissing to each other over their two-way radios; past a gleaming white missile, nearly invisible in the snow and dragged on rails as high as a two-story building. He ran past—knocking tanks and roadblocks out of the way, galloping over the heads of soldiers, flicking rifles off their shoulders with a tap of his hooves. Tiny capillaries burst in his throat and he tasted blood. Someone called from behind and he raced on, each foot cracking down on the solid earth.

"Stop, *please!*"

It was Stuart. Peter had left him a hundred yards behind, floundering to catch up. He hopped over to Peter, dangling one foot in the air. "I stepped in some *dog shit*." He lifted the soiled foot higher, as if to show it were permanently ruined. "I can't go anymore. My sides hurt." Peter was bent over, squeezing his own sides to keep his lungs from exploding. He looked at his watch. Twenty-five minutes left to finish the race. "Come on, we'll go slower."

"You go," Stuart said, scraping his shoe with a stick. "I can't do any more."

"Are you letting a little tiredness stop you?"

"It *hurts*."

"Look, you can't stay here alone. You see all the remarks around here? The people who wrote this stuff are sick, *sick!* Now come on. We'll do an easy pace." He checked his watch. He could carry the little bastard and still make it. He could do it. He could do it if they moved right away.

"I'm waiting for my dad."

"Who knows where he is! Let's go. You're coming, understand?" And he reached for Stuart's arm. The boy immediately collapsed on the ground, shrieked, and grabbed hold of a fence nearby. Peter began methodically peeling Stuart's fingers off, dragging him out of reach of the fence. He almost had him clear when Stuart yanked at his hair, making Peter look up and see in the distance a water tank painted with the most childish slur yet. A memory slowly rolled past him, turned and started back, gathered momentum, and finally smacked the center of his forehead with such icy force that he sunk to his knees like a slain elephant. Emblazoned on the water tank in bright yellow paint,

JEWS SELL YELLOW SNOW

Silly puffs of air came out of Peter's mouth when he tried to speak. His throat constricted from the astringent taste of his own foolishness and rage, and he struggled for breath. Finally his voice came in an abrupt fury: "YOU! You wrote all this! *You* those swastikas! *You* those sick comments! *You* your own father's car! *You*," and he stumbled toward the boy, grabbing him by the collar and twisting it down to the breastbone. "You little monster—you stirred up all this hatred, didn't you?"

Stuart tried to escape the choking grip; his sweatshirt was a large knot and he was hanging from it. "Nobody cared! Nobody was doing anything!" he pleaded in his defense. And when Peter rose up on his legs, the boy fell to his knees, cringing from a hand that struck his face hard, making his head ring against the fence post and blood spurt instantly from his mouth.

Peter stepped back, horrified. The boy, dazed and whimpering, lay inert against the fence, one shoulder cocked as if he were talking on the telephone. Peter looked closer and saw that he had not so much split the boy's lip as seemed to have unzipped it neatly along a wide line. Then Stuart parted his mouth and a bubble of blood popped, revealing inside the broken fitting of his braces.

"I'm going for help," Peter said, but only took a few steps backward, staring into the boy's mouth, transfixed and frightened by the deep welling of blood.

He found a patch of ice that he slammed with a rock, chopping frantically, shoveling the pieces into his scarf and then returning to Stuart.

But the boy, seeing the bundle coming straight for his mouth, screamed, "Don't hit me again!"

"Don't *say* that. I'm not going to hit you. It was an accident…" but Stuart raised his hands protectively and squeezed back against the fence.

Peter knelt down and studied the wound. He was in awe of its will to bleed. He kept fighting a strong urge to let himself be drawn deeper, much closer; he forced himself to turn away. After he did, he could still feel the pulling, the suction of a cooling glass on his skin. He had, for a moment, utterly lost himself in the boy's flowing blood.

"My mouth really hurts," Stuart said. There was a scared look on his face. "When's it going to stop?" He meant the blood, and Peter—gently this time—pressed the scarf to the boy's mouth, showing him how much pressure to use.

"You won't tell, will you?" Stuart asked.

"Shush now. Hold that on tight."

"I won't tell on you. I swear I won't."

Peter strapped the boy's legs around his waist, heaved the body onto his back, and then stood up and started running. He ran into a cornfield, crushing the brown, frosted stalks under the weight of the both of them. He forgot which way he was supposed to go, and Stuart kept turning him in the right direction, riding close like a jockey to his neck. His kidneys began to hurt from the strain and the bouncing, and he thought about how in two days he would be thirty-six. For five years, he'd been lucky and careful enough not to even have a cavity. If he slipped on a patch of ice now, he'd break both their necks.

"Hurry!" Stuart breathed in his ear.

Peter wrenched his head forward and kicked out his legs. He'd given over the rest of his body to the boy; only his chin bobbed freely. His shoulders ached enough to tear off in the next strong wind. He had fifteen minutes, a mile and a half to go. He had 370 million more breaths if he lived until eighty. He'd figured it out on his calculator last week. He could use most of them now. He could use most of his share and still hope for a decent life with whatever was going to be left.

The Horse Burier

THE SISTERS WANTED TO bury Lulu on their farm, so they called Henry's son, Landon, to do the job. Landon owned and operated a front-end loader with a backhoe. He mostly worked construction but took side jobs too, including horse burial. He worked nights and weekends to support his ex-wife and two kids. Several years ago he'd gotten into trouble gambling beyond his means—way beyond them—and Henry hoped that after a divorce, bankruptcy, and visits from mirthless men with snake-eyed determination, his son's problems were now behind him.

Still, it was clear his son had never disliked him more, and when he called Henry early in the morning, Landon's voice was low and begrudging.

"What do you need me for?" Henry asked him.

"Pipes," Landon said.

It was seven a.m. Henry had finished his first of two cups of coffee before he'd take his morning walk and then afternoon nap. His right hip had been replaced six months before, and though that side of him was good now, his left hip had started acting up. He couldn't sit for long without it stiffening and favored it on his walks. Before retiring a year ago from Western Waterworks, he'd crawled around in ditches checking water lines for the county, and if he knew anything, it was where all the water pipes ran across easements on private property.

"I can't locate anything without seeing where the grave is going to be. I'll have to go with you."

"I suppose so," said Landon.

"You don't want the same trouble again," Henry said.

"I don't need you reminding me of that."

Once, when digging a grave for a horse and working at night to beat a deadline, Landon had struck a water main. The damage interrupted service for two hundred homes, necessitated twenty man-hours of repairs, and cost four thousand dollars. Landon's insurance company had upped his rates so prohibitively that Henry was afraid to ask if his son was still paying the premium. Surely, he wouldn't be that stupid to go without. Then again, it wouldn't be the first time Landon had taken chances. He'd once jumped from the roof of a friend's house when he wasn't even drunk. He had landed on the target trampoline but had bounced into a shed, breaking it and his collarbone. On a Boy Scout camping trip, he'd decided he could wander off solo one morning and find a shortcut across a raging river, only to wind up clinging to a tree midstream for three hours until he was rescued.

He had not entirely outgrown such adolescent shenanigans at thirty-five years old, his latest being the ill-conceived construction of a zip line for his two sons across his junked-up backyard. The zip line had snapped and whipped back into the face of Jeremiah, his thirteen year old, resulting in eighteen stitches and unending teasing from the boy's classmates who nicknamed him Zipper Face. As with much of his life, Landon's actions had been well intentioned but poorly executed. Or maybe, as in the case of gambling, just poorly intentioned too.

Chad, Jeremiah's younger brother, had asked Henry recently what their father was a like as a boy. Henry froze up, completely unable to answer, fearful his own biases would come through and confuse or sadden the child. Every word he said to Landon now was so measured. "Your father was a funny little rascal," Henry finally offered, ruffling his grandson's hair. "Just like you." Chad waited for more. Nothing came and finally his grandson, puzzled at the brevity of his usually forthcoming grandfather, went off to play one of the two video games Henry kept at his house.

With the dregs of his coffee, Henry took a painkiller for his left hip, the pain having flared up while he sat and stared out the window at two hummingbirds fighting over the feeder. He had read that their hearts could beat 1,200 times a minute. Could his own heart even muster a couple beats per hour with all its despairing sludge? But that was the self-pity talking again. Meg had been gone for two years now. It was time to move on, as everyone advised him.

Until Landon called, the phone had not rung in three days. Even the telemarketers seemed to have forgotten him. Landon contacted him only when he needed a favor. Meanwhile, Jenny, Henry's daughter, the child he had always thought would dote on him, lived two thousand miles away in Rhode Island with her sculptor boyfriend; they barely scraped by on a rocky farm they'd gone into hock over. No, there was nothing to do but bury a dead horse. A dead horse who had loved and been loved by two old ladies who probably never felt sorry for themselves a day in their lives.

He knew these two old ladies. He'd been up to their farm a few times over his forty years living in Meldrum, a once sleepy rural Colorado town that was presently exploding as a bedroom community for Denver sixty miles south. While all around them other ranchers and farmers sold off their property to developers, the sisters held out. Now they were ringed by subdivisions, their land worth far more than they could pull out of the ground growing sweet corn and winter wheat. And by the looks of the fallow fields, he wasn't sure how much they were doing of that anymore.

He'd met them through his wife, Meg. Esther and Gladys were their names, and one winter they both came down with the flu. Though near death, they'd been unwilling to leave the farm. Meg, a nurse for county health services, had gone to check on their welfare after a neighbor worrying over them had made a call to the Senior Health Outreach. Fretting about her going alone on a February day forecast to have a blizzard, Henry had driven her up to the sisters' farm and waited in the car with the heater running while Meg went inside and checked their vitals. She couldn't persuade them to go to a hospital. They were proud to say they'd never been in such a place, not even when they were born.

She was able to give Esther, who was the sicker of the two and severely dehydrated, an IV, getting her fever down from 105 degrees with the help of a cool bath and aspirin. She also insisted on staying overnight to watch over them, telling Henry, who'd been reluctant to leave, to come back in two days. The snow had started falling so fast and heavy it was if a plush blindfold had been slapped across the windshield. When he did come back, he found both women on the upswing. Henry was quite sure Meg had saved their lives, or at least Esther's. The sisters, though embarrassed to be at the mercy of anyone's help, showed their appreciation with a month of homemade pies, dropped off at Henry and Meg's door. Henry would see Gladys run up, ring the bell just like his daughter had done playing ding-dong-ditch as a mischievous ten-year-old, and then jump back in their pickup before anyone could say a word to them. Over the years, he'd also seen one or the other riding their beloved mare, Lulu, along the dirt road in front of their farm, on the way to the little country store that had closed a year ago and been replaced by a 7-Eleven.

When she was dying, Meg came out of a stupor one morning to plead, "Promise me, Henry, promise me!" She spoke desperately. "I promise," he said. "Promise me!" she screamed, squeezing his hand with astonishing strength. Her eyes were wild and her forehead soaked with sweat. The nurse came rushing in. He'd never heard her speak with such fright about anything.

And what did she want him to promise anyway? He would never find out. She was dead two days later. That he would try to be happy? That he would marry again or never marry? That he would not show his disappointment in Landon any more than had been obvious over the years? If he could have figured this out, if he could have believed she was in the least bit lucid and wanted him to achieve some goal, some meritorious purpose, he might not be the miserable, aimless bastard he felt himself to be now.

"Thank you for coming," Esther said. The two sisters stood with him and Landon in the open meadow where they wanted Lulu buried. They'd camped here last night with a shotgun to keep the vultures and coyotes from scavenging the horse. The mare had been part of their lives for twenty-eight years, and well, *goodness*, Gladys said, she was going to have a proper burial and not be carted off to some rendering plant!

Henry nodded. Landon pulled his backhoe around to a slight rise in the meadow where the sisters wanted Lulu's grave. The sisters' farmhouse was a mile away, as required for the burial, and as far as Henry could tell there wasn't any water source close enough to be a problem. In the distance rose the Rockies, still snowcapped at the end of May. To the east, a new development of three-story homes with decks as big as his house's main floor marched toward the sisters' open land like a military campaign. He could imagine catapults firing burning bales of hay at the sisters in an effort to uproot them. Or maybe they were just savvy businesswomen, holding out until the money became so good they couldn't resist. Seeing them kneel beside the dead mare, its bulging, translucent eyes sightless in rigid death, stroking the blaze marking the horse's face and whispering last words into the still pitched ears, he couldn't help thinking they were also saying goodbye to the farm and perhaps all else. Near ninety, how much longer could they operate independently out here, no matter how fierce their determination?

Tears, involuntary, surprising, unwelcome, ran down his cheeks. The last afternoon of Meg's life the cancer had rendered her unable to speak at all. She'd been moved to hospice a month before. Landon had driven over every day after work, and Jenny had come from back East as often as she could, calling twice a day if she couldn't. They'd been devastated by her early death, he knew, just short of her sixty-fifth birthday. But she had not been their whole lives as she had been Henry's, and he hardly could think what to do with himself some days other than walk around the house talking to her, the loneliness so acute he clapped his hands over his ears and screamed *shut up shut up shut up!* at himself. He didn't hear her voice, just his, and he wished he would be crazy enough to hear her talk back to him. But it was just silence upon silence like a hollowed-out wind or a starless night seen through a porthole.

"Any problem?" Landon asked him.

"I'll be okay," Henry said.

"What?"

He realized his son was talking about something else entirely and hadn't noticed his tears. Henry turned away, wiped his face. The sisters, however, were watching him intently. "What problem?"

"The pipes. Am I going to hit any when I dig?"

"You're fine." The pipes ran through the neighbor's property to the eastern quadrant of the sisters' land. Where they wanted the grave wouldn't be a problem. He knew because he'd been up here a number of visits when retrenching had taken place. At one time, the water for the farmlands around here was pumped from a water tower. But that wasn't enough to handle the development, and now other aquifers had been tapped. Pipes crisscrossed the area delivering the water to a new treatment plant six miles south. "You're safe to dig."

Landon lowered the backhoe's boom and struck the ground with the bucket, scraping off the topsoil in deft strokes. Before he became known for his expertise burying horses, he'd once dug a hole too shallow and narrow. When he'd put in the horse—more like slotted it—the hooves had stuck straight up above the ground like tiki torches. These days he dug more generous holes, allowing the thousand-pound creatures to be laid to rest on their sides, if they fell in right. "Ten feet going to be okay?" he asked the sisters.

"That will be just fine," the sisters said in unison. They had told Landon they didn't want quicklime put on top of Lulu, just her buried deep enough to be safe from coyotes or dogs digging her up. They would plant grass on top and mark the grave when the time came. Lulu alone, Henry thought, would keep them from selling the place. How they loved that animal.

He had to admit that when his son was focused, no one could do a better job. You wouldn't think he'd be irresponsible enough to gamble away his mortgage payments and his wife's savings too as he did five years ago, and then a year later wonder why she was leaving him and petitioning for full custody of the kids. He had no idea about his son's present love life, if he'd even dated anyone since the divorce. Landon worked twelve hours a day to make good on his obligations. Henry couldn't fault his son for a thing now. He'd said as much to Landon, but Landon had just grunted in return.

"He's a good man, your son," Gladys said, as if reading Henry's thoughts. "He called us back right away when we came to him with our problem. Not everyone is so willing to bury a horse. We would have been out of luck if he hadn't come. You all…" Gladys turned away, looked blankly at her sister. Esther put her hand on her sister's thin shoulder. She finished her sister's thought, knowing it as well as her own. "You all have always been there for us when we needed you," she told Henry who nodded, though he shouldn't have taken credit for what was all Meg's doing. He swallowed hard remembering her up here with these two ladies in the snowstorm when they were sick. He couldn't get her to leave them for anything. He wanted her to come back with him and have her call an ambulance and make the sisters go to the hospital. "There's no forcing them," Meg had said.

"Then they're just being reckless," Henry had fired back, sitting in the car with Meg, the car's heater running at full blast.

"Maybe," Meg said, "but they have their principles and you got to respect that."

Principles, yes, that was the issue, wasn't it? He had a lot of time now to think about principles and whether his own had or had not done the job they were supposed to in his life. When Meg got out of the car that snowy afternoon, he wondered if he'd ever see her again—the radio was calling the storm the blizzard of the century. He did, of course, see her again, and her bond with these ladies and her respect for their implacable will, well, that will was the same in her. She was always prepared to make a sacrifice, even for two old obstinate ladies who wouldn't budge on selling their land any more than going to a hospital. Maybe that's what Meg had wanted him to promise. He'd show some spunk in the right direction when the time came.

Landon sat up in the cab, wearing coveralls and wraparound sunglasses, getting bumped around even with the stabilizers by the clawing backhoe lashing the ground with angry blows now that he'd hit the heavier clay soil. Such work was nasty on the back and kidneys, and Henry wondered how long Landon could do this without incurring some kind of disability.

At the height of Landon's problems, with not enough money even to pay for his kids' soccer registration, he had asked for a loan. Henry took care of the soccer registration and made sure the family had food and weren't foreclosed on, but he wouldn't loan Landon any extra cash because he feared his son would gamble it away. Landon said he had to have it. Henry told him he should have thought of that before. One night two men came to Landon's house, and unlike in the movies when they might have hit him across the kneecaps with a crowbar, these "associates" calmly requested Landon, in front of his wife, Linda, sign over the title to his Ford truck. It was either that or they'd take Landon and do to him what did happen to such people in movies.

Somehow, with the help of an ex-cop he knew, Landon got the gorillas off his back, because he still owed them far more than his truck was worth. But he also never forgave Henry for not loaning him the money when it could have stopped the men from stripping him of his truck and his dignity in front of Linda. He blamed Henry for that humiliation and for Linda's leaving him. But Henry had not made Landon gamble for days at a time and show up sleepless in front of his worried family. Henry was not the one who lost money at casinos in retooled Colorado mining towns—savings that Linda had put away for the kids' educations.

Meg had prevailed upon Henry to please, for the sake of family peace, make a good-faith gesture of giving him a loan. She called it a symbolic act, if nothing else. Henry refused; he was adamant in his opposition; he didn't believe in symbolic acts that had no force behind them; it was time for Landon to face facts. Meg wanted the loan to come directly from Henry, but eventually she gave the money to Landon herself. It was too late by that point to save the marriage or get back his truck. For all Henry knew he had gambled away that money too. What he did know for certain was that Landon had not used the word "Dad" once, or even addressed Henry by name, for over four years, ever since his divorce. He was just "you."

The hole, finished now, had a mound of dirt beside it. Landon got down from his machine and came over to where Henry and the sisters were standing. "She's too big for me to get inside the loader, so I'm going to have to push her in. You good with that?"

"We're okay with it," Esther said. "But we don't want to watch you pile dirt on top of her. We're not delicate about it. We just want to remember her all clean."

"Fair enough," said Landon and climbed back up. He turned the equipment around to use the front loader. Lulu lay about five feet from the pit. Landon inched the loader forward, slowly nudging the animal until he pushed her into the grave. She landed with a thump on her right side, her legs sticking up at a slight angle against the south wall.

The sisters came over to Henry with a paper grocery bag they'd been holding. "Here you are," they said, handing him the sack. Inside were a bouquet of daisies and a legal-size envelope with Lulu's name printed in blue marker on the front. He looked at the hole, he looked at the horse that now filled it, he looked at the sisters. He realized they wanted him to somehow get down in the ten-foot hole and respectfully place the letter and flowers on top of Lulu. "We'd be so grateful," Esther said.

"Landon," Henry called up to his son, who was waiting for the sisters to walk off so he could start filling in the grave.

"What?"

"Come down here."

"Why?"

"Please."

Landon shut off the motor and lumbered down from the cab.

"Excuse us a moment," Henry said to the sisters, whose firm smiles clearly indicated their expectation that the bouquet and letter would be laid by a kind and tender hand on Lulu.

Henry guided Landon a few feet away from the sisters. Holding the daisies and the note, he felt as if he might be courting someone rather than burying a dead horse.

"What's wrong?" Landon asked. "I've got to get back soon."

"Listen, they want us to put these with Lulu."

"So throw them in there."

"That's disrespectful. I think it's really important to them."

Landon glanced over at the sisters. They had turned their attention to the grave and were peering down at Lulu in her final resting place.

"Well, what do you want me to do about it?" Landon asked. How he wished his son could say one sentence to him without contempt.

"I'll have to get down there," Henry explained.

Landon looked away. His eyes were bloodshot from lack of sleep. His son wasn't a drinker, never had been. He'd gotten so drunk one time when he was sixteen that he'd wound up with alcohol poisoning and never touched liquor again. Instead he'd turned to gambling, telling Henry two years later when it came time for college and he refused to go that he wanted to be a professional poker player. Henry had ridiculed the idea, which he dearly regretted, because his scorn infuriated the boy and only made him more determined to prove Henry wrong. Well, he hadn't been wrong, just tactless, and now his six-foot-three, two-hundred-fifty-pound son spent most of his days squeezing his frame into a cab meant for a man half his size. "I'll lower you down there. It's the fastest way. We can't walk a mile back and get a ladder," Landon said.

Henry looked at the front loader. His bones ached at the thought of getting inside the bucket. "Okay," he agreed.

They walked over to tell the sisters.

"We hope it's not putting you out too much," said Esther, pulling at the cuffs of her jacket, its suede collar worn with holes.

"No trouble at all," said Henry, thinking how could he say otherwise to these two?

Landon got back up in the cab and Henry lay down in the bucket, folding his arms across his chest like a dead man. On his way down to a dead horse. "Careful now—"

Landon jerked the bucket up, rolling Henry toward the back. Henry closed his eyes, fully expecting Landon to drop him from an unnatural height, but his son lowered him smoothly as far as the loader could reach. He had to jump down a couple feet to the ground.

He squeezed in between the horse's back and the right wall of the grave, then placed the flowers and envelope on the horse's neck, giving the stiff creature a pat. "Done!" he shouted up.

And here, when he tried to turn around to walk back to the loader, is where he slipped and felt something pop. He fell flat upon the horse's neck.

Landon called down. "You okay?"

"I don't think so," said Henry. He was unable to move. The horse smelled of rot. Flies buzzed Henry's face. Coarse hairs from the animal's mane probed his nostrils like toothpicks.

"What's wrong?"

"I—I can't move." He had to save his breath. Even talking was painful.

"Get back in the bucket," Landon said.

"I can't," Henry protested. "Have the sisters call for help."

"They left," Landon said.

"Left?"

"They didn't want to see the dirt piled on. Listen, just drag yourself into the bucket, and I'll get you out of there, okay?"

"You don't understand, Landon. I *can't* move." It wasn't that he didn't want to; his will had nothing to do with it.

"You sure?"

"For God's sake, I'm certain."

"Okay, then," Landon said.

"Okay *what?*"

And then Henry heard Landon raising the loader's bucket up. What was he doing? Leaving him here?

Then he knew. Of course. What else would he expect? It was very simple—he would tell anyone who would listen. It was clear as day once you thought about it. You didn't have to be a psychologist. You just had to know what it meant to be a father, and how you could love your son but let crap get in the way of that. Those little moments when your son failed a test and you rejected his miserable excuses for not trying harder. Or when he left your tools outside in the rain to rust, and you made him carry them (and a brick too, just to make the point) back and forth from school to teach him a lesson. Or after he came to you in tears at ten years old, so young then, saying that the kids at camp had ridiculed him about his milky white skin and girlish breasts. He tried to tell you about it, but all you could say was *go talk to your mother*, to hide your own disgust. Was it any wonder, Henry would ask himself when the ground turned hard with the first frost and the sisters died within months of each other and their land was sold off after a contentious probate hearing involving dubious relations who claimed to have known them, was it any wonder that he would look up and see the bucket above him ready to deposit its payload? Clods of dirt escaped from its teeth, raining down on him like baptismal fire, stinging him with their spite, dusting his eyes and pillorying his mouth, until he screamed for mercy and his son said, "It's okay, Dad. Just a little more."

Navajo Café

THEY HAD LEFT THE Grand Canyon early in the morning and driven onto the Navajo Indian reservation in search of a Navajo taco. A friend of Owen's had urged him to make sure he stopped out West for a Navajo taco: a large wheel of fried dough, like a popover, smothered in beans, green chiles, lettuce, tomatoes, and cheese. Except that Devra, Owen's ten-year-old daughter, refused to touch her smaller child's portion, now that it had finally arrived. She said it looked like a cow pie. It did look like a cow pie, Owen agreed, only a good cow pie. Still, she'd gone into a sulk, stubbornly refusing to eat or even talk to him.

She had grown increasingly pouty and uncooperative on the trip. Last year's vacation had been so easy that he should have known not to expect the same results this year. But he thought she would be old enough for a cross-country trip (they lived in Connecticut) to see the West: the Grand Canyon, the Painted Desert, Monument Valley, Yellowstone, the Rockies, Carlsbad Caverns, Stuckey's. They'd planned a mule ride into the Grand Canyon, down the Bright Angel Trail. At the last moment Devra became frightened and wouldn't stay on her mule, kicking at the indifferent animal, who was evidently used to temperamental children and just continued urinating without pause. Finally, Owen had to lift her off; they were holding up the mule train. He settled for a cup of hot chocolate and an "I Hiked the Canyon" T-shirt in the visitors' lodge.

She had been hysterical like this once before, two years ago, when the sock incident happened. It was the anniversary of her mother's death. Owen had been walking by Devra's bedroom when he overheard her say to her friend CeeCee, who was spending the night, "I'll trade you one divorcée and one old maid for a widower and an adulteress." Her friend had asked, "What's the adult dress look like?"

Where did she learn these things? Owen had wondered. He carefully supervised her TV watching. He could understand the widower—Owen had been referred to as that—but the divorcée, the adulteress? "Deal," CeeCee agreed, and then there was so much squealing and giggling and howling that he opened the door to see what was going on. They'd stuffed socks with toilet paper and put rubber bands around the toes to make heads. About thirty sock dolls were on either side of the bed. In the middle was a Dutch oven filled with steaming water. One drenched sock doll tied to a stick was being dunked in the water. "What are you doing?" Owen asked, more incredulous than angry. But they took his tone for a scolding and both burst into tears, cowering together in the corner as if they'd committed the most shameful act possible. "You didn't knock, Daddy! You didn't knock first!" Devra screamed out through her tears, shaking all over, this one pitiful comment her only defense against a torturous punishment she seemed to believe would result from the evil deed. Her little friend was so frightened she began hiccupping, choking on her tears. "It's okay," Owen reassured them. "It's all right to play. Go back to playing. I was just wondering if you wanted some popcorn. I didn't mean to barge in," and he left the room quickly.

Downstairs, the image of all those puff-headed sock dolls, with wadded up toilet paper and rubber bands twisted around their necks, stayed with him. He put some oil in a pan for popcorn. Suddenly CeeCee ran down the stairs, grabbed the front doorknob with both hands, and dashed out before he could catch her. Owen went back upstairs, as nonthreatening as he could make himself, picking up a plant from the hallway so it would look as though he were on his way to water it. He knocked on her door. No answer. He opened it and came in with the fern. She was already in bed with her pajamas on, the light turned off. Two hours before her bedtime, it was only seven-thirty. She kept her face pressed into the pillow, still trembling, and pretending to be asleep in the midst of her violent shivering. He stroked her hair, which had always calmed her before, but now only made her dig her face harder into the pillow, filling him with pity and sadness and a terrible helplessness at not knowing what to do. He sat with her for an hour. Even after she was asleep he had to unclench her fingers from his pant leg. On the way out, he picked up one of the sock dolls.

He examined it carefully, unable to see why she had been so terrified at being caught; it wasn't the first time she'd been a little mischievous...a couple of rolls of toilet paper gone, but no big deal. Then he suddenly saw that these weren't the socks he washed every week at all; these were Amanda's socks, her mother's. Devra had taken them from one of the trunks Owen had packed after the accident. She'd opened the trunk, and made puppets from her dead mother's socks, meaning to punish and drown them in hot water. No wonder the poor child was frightened. Caught playing a harmless game, in her mind she must have connected it with all sorts of horrible malevolence. Owen went back upstairs and sat by her bed so he'd be there if she woke up, wondering if the game were some unconscious anger Devra needed to express against her mother for abandoning her.

"I heard a story about a little boy who also wouldn't eat his food," Owen told her now, trying to get her to take a bite. Devra was watching some Indian children at a table on the other side of the café. They were sipping Cokes and eating hamburgers. In fact, he saw no one else eating Navajo tacos. An old Navajo woman came in wearing a squash-blossom necklace against a blue velveteen blouse, and long, flowing skirts. "That's a traditional Indian outfit," Owen pointed out to Devra. A Navajo man in the booth ahead glanced around at Owen. He looked young, educated. Owen thought perhaps his remark had been patronizing, but he didn't see any harm in identifying the way a different culture dressed. It wasn't as though everyone in here looked the same. Their waitress, for instance, appeared a typical enough American teenager—her hair layered fashionably on the sides, and she wore a gold chain instead of Indian jewelry around her neck.

"There's this little boy named Stanley," explained Owen, hoping the story would distract her enough to eat. "Stanley is five years old and has never said *a single word*." Devra, in spite of herself, turned toward him with interest. "One day he's sitting at the breakfast table and he says out of the clear blue, 'The oatmeal is lumpy.' His parents are very very happy. 'Stanley,' his mom says, 'you spoke, darling! Your first words! We're so pleased!' After the excitement dies down a little, Dad leans over and asks, 'How did this happen, son? I mean, you haven't spoken a word for five years and suddenly you talk. Not that we're finding fault, but why is that, son?' And Stanley looks at them with a very serious face and says, 'Up until now things have been just fine.'"

Devra stared at him.

"Well, *I* thought it was funny," said Owen, not knowing whether she didn't get it or she just had better taste than he did. "Okay, Miss Silent Puss, I think we'll call it a day since you insist on being such bad company.

I'm not going to waste my breath trying to get you to eat—or talk. You have no reason to behave this way."

"I do, too."

Her first words in an hour. "And what is that?"

She didn't answer him. She continued sitting with folded arms. Her hair was too long and he wished she'd agree to have it cut. One day some demonic meatball would yank it back on the playground and she'd be in a wheelchair the rest of her life. She was small and thin for her age, with green eyes that could be impenetrable or determined, as they were now, or so glassy and ethereal that he worried where her mind went. She was at a stage where she wouldn't let herself be seen undressed, or wear shorts unless she had tights underneath. When he asked her why not—she had such cute legs—she broke into tears and said they were ugly green celery sticks and not part of this world. They belonged to Udau, a mythical playmate she used to blame everything on, whom she hadn't mentioned in years.

He asked the waitress for the check. "She had a big breakfast," Owen said, excusing Devra's untouched meal. "You don't have to wrap it," he added, although the girl hadn't given any indication of doing so. While she went to make change, the Indian in the booth in front, who had glanced at him, stood up and stretched. He wore a leather vest over a faded pink union shirt, wraparound sunglasses, and on his wrist a heavy silver bracelet embedded with a fat piece of turquoise. He kept nodding at Owen. It was peculiar. None of the other Indians gave him a second look, while this one seemed ready to dance with him. Finally Owen felt uncomfortable enough to say something. "Excuse me, do you know how far we are from Flagstaff?" The Indian just stared at him uncomprehendingly, rolling his shoulders back. His neck was muscular and loose, cracking freely. Owen listened to the bones popping, the Indian sucking air through his teeth—his thumbs hooked at the waist around empty belt loops. "Flagstaff, Arizona?" Owen repeated. Maybe he didn't understand English. Or was slow. Or on drugs.

The Indian came over to their table. He squatted down so his chin was even with the edge. He took off his sunglasses, looked deeply at Owen, then at Devra, then back at Owen, and then sang in a warbling voice:

"I got those walking talking crying Yiddish blues. Oh, baby, ain't I so low. I got me backaches and sideaches and bellyaches and heartaches. I got me the way way way *way* down walking talking crying Yiddish blues. I got the meanest old mean, I got the hurtest old hurt, I got the troublest old trouble, I got me those walking talking crying Yiddish blues."

"Jesus!" said Owen.

The Indian stood up, clasped his hands behind his neck, yawned, stretched, sucked air, and then, without turning his head, pointed a stiff finger over his shoulder. "Flagstaff, that way," he said, and ambled out the door. Owen looked around the restaurant. The other Indians were ignoring them. The waitress was leaning over the counter, eating a piece of custard pie. She'd forgotten his change.

"Oh, Lord!" Owen said.

Devra sat impassively, unaffected by the performance. "Don't notice me," said Devra, and slumped farther down in her seat.

They drove on a two-lane road that cut across the northern part of the reservation. Really strange. Devra sat in the back reading a book. He would let her be moody today. Tomorrow, right away, he'd put his foot down and make it clear they weren't having any more of this nonsense…or they were going home. He suspected much of her behavior was because he'd asked her in a roundabout way what she would think of his remarrying. One morning at breakfast he'd hinted, "Would you like to see more of Peg around the house?" He regularly spent two nights a week with Peg, always feeling a little guilty when he dropped Devra off for the evening at her grandmother's. "Where?" Devra had answered cagily, lifting her eyes toward the bedroom. "Just around the house," said Owen, unable to bring himself to be more definite. Devra had shrugged, making him feel ashamed and uncomfortable, as if his desires were unfair to her. A therapist he had been seeing, a woman in her sixties, asked him why he felt this way when he brought up the subject later.

"Because I feel guilty?"

"Do you?"

"I wasn't even there. It was a plane crash. I had no control over it."

"Control," the therapist repeated.

"But I didn't."

"Then that must not be it."

"Maybe I want to be sure she likes me."

"Are you afraid she doesn't?"

"No, I know she does. I'm her father. She has to like me."

"Oh, come now, Mr. Timmerman. That's never stopped children

before."

The woman could be brutally observant. "I mean, she doesn't have a choice."

"Oh?"

"Choice in a different way."

"You mean she doesn't have a mother. You're her only choice."

"Right. I have to be both to her."

"Impossible, Mr. Timmerman. You're only one person. And if you continue trying to be two, you'll continue to be disappointed and indecisive, as you are now. You can take responsibility for your own actions, but not for those of someone who isn't alive."

Owen had squeezed the rubber ball he'd gotten in the habit of holding during the sessions. "Control, Mr. Timmerman. Control is not your life's work."

It was getting dark and they were almost clear of the reservation. He'd pointed out what sights there were to Devra—the octagonal houses of logs and mud that were called hogans, the mesas, the sheep grazing near the road, but she'd kept her nose in a book. He felt invigorated by the open country, the expanse of earth, the hard, red rock and quiet authority of the land, the yucca plants with their white stalks full of blossoms shooting into the clear sky, while everything else seemed to hug the ground—a terrain that favored views from the belly, the hogans popping up occasionally like round loaves of bread.

He glanced in the mirror at her now and thought that things might be all right. He had nothing more to go on than the excitement brought about by the drive—the possibilities in this unwalled land—that he could give her a comfortable life—no, more than that: a hopeful one. He knew he could be a good father and that she loved him and that he would never stop worrying about her. He would always struggle with himself against trying to reach inside and fix in her a view of the world, a view that wheedled against despair, that countered all losses, and that tried to insure an impossible equity. Probably what she needed, even as a ten-year-old, was for him to stop fussing over her, to take a breath free of his inspection, to fail on her own without feeling as though nothing else could go wrong because something too terrible had already happened. He had to admit, though, that if he worried about dying and leaving her alone in the world, his greatest fear was that he had no one else. He had made it through the worst parts of her mother's death by thinking, with a cold assurance that made him wince now, there's still Devra left. A day hadn't passed when he hadn't bargained that they can take anyone, but not her, a feeling that had started the moment he touched her and held her weight in his arms, her presence a vivid connection for him to a self deeper than any other—not from his mind, but from his heart to her baby heart.

"Are you hungry, Dev?" The calmness in his voice made her speak up unguarded and say yes. He turned around and was about to say they would stop for dinner—no more Navajo tacos—when there was a dull thud and she screamed "You hit him! You hit him!" Her scream continued as Owen, moaning reflexively, pulled the car off the road.

He unfastened his seat belt and told Devra to wait in the car, but she screamed so desperately that he took her in hand and went running down the road, terrified of what he would see, the low moan still rolling in his throat, a sudden shame that his bowels might erupt—his fear was this penetrating. He squeezed her hand.

An old man was sitting up beneath an embankment where he'd evidently tumbled after being hit. "Are you hurt?" Owen asked. The old man was an Indian, his face deeply wrinkled in the dim light of a bar back from the road. He reeked of liquor. "Didn't you see me?"

"He doesn't speak English," said an Indian woman who had come up from the parking lot. Her friend had gone inside to call an ambulance.

"I didn't even see him coming. Where was he?"

"Over there," she said, and pointed across the road. "He sits over there when he drinks too much."

"Did you see him cross?"

The Indian woman hesitated. "No."

Owen couldn't believe this was the same man he'd hit. Sixty miles an hour. He remembered glancing at the speedometer before looking back at Devra. The man should be dead.

"I saw the whole thing," a truck driver said, running over and out of breath. He had pulled his rig into the parking lot of the bar. He was white. He leaned over and shouted in the old man's ear. "Your leg hurt, grandpa? Can you stand up?"

"Maybe he shouldn't—"

"That's it. Lean on my shoulder." Once up, the old man wobbled unsteadily, although it could have been from being drunk. The truck driver helped him sit down again, and the old man went back to rubbing his leg.

"His leg?" Owen asked.

"I think he's all right."

"I was going so fast. I don't understand why he's—"

"These guys are loose as a goose when they're drunk like this. He rolled with the punch. Must have been like being hit by a big plunger."

"But anybody would be…should be…"

"Look, don't argue with luck. You hit the loosest, highest old Indian around."

Owen bent down and held Devra. Both of them were shivering. The desert air chilled quickly at night, and he was trembling anyway, now that it was starting to sink in, how lucky they'd all been. They stood silently around the old man and waited for the ambulance to arrive. Owen desperately needed a drink from the bar, but he didn't want alcohol on his breath. Trucks flew by on the highway, sucking them in their draft.

A siren came from the distance, then a police car pulled up. "Listen," the truck driver said. "Don't let these guys push you around. They've got no authority over white people."

"Who are they?" Owen asked.

"Navajo police. You're right on the border here, so it's still their jurisdiction, sort of."

The Navajo cop came over. He was a short man with straight black hair that lay flat over his forehead. He said something in Navajo to the old man. They carried on a conversation for a while, and finally Owen couldn't stand his own silence and said he'd been driving the car. The cop looked at him, then stated in a voice without accusation, "He says you didn't have your lights on."

"Yes, he did," the truck driver put in before Owen could answer. "I saw the whole thing. Grandpa here walked right in front of him."

The Navajo cop didn't say anything. Owen kept silent, too. He actually had no idea what had happened, except he was sure his lights were on. Then he'd looked back at Devra, and thump—not the sound of glass shattering or metal denting or stone crumbling or even rubber bouncing, as the truck driver imagined, but of flesh thumping, an unnatural sound—a simple, muffled, almost polite noise.

An ambulance arrived in tandem with a state police car. The state cop, a young, reedy kid with a Western twang, immediately came over and asked what had happened. Owen explained, and the cop kept nodding in such a way that Owen knew the kid had made up his mind about any accident involving an Indian even before he got here. The truck driver repeated his version of the story, how the old man walked dead drunk right in front of Owen's car. The Navajo cop listened but didn't interfere. "Let's look at your car," the state cop said. Owen asked the truck driver to watch Devra; he didn't want her walking down the dark highway unnecessarily. She sat down alongside the old man, who was being examined by the ambulance crew.

The cop shined his flashlight on Owen's Connecticut license plate, wrote down the numbers, then went around front. He didn't ask to see Owen's driver's license. "There you go," he said, pointing to a small crack fanning out like a seashell on the passenger's side of the windshield. "You must have got him when you swerved."

"What do you mean?"

"I don't see how he could crack your windshield here unless you swerved."

Owen didn't answer. The other possibility, he knew, was that the old man was already past the car—not stepping in front of it, as the truck driver claimed, but grazed by the car as Owen sped by.

Walking back, the state cop told him these accidents happen all the time. They were on the line, just across the border of the reservation. Liquor wasn't allowed on the reservation, so bars were built at every entrance and Indians came out here and got drunk and then killed themselves on the way home along the dark highways. This was the third pedestrian-auto accident this month; the other two hadn't been so lucky. "How fast were you going?" the cop asked. Owen tensed up. "About sixty," he said. The cop shook his head. "One acrobatic Indian."

"Do you have to make a report?"

"Not unless you want it for the insurance company."

"Insurance company?"

"Your windshield."

"No," Owen said. He just wanted to get out of here as fast as possible. "Is there a motel nearby?"

"About ten miles ahead."

He thanked the cop and then said goodbye to the truck driver, thanking him also for stopping. The old man still sat against the embankment, next to Devra. He had been saying something to her as Owen walked up.

The Navajo cop helped the old man into the police car; he would take

him home. Not a word had been exchanged between the two police. "He'll
be all right, won't he?" Owen asked. No one answered him. Only Devra
and he were left. Everyone else had left as quickly as they had appeared.
Owen suddenly regretted not apologizing to the old man, but he'd been
too worried about fault and blame to do what seemed decent and natural.

Devra rode up front with him. He was glad to see she understood
how he felt. He couldn't take her acting up now. His back was tense as
steel, his legs locked; he forced himself to shift the car into gear, then
slowly pull onto the road. Gradually he increased his speed until he was
confident enough to do what felt like a reckless forty miles per hour. A
truck bore down from behind. He hugged the right side of the road until
the double trailer passed.

"I saw that old man say something to you."

"Yes."

Owen laughed. "He must have thought you were an Indian."

Devra was silent.

"He did speak Navajo to you, right?"

"Didn't."

Owen shifted his eyes, not turning his head from the road but trying
to see her expression. "Come on, Dev, he couldn't speak a word of English."

"He could. If he wanted."

"All right. What did he tell you?"

"Lots of stuff."

"Like what?"

"Just stuff." Devra moved in her seat. "He told me not to tell most
of it."

"That's fine. You should keep secrets."

"You don't believe me."

Owen considered a moment. "No, I suppose I can't. Not this time."

"He said you wouldn't."

"Fine," Owen said, wanting to let the subject drop and not appreciating
when she played fancifully with the truth, perhaps having heard the
old man say words and then just supplying her own interpretation. He
sometimes sensed that she might tease men when she grew older, learn the
fine art of deceit—with all its attendant self-mystery.

"I could tell you one thing."

"If you want."

"He asked me if I was scared."

"Did he?"

"He said not to be. I wasn't supposed to be scared. It was a mistake and I could stop. My being afraid."

"And what are you afraid of?"

"Everything."

"There must be *something* you're not afraid of."

"No," Devra said with certainty.

Owen reached for her hand. "Are you going to listen to this old man then and stop?"

"Yes."

"Well, I'm glad for that."

She fell asleep before they reached the motel. After he registered and put her to bed, he went outside to get ice. But the machine was broken, so he returned to the room and sat on his bed, spreading out the *Navajo Times* and rubbing his feet through his socks. He watched her sleep with the pillow pulled tight around her ears like a bonnet, a new pose, probably a superstitious one. She'd once spent a week refusing to bathe, wearing a necklace of Puffed Wheat that supposedly belonged to Gulada the Taradiddle Queen. The funny thing was that he could watch her all night. Stare at a sleeping child with a pillow over her head. That's all it was. A child at rest. Reduced respiration. Accelerated gamma waves. Temperature decline. Held limbs. He wouldn't do it, though. He wouldn't watch her. They both needed to rest.

Seeing Miles

NOAH STARED AT MIMI'S picture, taken at his bar mitzvah twenty-five years ago. She was his cousin, a second cousin, and she and her family had come out to Milwaukee from Brooklyn for the occasion. He remembered being smitten at the ceremony. She had dark silky hair and large brown eyes flecked with gold. Slender and tall, her face had an oval shape like a prized portrait, and her hair was tucked behind her small, well-articulated ears—carved as if from soap. Her throat had a long white curve, and she sat very still in the second row of the synagogue as he read from the Torah and led the congregation in blessings. At the end of giving his bar mitzvah speech, he'd thanked his parents for being so supportive and then thanked all his relatives and friends for coming. He looked at Mimi and said, "And thank you." It was a bizarre and spontaneous moment for him in a life so far of calm, reasoned, and practiced application. Nevertheless, she just continued to stare unwaveringly at him on the bema. But he was a goner. It was his first experience of painful desire, a fervor that threatened to swallow his flesh. Nor did it hurt that he was just entering puberty, and Mimi, fifteen, was obviously there already.

She had hung back at the reception while he danced the box step with skinny and mostly undeveloped girls from his seventh-grade class, and Mimi's remove and mystery gave her a kind of regal aloofness that only worked him into more of a frenzy. She had declined to dance with him, explaining, "I'm not a good partner. I like to lead."

"That would be fine."

"Thanks, but no."

At one point, he saw her standing alone by the presents and went over to her. "Pick one," he said.

"What?"

"You can have one."

She smiled at him, straight white teeth, free of braces. "You're silly."

"I'm serious." He felt desperate to give her something.

"I can't take your presents."

"Just one."

"You *are* serious."

And then her father, Uncle Irv, had come up and congratulated Noah on his excellent reading of his haftorah, and that was the end of the exchange. He'd been ready to give up his newly gotten gains to her, the tower of gifts and gelt for becoming a man. My kingdom for your hand. *I'll marry you someday*, he thought.

He'd seen her a couple times afterward, at a wedding and then an anniversary party for her parents where she wore a wool plaid cap, like a cabbie, and baggy corduroy pants, and seemed inappropriately dressed for the occasion. Still, he couldn't deny that every time he saw her the same feelings flared up, though evidently not on Mimi's part. Her eyes, almond shaped and impenetrable as to her own thoughts, remained curiously distant. And soon he lost touch with her.

Now he was driving to the Denver Hyatt. Mimi was coming in from New York for a social workers conference. Noah himself was a psychologist with a practice in Denver, which would give them something in common after all these years. All that was good. He had brought with him the picture of her at his bar mitzvah. Of course this was twenty-five years later, and she was now a he. Miles. Mimi had been gone for two years.

Miles told him he would be wearing a blue short-sleeve shirt and yellow tie and Noah had spotted him right away standing beside the fountain. He wouldn't have thought for a moment Miles stood out from any other man, professionally attired and waiting to meet a lunch partner. With his dark cropped hair, he was shorter than Noah remembered him as Mimi—a taller girl but on the shorter end as a man. Above all he appeared neat. Well groomed, spotless nails, and with a firm handshake in place of a hug.

"My mother has been a lot better about it than my father," Miles said when they sat down at lunch. He had ordered a steak to Noah's Caesar salad and was taking sturdy bites. "Irv can't really look me in the eye, but Mom asks me how I'm doing. She never says anything specific such as 'How's the hormone treatment going?' or 'Your voice is getting deeper,' but she does remember to call me Miles, which my father won't. He just avoids my name all together. I think fathers have a harder time giving up their little girls. A mother just accepts her child regardless."

Noah thought of his own daughter, Leah, twelve, and indeed he did have a problem imagining her transforming herself into Leon. He craved her daughterness.

"You just learn to live with people's reactions—those who knew you when. Actually, I have more confusion with people I meet now. Do I tell them about the before? Or is the before no longer me? Will they feel tricked once they find out? Or worse. I had at least one person in my caseload who learned I'd undergone reassignment. This individual, who was a bit unstable anyway, threatened me."

"What'd you do?"

"I forwarded a copy of the letter, which said some god-awful things about making me back into a woman, to the police. I can't say it didn't shake me up. In any case, I have to consider every time how relevant it is to explain about my past. This may be the hardest part of gender reassignment—other people."

"I can only imagine," Noah said. He searched Miles' face, with its thin shadow of beard, to see if he had any inkling of what Noah had once secretly thought about him as a her. He'd been riveted by Mimi, by her elusive sylph beauty, her slender jaw and sinuous lips that reminded him of graceful Arabic script. He could still see a delicate handsomeness in the man now.

"And how about you?" Miles asked him. "Did you bring pictures of your family?"

"I did," said Noah, and took out the leather folio and showed him photographs of his wife, Rose, and of Leah.

"You have a gorgeous family," Miles said.

"We've been trying to have another child," Noah told him. He had no idea why he'd admitted this to Miles. They rarely told anyone. After so much time the pursuit no longer felt new or promising. And they were thankful for just having Leah when he knew many couples who weren't even that lucky. Though he knew, too, that Rose felt more frustrated than he. For him, Leah's large and sometimes histrionic personality more than filled the house. She was enough. Just as he had always chosen to believe that he, an only child too, was enough for his parents. But Rose had spoken of the joys of a large family, having four sisters herself, and lately the subject, as she turned thirty-eight, like him, had become a line signifying their places on opposite sides of a stubborn marker. More than once he'd indicated he'd like to have a vasectomy and be done with it. "It," of course, was the pressure of making a baby, which had lately morphed into the pressure of performance.

"I'd like to have a family someday," Miles said. "That was the hardest part of my decision. Bye bye to my reproductive organs."

"I can only imagine." Noah realized he'd uttered these words twice now and must have sounded like a dazed observer at a sideshow. He should have been less unsettled by Mile's bluntness—what had happened to his professional training after all? He'd worked with gay men and women, even transgender patients, though not someone who'd elected to have sex reassignment surgery. Yet he felt a personal reaction to everything that was being said. As if he were channeling the family's regrets.

"I'd be glad to adopt, if I met the right woman. Of course, that's a problem in itself." Miles smiled broadly. "I mean, am I a straight man now who dates heterosexual women, or a man, formerly a woman, who still likes lesbians? And would any of them have me?"

"You had a partner before?"

"Helena." Miles bent his linen napkin into a frown that drooped from his mouth. "End of a five year relationship."

"You must have wanted to do this very badly."

"What you're really asking is do I have any regrets?"

Noah smiled. "You're a good therapist, I can see."

"I am, more than I get paid for. But to answer your question, well, let me put it this way. I'd look in my closet at the pantyhose I was supposed to put on for corporate America before I became a social worker and it would make my skin crawl. I never felt comfortable in women's clothes or a woman's skin. And frankly, I'd always wanted a penis. Now I have one. Would you like to see it?"

"Pardon?" Noah said, flushing.

Miles reached out to touch Noah's hand. "I'm only fooling with you, cousin. Consider it transgender schtick."

But was he? After lunch, Miles suggested they go for a swim. The hotel had an indoor lap pool. "I love to swim," Miles informed Noah. "That's the one sport I used to do competitively. Why don't you join me?"

"I don't have a suit."

"I always bring an extra." They were standing in the atrium of the hotel under the vast open glass panels, surrounded by a mauve forest of sofas, chairs, and wall hangings. "Unless you have to get back right away."

"No," said Noah, because he didn't want to seem...what? Rude? Uptight about swimming with a transsexual? "Sure, let's do it."

They went up to Miles' room, discussing the conference on the way. Miles' presentation tomorrow was part of a panel called "Living with Your (non) Transgender Parents." His own experience with his parents' semi-denial was not atypical, he said. "I can certainly understand," he admitted. "How would you feel about your child becoming a different gender in the middle of her life? For one, you're asking parents to give up any illusions about carrying on the family name in a genetically natural way. It's one thing not to have children; it's quite another to willfully, as in my case, undermine the very capacity to do so. No wonder so few doctors will do the operation. They're asked to perform an irrevocable procedure that is based entirely on a state of mind, something they're supposed to believe in called gender dysphoria, that either removes the sex organs or constructs entirely sterile ones. I mean, I have a respectable penis, thanks to the wonders of phalloplasty, but heaven help it to squirt out a single sperm. I sympathize, I do, with my parents, with the doctors...with everyone. Do you want to change in the bathroom?" Miles asked, starting to get undressed. He threw Noah a suit.

He did. He hadn't prepared himself after all. Not for the forthrightness of Miles' remarks. If anything, he thought he'd have to draw Miles out, as he would a struggling client, a gentle questioning to establish trust. But Miles was a runaway train—*I have a respectable penis.* Had Noah ever said anything like this to anyone? And how big *was* Miles' penis anyway?

In the bathroom, Noah held up the suit, small, but he could fit into it. At least it wasn't a Speedo.

"You okay in there?" Miles asked.

"Fine," said Noah.

"Suit fit?"

Noah pulled at the crotch of the tan nylon trunks. "Just great."

When he opened the door, Miles was standing there in the hotel's white bathrobe cinched tight and with flip flops.

"Not bad," Miles remarked, eyeing Noah's suit. It was almost as if his cousin had been expecting this moment.

•

Miles, as he'd hinted, proved to be an excellent swimmer. Noah watched him glide effortlessly back and forth in the pool, making smooth flip turns at the wall and then shooting forward with submerged musculature into the next lap, silent as an eel. Meanwhile, Noah stood in the water's deep end supporting himself with his elbows on the ledge. Rose, a strong swimmer herself, had tried to encourage him to go with her to the community pool. He agreed that he needed exercise and too often got stuck in his head, the profession's occupational hazard, and that he should follow his own advice to clients to get out there and stir up some endorphins.

"Want to sit in the hot tub?" Miles called to him from across the pool. They were the only ones in the pool. They'd come down on the elevator and passed through a throng of conferees registering for the conference. Noah had followed Miles assuming he knew the best way to the fitness center, but now he wondered if there hadn't been a more direct—and private— route. In the popularized argot of the profession, he would have considered his cousin's behavior—the eagerness to change clothes in the openness of the hotel room, the strolling through the lobby, the offer to view his respectable penis—an exhibitory overcompensation for his fears of being insufficiently masculine. The catch was that, overcompensation or not, it was making Noah feel like the lesser man.

"Sure," said Noah, and boosted himself out of the water. The trunks clung to his thighs. It was odd…he almost felt as if he *were* thirteen again, wearing this small suit, self-conscious about his changing body. Except presently his body was changing against his will—or lack thereof—into a sedentary salute to middle age. Miles, by comparison, showed all the signs of rejuvenation, if not outright youth.

In the hot tub, he got a good look at Miles' chest, which had just a little extra padding, as if filled with a layer of down, but not so much that you'd think *I'm staring at a former woman's chest*. He could see no signs of scars. The nipples appeared a bit asymmetrical and larger than they might (although compared to what?). In a moment of strange elevator intimacy, Noah had confessed on the way down to the pool that he'd had a crush on him—on Mimi, that is. He hadn't gone into the extent of it via his hormone-erupting, thirteen-year-old psyche at a religious rite of passage overseen by a God in whom he'd later stop believing. Or that he'd mentally unzipped her pink dress and never dreamed he'd have to unzip her skin to find the real person. He'd simply said, "I had a pretty good crush on you as a teenager." And Miles, standing up straight and thoughtful in his terrycloth hotel robe with its Hyatt insignia and his navy blue knee-length swim trunks, as if he were a boxer having a centering moment before he entered the ring, turned to him and said, "Admiration accepted. And returned."

Miles caught him staring and smiled. Noah quickly turned away, embarrassed by his curiosity and gawking.

"Enjoying yourself?" Miles asked.

"What do you mean?"

"The swimming."

"Oh. I am," said Noah. He had to keep flattening down his ballooning trunks.

"Is something troubling you?"

"No," he said, though he knew from his own experience with clients that he'd responded too quickly to be credible.

Miles extended one leg—hairy, Noah noted—and tapped his big toe against Noah's chest. "Sure?"

"Well, we're struggling a bit right now. Rose and I. But it's nothing serious."

"Want to tell me about it?"

"I think it's about the direction of our lives."

"Sounds like a traffic problem."

Noah laughed. "In a way. Rose would like another child, as I said."

"Actually you said you *both* wanted a child. Is that not accurate?"

"She more than I. I think she believes this is the way to move forward. I'm not so sure."

"You've been married, what? Fifteen years?"

"Yes."

"So that's a lot of time together. I envy you. It's an investment worth guarding."

"That it is," said Noah. And then thought how strange to be talking with his cousin in a hot tub about the intimacy of his marriage, his cousin who had just told him he had a respectable penis, and with whom, ironically, he felt completely honest in a way he rarely enjoyed these days. "I guess we'll just have to see what happens next."

"I couldn't agree more," Miles said. "I'm a poster boy for what comes next. And you want to know something? It's always a work in progress. Somehow the definitiveness of next, despite my certainty of its permanence each time, still eludes me."

They went upstairs to change, and again Noah used the bathroom, while Miles dressed in the less private confines of the room. Noah looked at his shriveled penis in the mirror, always to be counted on after swimming, but especially in a tight suit. He stretched the appendage, but it quickly retracted into its accordion mode like the face of a preternaturally wrinkled Chinese Shar-Pei dog.

"All right if I just rinse off in here?" Noah called through the door.

"Go ahead. I'll do the same after you finish."

He saw Miles' travel kit on the back of the tub once he opened the shower curtain. He knew all about confidentiality. What could be more important in his profession? You went to jail, after all, to protect a client's privacy. Or told yourself you would, if it ever came to that. Yet, he couldn't stop himself from looking in the bag and picking up the prescription bottles. Lexapro, Wellbutrin, Ativan…the whole gamut of depression and anxiety treatments. It didn't surprise him. What did was the sudden pang of tenderness he felt for Miles and his vulnerabilities. He could recall when he'd first seen Mimi, and she looked so alone, maybe the loneliest and prettiest girl he had ever seen, a deadly combination for someone like him who was keen on others' wounds and on his way to becoming a psychologist, the seed watered.

"You need anything, just take it out of my toiletry bag," Miles said, and Noah drew his hand away quickly, as if Miles could see him. "I mean, deodorant or something."

"Thanks."

"Want to shower together?"

"Huh?"

"Noah, Noah," said Miles. "Just kidding."

"Oh, yeah," Noah said. "Transgender schtick. Right."

He showered and dressed, and after Miles did the same they went down in the elevator. He was already planning what he would say to his parents who'd want to know how the visit with Mimi went, wondering if he would tell them the truth. He still couldn't believe Uncle Irv hadn't told them about Miles. Oh, yes, he could. Repression could be a formidable force. He'd once had client who, in trying to convey the degree of denial in her family, explained that when she was fifteen she'd had a miscarriage, literally in front of her parents. They'd all been sitting on the sofa in the living room watching TV. Four months pregnant and wearing baggy shirts to conceal what she'd been starting to show, his client, faint and weak, had gushed out a bloody clot. She'd run to the bathroom, but there was no mistaking what happened—the back of her shorts soaked, the blood right in front of her mother and father. They'd said nothing. She'd quietly cleaned up "the mess," and that was the last ever spoken about it.

So it was no wonder Miles was still invisible and Mimi would live on in the family memory until the generation died out. Noah still had the sense that he was on a mission, a counteragent to the family secrecy. And Miles seemed grateful. He'd thanked him profusely for taking the time to meet.

"Of course," said Noah. "I want to keep in touch."

Miles tilted his head. "I'd like that."

When he got home, the lights were off inside. Rose had left him a note that Leah was at a sleepover and that she herself had gone upstairs to think—code for napping. His wife adored naps. Whereas such naps led to insomnia for him, Rose could wake up from a luxurious repose, stretch happily, murmur indolently, and be asleep four hours later without interference. *Disturb me*, the note said.

He went into the bedroom. The sound machine whirred away. They'd gotten hooked on white noise, operant conditioning: as soon as the machine went on, they both became sleepy and reported to their dream quarters. It all seemed like such normalcy now after seeing Miles.

He lay down and curled up against her, and she pushed back into him. He felt the warmth of her buttocks through the thin fabric of her nightgown. He pressed his lips to the soft nape of her neck and then kissed her shoulder, biting her lightly until she said "Mmm." Then she turned around and faced him. "What was it like?"

"Different."

"Your father called. He wanted to know how it was seeing Mimi. If she's married yet or has, as he put it, a beau. He doesn't have a clue, does he?"

"No," said Noah, "and I'm not sure I'm going to tell him. If Miles' own father wants to keep it a secret, why should I say anything to my parents? It's unlikely they'll ever see Miles again, and everyone will go to their graves—this older generation—content with the perceived status quo."

"What's he look like? Like the photograph still?" He had shown her the picture of Mimi at fifteen and explained his adolescent crush. She'd had similar sentiments for one of her boy cousins, but nothing had happened there either…well, nothing, except a game of strip poker. Rose won, cousin lost, end of story. As much as she remembered at least. It was her first sight, given her family of four sisters, of a penis, which had a dampening effect on her crush: her cousin's angelic face came with one of *those*?

"I can still see her in him." He thought of the way Miles canted his head as they were saying goodbye—much the way Mimi had looked at him when he was thirteen and sent his heart then, and another organ, soaring, as if she wanted to study Noah from a cockeyed angle and to look pretty while doing it.

"You smell like chlorine."

"We went swimming. I guess I didn't get it all out of my hair."

"You went swimming? With Miles?"

"And I showered in his room afterward."

"Oh, my." She was unbuckling his belt as she said this, her hand slipping under the band of his underwear. He remembered standing in front of Miles' bathroom mirror, examining himself and his manhood, trying to decipher what it meant that Mimi had once been the object of his earliest masturbatory fantasies when he was thirteen. And those weren't the only ones. In the related category of his rescue fantasies, he'd saved her from burning buildings, muggings, sexual maraudings, and, ironically, considering Miles' prowess as a swimmer, drowning. Her eternal gratitude was his dying reward. Breathless, sacrificing himself, he'd come. Le Petit Mort, as the French called orgasm, so willing with their philosophical fatalism to commingle sex and death at any opportunity.

Had he always wanted to save people?

"Ohh," Rose cried.

"You all right?"

"Yes, yes, go…don't stop." He'd thrust into her hard, skipping their usual foreplay, bunching her nightgown up around her neck, and with his fingers splayed across her chest, pinning her down. Her cries echoed through the empty house. So rarely did they have it all to themselves. He heard his own moans, too, reverberating in his throat, his breath coming faster, his desire swift, heedless and unstoppable, and then Rose slapped him across the face, the resounding bite of her hand stinging his flesh, and he came instantly.

He rolled off her. They lay there next to each other, spent and looking up at the ceiling. He was reluctant to speak, and Rose's breathing filled the silence. Finally, he asked, "Why'd you do that?"

"You…"

"What?"

"You said his name."

She had never slapped him during sex or any other time. It was so unlike her. So unrestrained. He'd burst forth at the touch, but now he couldn't tell if the slap had been simultaneous or if his coming had preceded it. "I think you imagined that," Noah said. "Just because we'd been talking about him."

"I didn't. You called his name. It bothered me."

"I wasn't thinking about him." Or was he? Was he thinking that he hadn't told Rose about Miles' bragging about his new penis or about the sudden kiss on Noah's cheek that took him completely by surprise as they were saying goodbye and how he couldn't get over how soft it was, *Mimi's* kiss, as if Miles purposely had turned himself into her for a moment just to confuse him.

Noah propped himself up on one elbow and looked at Rose, her flushed face and chest, her still-erect nipples, her eyes a green bemused cloud. "Well, whether I did or not, I'm sorry."

"Me too. Did I hurt you?"

"No. I was just…surprised."

She kissed the tips of her fingers and touched them to his cheek. "I wanted your attention. On *me*."

The phone rang. He got up to answer it because it might be Leah. One day, when she was older, he wouldn't feel the need to jump for the phone every time, but now he imagined terrible scenarios in the span of milliseconds. It was a hang up, a Denver number on the caller ID, and he wondered for a moment if it might be Miles.

When he came back to bed, Rose was lying on her back with her knees pressed against her chest. The doctor had told them this position didn't help. If she was going to get pregnant, if they were going to have another child after trying all these years, the little fellas would swim up in her regardless and do their job, the doctor said. But Rose did it out of habit or superstition and Noah accepted the practice without comment. "Wouldn't it be ironic," Rose said now, speaking into her knees, "if after seeing Miles, it finally *did* happen?"

Noah lay down beside her and placed his hand on her flat belly after she unfurled herself. He felt the warmth there, felt something stirring, felt, he was sure, a magnificent and mysterious transformation taking place. And he felt, too, Miles' faint lips against his cheek, the same cheek that Rose had slapped, as if to startle a new life into being, neither him nor her but faceless creation.

Goodness

THEY'D ARRANGED FOR A private wine tasting. It was their thirtieth anniversary and somehow—somehow!—they'd never been to Sonoma. You must go! friends told them. It's beautiful there! Wine country! You won't regret it!

Neither of them were big drinkers. (That doesn't matter, everyone insisted. It's *wine*.) In fact, they knew little about wine and didn't care to know a great deal more. Larry, their corner liquor store clerk, had always advised them on the "fruit-forward" wines they preferred. He'd talked them out of the Merlots (Hadn't they seen *Sideways?*) and dismissed outright any Rieslings as kids' soda pop, and *forget* about the so-called table wines, even though Alan had always liked Chianti with Italian food.

Larry, who visited Sonoma every year, had persuaded them to sign up for a private wine tour. It *did* cost, but then again, how many times did your thirtieth anniversary roll around?

The pressure fell somewhere between guilt-tripping them and a motivational session. In the end, they agreed to the private tour, as well as the upscale inn with its ten luxury suites. They chose the Zen suite that included its own meditation garden with river stones smoothed by the ages, a burbling fountain, Asian vases, and a two-person shower bigger than their bedroom at home. Now that he was retired, Alan worried they couldn't afford the trip, let alone the four-hundred-dollar, all-day private tour. But Larry swore by this company. "Do you want to be stuffed on a bus with a gaggle of tourists, fed a bland box lunch and herded into one of the big commercial places like a trip to Costco? Or do you want to be chauffeured around in a Tesla and given the royal treatment?"

Alan wasn't sure he cared. It was only wine, after all, a sentiment he knew was blasphemous and worthy of a beheading in Larry' eyes.

"How many times will you have this opportunity? This should have been knocked off your bucket list a long time ago." Larry blanched. "Oh, Jesus, I'm sorry."

"It's okay," Alan said. "You're probably right."

A year ago on a trip to Costa Rica, Alan had suffered a massive heart attack, requiring evacuation by helicopter. He hadn't traveled anywhere since. His doctor assured him he was good to go: "It's understandable you're concerned, but you're perfectly fit to travel. And it's California, not international, so that should ease some of your worries. Consider it a trial run. Trust me, it will do you good."

The Costa Rica trip had been their first big vacation since Alan retired from the Denver Building Department. Donna had left her high school teaching job two years earlier and been eager for him to do the same so they could travel. And when they did, on the Tarcoles River Crocodile Tour, enjoying the rewards of all those years of working and limited vacation time, he got struck down as if someone had thrown a spear from the jungle banks. He didn't know how to reconcile what had been promised—the joys of his golden years—with what actually occurred—near annihilation on a crocodile-filled river. He became so depressed that Donna made him see a therapist. He was on medication now, and he still went weekly to see the therapist. By all outward signs he was doing better. And yet he woke up every morning not meditating on a Sanskrit word or the sensation of his breath, as recommended in his survivors support group, but visualizing and urging the traffic of his blood through his heart's bypass.

"You'll enjoy yourself once you get there," Donna assured him, as if he were a child afraid of going to sleepaway camp. Come to think of it, he'd never adjusted to sleepaway camp either. While the other kids flourished and forgot they even had parents, he wrote plaintive letters throughout the session asking to come home.

He knew other men who'd had their brushes with death, some of them heart attack survivors like him, but they—often literally—thumped their chests with pride. *Never felt better. Makes me appreciate every single day as if it were my last.* The swagger in their voices! A triumph of nerve over the inexorable forces of fate. Meanwhile, Alan could barely contain his jackrabbit fright when anyone asked him how he felt since "the event."

"Don't compare yourself to anyone else," Donna encouraged him. "You're making progress."

And wasn't wine good for the heart?

•

They'd flown the two hours or so from Denver to San Francisco, rented a car, and arrived in Sonoma just in time for the inn's late-afternoon wine tasting.

One couple from Oakland had come over just for the weekend. The man, tan, wearing a golf shirt, worked in finance. "We make a run out here every couple months and bring home four or five cases—particularly a Syrah we can't get anywhere else." Alan already felt uncomfortable. They lived in a nondescript suburb of Denver and had little experience with cocktail chatter, let alone how to banter with wine enthusiasts. "I actually like nutty," the man said. "Not oxidized, of course." He winked at Alan.

"Of course," Alan agreed.

"When there's just a bit of an oaky flavor it can be a positive. You don't want it to cross the line, however. Which wineries are you visiting?"

"We have a private tour tomorrow," Alan said, puffing up a bit.

"Nice."

"I think it will be."

"Your first time?"

"Yes, how did you know?"

"Just a guess. Enjoy yourself."

"We will."

He walked across the room to Donna, sitting on a loveseat in a quiet corner. "Try this," she said, handing him a glass of red wine. "I believe its nose has that nouveau flavor and velvety essence of a Beaujolais, though you might actually find it more herbaceous." She broke into laughter.

"Shh," said Alan. "They'll think we're making fun of them."

"Aren't we?" She was already tipsy. "I'm going to scarf down some of that cheese."

"Scarf?"

"That's the right term for these gatherings, isn't it? Also, 'guzzle,' I think I heard someone just say, *I'm going to guzzle this Bordeaux until I vomit!*"

"I'm sure you did not."

She gave his belt a tug. "There's only one thing to do after all this imbibing."

"What's that?" Alan asked.

"It involves our extravagantly overpriced suite with its enormous bed and the one-million-thread-count sheets. I'll let you think about it on the way there." She took his hand and led him away, but not before she conspicuously knocked back a glass of Pinot Grigio to the disapproval, Alan sensed, of the other sipping guests.

The regular driver, Skip, the man Larry knew personally, called early the next morning. He had a family emergency and couldn't make it. He was sending his colleague, Dean, to be their wine concierge for the day. Just as knowledgeable, Dean would also chauffeur them to the private tastings in his Tesla. "I'm terribly sorry," Skip said. "My mother isn't well."

Donna took the call. Alan could hear her making a lot of sympathetic noises. They'd both gotten up early, showered, and dressed casually for the occasion, Donna in denim leggings and a light blue pullover—it was colder than they'd expected—and Alan in khakis and a windbreaker. They'd stuffed themselves on the lavish breakfast fare of strawberry French toast, green chile quiche, smoked salmon, poached eggs, and orange mimosas. Alan wasn't overweight, but the gorging nevertheless caused him a moment of angst about endangering his heart.

"Will it be the same tour?" Donna asked on the phone. Alan heard a string of uh-huhs and then Donna saying, "Okay, I hope your mother feels better," and then some more uh-huhs and finally Donna's goodbye.

"What did he say?"

"He says it will be all the same. He'll personally check in with our new guide."

When Dean showed up, about thirty-five years old, Alan guessed, he quickly reassured them everything would go as planned. "The only difference," he said, pointing to where he was parked, "is that I drive a black Tesla and Skip's is white."

"I've never been in a Tesla," Alan said.

"Well, you're in for a surprise."

And off they went. Except not. For some reason Dean couldn't find their first stop. After repeatedly entering the location into the navigational system of the Tesla—the screen was like an IMAX compared to the one on their Hyundai—they kept getting lost in the wooded hills.

Donna, always obliging, said, "It's very pretty countryside."

Dean pulled off the side of the road and called Skip. A number of complicated directions ensued: north, south, a mention of a dirt road, a blue sign for Mantoni Brothers, and then Dean saying, "I think I got it."

But he didn't. "I am so sorry," he said. They were up in an exclusive area with long driveways back to homes hidden in the woods.

"Let's do that then," Dean said, on the phone for a third time with Skip. Alan wondered how Skip's mother was doing and why Skip had so much time to confer with Dean about being lost at their expense. "We're going to a *much* better place," Dean assured them after hanging up. "And Skip is going to cover it. You'll love this vineyard. Do you know the director Richard Reimann?"

"I don't think so," Alan said.

"Ever heard of *Hellride?*"

"I missed that one."

"How about *Doom Tower?*"

"Nope."

"You must know *Final Days* and *Final Days Retour?*"

Donna piped up, excited. "'Retour' as in French for 'return'?"

"No, *re*-tour, like in re-up for another tour of duty."

She sighed. "I guess not."

"Are these popular movies?" Alan asked. He meant escapist films.

"They've made *millions*," Dean said. "Richard lives here in Sonoma when he's not in LA. There's a chance he'll be at home. His assistant is going to meet us up there and bring Richard's labels. You won't believe the quality of these blends. I have to tell you, it's a blessing in disguise we never found Mantoni Brothers. Nobody gets to go to Richard's house. There's private and there's *private*. This is going to be sweet. And Skip is taking care of it all. Is the music okay?" Dean asked. "Because I've got jazz, classical, rock, alternative rock, blues, country—"

"No country," Donna said. "Maybe some classical. I may be getting a bit of a headache from driving."

"Totally understand. We'll be there soon." He floored the Tesla on an open stretch of road to demonstrate how it zoomed from zero to sixty in 2.8 seconds—nicknamed "the insane mode." Alan was thrust back against the Tesla's leather seat as if on a space shuttle.

The rutted, narrow road to the house wound up through verdant vineyards, immaculately tended. At the very top stood the director's house, teetering on the edge of the hillside as if in some beanstalk part of the sky and breathlessly open to the valley below. The entire front of the home was glass, with a balcony stretching its length, the sun glinting off its steel railing.

The movie director's tall assistant, Lila, met them inside. Her long brown hair fell over the front of her blouse when she bent down to grab a box. Straightening up, she tossed her hair back with a flourish and extended her thin hand. "*So* glad you're here," she said.

They sat around a table. Alan couldn't stop staring at the view outside the house's front wall of glass, the sublime airiness of the director's retreat. Lila unpacked wine glasses from a box, along with three bottles of red wine. A cooler held the whites. They came from the director's store in town that sold his private label. "Usually," Dean informed them, nudging them again at how special this was, "you have to sample the wines at the store. No one actually gets to enjoy the vintages in the splendor of Richard's home, right, Lila?"

Lila stretched her long neck and nodded.

On the adjacent wall to the kitchen, in Alan's direct line of sight, were posters of the movies that Richard Reimann had directed: buildings in flames charring their inhabitants; women and children running from slimy aliens; commandos attacking a Middle-Eastern-looking compound; a frothing dinosaur with a victim's legs wiggling from its jaws.

"That's right," Lila was saying to Donna, after pouring them each a taste of wine, "swirl it around, let it settle a bit, stick your nose in and smell those berry flavors with that touch of Asian spice. There's no better place to grow grapes for this Pinot Noir than right here in this ancient volcanic soil."

Alan took a sip. He didn't know the protocol. Was he supposed to spit it out into the dump bucket? But why waste good wine if it was so outstanding?

"Well, well, well," said Lila. "Look who's here."

A short, muscular man in jeans and a sweaty gray T-shirt and at least a day's growth walked in with a tennis racket in hand.

He nodded at Alan and Donna.

"Richard, this is Alan and Donna, all the way from Colorado. And this"—Lila twirled her hand as if introducing him on stage—"is Mr. Richard Reimann."

"Hi there," Alan said. "Great house."

"I like it," he said. "And then I don't. And then I do again."

"I get what you mean," Donna said, who sounded convincingly like she did.

Alan raised his glass. "Thank you for letting us come into your home."

"The pleasure is all—" He turned away abruptly and went into the bedroom off the kitchen. When the door opened, Alan glimpsed a massive bed with a steel frame and headboard.

Alan suddenly felt uncomfortable, like a lookie loo who'd come to gawk at the famous director's house. Meanwhile, Lila had poured another red wine, this one a "Cab," with "a hint of ginger and green peppercorn." He also noticed for the first time in the table's center a sheet of quality paper stock with elegantly printed lettering listing the outrageous prices—some into the hundreds—of the wines they were sampling and no doubt were expected to purchase. He tried to catch Donna's eye, but she was savoring the cab's taste and making increasingly stronger *mmmmm* sounds.

Dean, who had been in a corner talking on his cell phone, came over and sat down with them at the table. He spoke in a low confidential voice. "The wine? A sideline for Richard but like everything he touches, a huge success. His is a multifarious mind of broad ambition," he intoned. Alan bent over to hear him better. His hearing wasn't what it used to be and he sometimes had to fake it. "Also noteworthy," Dean continued, "the man enjoyed a wild youth. Kidnapped while running guns and hashish in Afghanistan. A stint as a professional boxer—welterweight, twenty knockouts. Cliff diver in Hawaii. Saxophone player in a jazz band. Most impressive of all?—you seem like educated folks so you'll appreciate this—a PhD in literature from the University of Mississippi. Dissertation on William Faulkner. Did *all* this before turning to screenwriting and directing and making his millions." Dean looked over at Lila who was waiting to pour them another wine. "Am I telling tales out of school here, Lila, or just the god-honest impressive truth?"

"You're telling it, Dean," Lila said. Alan stared at the director's bedroom door, expecting him to burst out in a flaming hoop.

"He's in his element up here," Dean said. "He *hates* the whole LA scene."

"Does he have a family?" Donna asked.

Dean put a finger to his lips. Alan strained to hear his answer. "Three children. Divorced twice."

Then, as if on cue, Richard Riemann reappeared from his

bedroom—showered, bare chested, and wearing a sarong around his waist, aqua with blue sea turtles. A joint in his hand. He offered it to them.

Theoretically, this was a wine tasting. And though Alan, recent heart attack victim, retired assistant building engineer and admittedly a cautious person, deduced the courteous thing was to accept the joint, despite having not smoked since, oh, forty-plus years ago in college, he still had trouble letting go of the idea that they were supposed to be urbanely and snobbishly sipping fine wine and not getting baked.

"Thanks," Donna said, not hesitating. She looked at Alan, beseeching him with her eyes to join in and enjoy himself, loosen up, have fun. He knew that look. She had been giving it to him ever since his heart attack.

"I think I'll pass," Alan said.

Donna, Lila, Dean, and the auteur in his sarong all passed around the joint as if old friends. Alan knew none of the director's movies, though he had read lots of Faulkner. At one time, he'd strongly considered becoming an English professor. But he'd given up on the idea after his father insisted he study engineering and refused to pay his son's tuition for a career gamble as some ivory tower professor. Which was another way of saying he had no respect for Alan's choices.

"I hear you like Faulkner," Alan said out of the blue. It was all he could think to say. Everyone, including Donna, who had the joint in one hand and the newest wine—a Grenache—in the other, stared at him.

Richard Reimann raised one finger and disappeared back into the bedroom. When he returned he put a letter typed on cream-colored stationary in front of Alan. From the way Reimann handled the letter, holding only the very tips of the corners, it was clear Alan was not to touch it or even breathe on it. The single-spaced letter, with capital X's over what looked like a few misspelled words, was written by William Faulkner, the great man himself, to a department store owner in Oxford, Mississippi. Something about money and a disputed bill (Alan, reading fast, tried to get the gist of it while Reimann hovered).

"Is this incredible or what?" Reimann said.

"It *is*," Alan agreed, unsure of exactly what he was reading or why it might be incredible. In both content, a bill dispute, and form, those x'd out words, the letter appeared quite prosaic.

"*Typical* of Faulkner," Reimann said.

"How so?"

"How so what?"

"You mean typical of Faulkner's money problems?"

Reimann gave Alan a disappointed look. "Hmm," he said, and picked up the letter by its corners and went back into the bedroom.

"I am so fucked up," Donna said, rubbing her temples.

Lila was packing up the used glasses and the half empty bottles of wine. Alan felt he had failed any number of tests: he had not one intelligent thing to say about the wines, let alone the money to afford a single bottle; he had no doubt proved himself timid in front of Donna by failing to participate in the festivities. His father's favorite word for his son, "pusillanimous," came back to him—or maybe he was just feeling sorry for himself. And of course he'd somehow missed the deeper significance, assuming there was one, of Mr. William Faulkner's complaint to a department store owner.

But he would not let a heart attack define him for the rest of his life. "Pass me that joint," he said to Dean, who was sucking on it. "I just want a toke." Did anybody say "toke" anymore?

He took a puff, then announced, "I'm going to have a last look outside before we go, if that's okay." He wanted to see the magnificent view below from the balcony, fill his lungs with the California air and imagine he was sleeping in the shade of endless grapevines, a boy again starting his life over.

"Absolutely," Lila said. "Go enjoy. No rush."

He walked around to Donna and squeezed her shoulder. "Happy anniversary."

"You too, sweetie." She patted his hand absently.

"Do you want to come outside with me?"

"I think I'll just stay here."

He stepped onto the balcony, leaned over the railing, and took in the view a good thousand feet below. Dean, in his tutoring while in the Tesla, had said if you see birds on the vines, that's a sign the grapes are ripe and ready to pick. And sure enough, staring down, Alan saw birds landing on the sweet plump bounty.

It was only an instant later—and he would remember it as maybe the most endless instant of his life, outdoing even that of his heart attack—the birds exploded into the air like a storm cloud. Alan felt a bump, followed by a sharp shaking, and then an abrupt hitch. The balcony had cracked at its threshold, an extensive deep fissure that separated him from the sliding glass door and interior of the house. Afraid to move, he heard shouts inside. He turned his head slowly to see everyone scurrying frantically, and then his loving wife of thirty years begging him with her hands out to stand absolutely motionless.

Earthquake, she mouthed.

He wouldn't move, he told himself. Goodness, he was high—utterly and hopelessly high.

Somewhere south of Sonoma, the epicenter of a quake had set him here in mid air, as precarious a position as the gods could dream up for a mortal. The crack looked as threatening as the scar down the center of his chest. If he could ever take a step, he would have to inspire his heart to jump over it.

Donna was crying and alternately pleading for him to remain completely still, help was on the way. He could see she wouldn't even open the sliding glass door for fear it might disturb the delicate balance. The wind whipped around his face and sirens wailed in the distance. Beneath him, rows and rows of vines stretched with ruler-like order in the afternoon sun, their sap flowing. Time passed through his fingertips like electromagnetic waves into the great oceanic blue and viridescent marriage of earth and sky.

He was free all right and nobody could tell him otherwise.

Q12081011

MR. CHESTER TOLD DAVID he would not pass tenth grade unless he passed gymnastics. "You can do it, boy," he said. "Just tuck your head under and let the momentum carry you."

David shook his head. "I can't."

"Can do," Mr. Chester said. "Repeat after me. Can do."

"Can do."

"*Can do*," Mr. Chester said. Several girls from the other side of the gym looked over. Gymnastics was coed, which made the activity particularly embarrassing.

"Watch me first." Mr. Chester crouched down on all fours to show David how to position himself for a forward roll.

The girls pranced around in their blue uniforms, locker keys dangling from their wrists on red and white lanyards. What soundless rhythm they moved to fascinated him—their easy laughter and the pleasure they took with their bodies turning somersaults and cartwheels in space.

"Pay attention, David," Mr. Chester said. He rolled forward and hit the front of the mat with a heavy thud.

David crouched down but couldn't make himself roll.

"I'll give you a push," Mr. Chester said. But as soon as he reached down, David jumped up and backed away.

"What's the matter, son?"

"I don't feel well," David said. The thought of being pushed over by Mr. Chester was frightening.

"You'll have to make the attempt," Mr. Chester said. "I can't pass you unless you make the attempt. There's nothing wrong with you and no reason why you can't do a forward roll. Everybody can do a forward roll."

•

"I'll go first," David's father said. Home from work for the first night all week, he had bought a mat to help David practice his gymnastics. David's mother stood against the wall in the rec room. His twelve-year-old sister, Tina, did flips, splits, cartwheels, handsprings. What a showoff, David thought.

Change fell out of his father's pocket when he did a lumpy roll across the mat. He stood up, red faced, his neck swelling over his collar. He was out of breath. "See? Nothing to it."

David's mother remained silent. His father loved to watch sports on TV. He couldn't understand David's lack of interest and two years ago had forced David to try out for the junior high basketball team. After everyone did a set of layups, the coach took David aside and said he could be a manager. "A player manager?" David's father asked that evening when David told him what had happened. "That's terrific. Like Pete Rose—only in basketball, right?" David nodded because he didn't want to disappoint his father. But when the first game came and his father arrived wearing a red sweater, the school color, with a scorecard in hand, and sat in the second row behind the team, all he saw was his son conked on the head by one of the basketballs that David hustled to collect after the players' warmup. "You don't even suit up," his father said on the way home. He sounded disgusted. David sat with the players' sweaty towels in a gym bag on his lap. Part of his job was to take the smelly towels home after the game and wash them. He thought about how wringing wet they were, the ten pounds of sweat he had to lug back with him. "They don't let you suit up?"

"I'm not a player. I'm just a manager."

"Christ, they don't even let you suit up," his father repeated. "Maybe you could at least ask them to let you suit up."

The following summer he went to work as an errand boy in the accounting firm where his father was a senior partner. Fran, the head secretary, was always polite and respectful and called him Mr. Lorber, like his father. Bringing his father back a corned beef sandwich one day, he walked in on the two of them embracing and it was so upsetting for everyone that David began to laugh ghoulishly, the kind of laugh he had when he watched *Creeper Feature* by himself on Friday nights and was scared out of his wits, and then he ran out of the office until his father chased him down.

"Your mother and I...we have some problems," he said to David, out of breath. "It isn't anything that can be helped."

"I don't want to work with you anymore," David said. "I don't want you to *push* me anymore."

"Of course, of course," his father said and David knew they had struck some kind of bargain, a bribe. His father could be made to squirm like everyone else. It was a sad revelation, the sudden power he had over him that made his father a frightened giant. "We don't need to tell anyone about this," his father said. David kept his face blank. He'd traded a piece of something solid and clean clutched deep inside him, something he had started out with, something everyone started out with. Gone now. "Promise?" David put his head down and nodded.

His father was on his hands and knees now, trying to align David's limbs for a forward roll. His mother stood above them, her hands spread over David's head, as though in a tense prayer. She couldn't stand noise of any kind—anyone else's noise. David was embarrassed to have friends over because she would shout down at them to "Shut up, your yelling is driving me crazy!"—when they weren't yelling at all, when they were playing quietly. The least disturbance from David or his sister produced hysterics way out of proportion to the wet towel left on the bathroom floor or the radio turned up too loud. He was frightened of his mother and tried always to be in a different part of the house than she was. In the morning he made sure he woke before she began slamming drawers or banging pots around in the kitchen, which happened all the time like some deranged percussion symphony. His sister, meanwhile, frozen with fear that she was somehow responsible for such rage, tried even harder to please, but would collapse at the slightest criticism or disappointment—if the peach in her lunch had a bruise on it. At twelve, she had already started wearing makeup and would stand in front of the mirror in the morning dabbing at her one or two pimples with cotton and alcohol. "That isn't good for your skin," David had warned her, trying to be helpful. Bad skin was an adolescent affliction he had been spared. "Please," she said with unbearable frustration at the intrusion. "I have to get this *done*." She was convinced if she only worked hard enough on the pimples she'd shrink them out of sight. David's heart went out to her, but his own frustration took the form of a chronic passivity and he just shrugged and walked past.

"Make your body into a tight ball and just roll." His father gripped David's shoulders, ready to throw him forward. At the other end of the mat was Wayne, their basset hound, his MY NAME IS WAYNE. PLEASE

RETURN ME TO…and other tags jiggling from his collar as he tried to come forward, restrained by Tina, to slobber on David for good luck. The will of the entire family pressed down on him. He had to do this for them. If he failed gym, he failed tenth grade, he failed his family, he failed God, whose latest incarnation for David had taken the form of Q12081011, a newly discovered quasar seventy-three billion trillion miles from earth. He tried to picture how far away that was—as far as he would have to roll.

"One…two…"

He grabbed onto his father's knees. He grabbed on with such force that his father cried out in pain.

"So," Rabbi Greenberg said. "You're wondering why I wanted to see you, David."

"No," David said. He knew why. His father had asked the rabbi to speak with him. He heard his father making the call after they gave up practicing gymnastics. *We can't do anything with him. He stays up all night and plays with that telescope we should never have given him. He mumbles when you ask him a question. And he's got some kind of phobia about gym class. Maybe you could just talk with him. He respects you. See what's up with him. We're ready to take him to a doctor, a psychiatrist, you know.* David had crept away from the closed bedroom door. He was becoming an expert at moving around the house with stealth. No one knew where he was, whether he was even home; no one could see him, he had become so adept at slipping around corners. Not bad for a mortal, he would say to himself as he disappeared behind a doorway, just missing being seen by his mother, father, or sister.

There were pictures on the wall of Rabbi Greenberg accepting an award from the United Jewish Appeal. Pictures of the rabbi, his wife, and daughter Lynn in Israel. Pictures of the rabbi at a Purim celebration in the synagogue, waving a noisemaker, a huge smile jumping out from his gray beard. David remembered a conversation he'd had with the rabbi two years ago, right before he was bar mitzvahed and was reading obsessively about the Holocaust, a subject that haunted him until astronomy became a more abstract yet purer contemplation of heaven and hell.

"What would happen," the rabbi had said, making time to talk with him, the first adult who took him seriously, "if there were neither one?"

"You mean nothing afterward?"

"No. That I didn't say. Not nothing. I said if there were neither heaven nor hell."

"I'm sorry. I don't understand the question."

He didn't. It was hard enough to imagine nothing—like trying to take an egg apart, empty out the yolk, and put the shell back together. Inside there was not nothing but rather the missing egg...which still existed, even if it wasn't inside anymore; it was an egg missing its insides, an eggless egg.

"What else could there be then?"

"Let me put it to you this way," the rabbi said. "Suppose you have two rooms. One is blue. The other is blue. One has good, comfortable furniture. So does the other. One has a nice fruit basket on the coffee table. Funny thing, so does the other. You look closer, you see these two rooms are exactly the same, same color, same furniture, same size, same fruit basket, same temperature, same scratch on the wall. But you know one is heaven and one is hell! You've been told this. How do you know when you're in one you're not, in fact, sitting in the other?"

"That's easy," David said. There was a knock at the rabbi's door. He was glad when the rabbi told the person just a minute. "You tie a string from one to the other and follow it back and forth. Two objects can't occupy the same space at the same time. This proves their separate existence."

"Ah," the rabbi said and stood up to answer the door. He had put his hand on David's shoulder. "Maybe you're right." But David had gotten the impression that his response was the correct wrong answer, the one the rabbi had expected but not wanted.

"What have you been reading?" the rabbi said now.

"Astronomy."

"No more Holocaust literature?"

"Not right now."

"You have anyone to tell your thoughts? Teachers at school? Any smart friends?"

"No."

"I would have been interested."

"I didn't want to bother you," David said.

"You mean you didn't want me to bother you."

He supposed that was true. Everything he did now he thought of as secret. As soon as he came home from school, he locked his bedroom door, read his astronomy books until late at night and then took the lens cap off his telescope and tracked the progression of Sirius or Canopus or Arcturus and the loneliness vanished.

"So what's doing with you? You're going to let some nudnik gym teacher keep you from passing this year?"

He told the rabbi about the gymnastics class.

"Let me understand," he said. "He won't pass you in gym because you won't do a forward roll?"

"Can't. Yes."

"What kind of Minnie Mouse business is this!"

Rabbi Greenberg stood up and stormed around the office. David had never seen him so upset. Finally, he told David to go home, he would take care of this personally. David left a little in awe of the rabbi's wrath.

But later that evening, the rabbi called and told him the gym teacher just wanted to see David try, he was refusing even to try—or he would need a medical excuse, which might be arranged also.

"No," David said. "I prefer not to," he added, quoting a character he had liked in a story from his literature class.

"So," the rabbi said. "I see this is your choice, what you wish."

"I didn't think so. Maybe it is." He thought about the moon circling the earth, the earth circling the sun, the planets circling each other, the galaxy rotating round another galaxy, the entire universe passing through a white hole to another universe and all of it repeated ad infinitum on a microcosmic level with subatomic particles, nothing stable. "I won't do it," David said. "I won't roll forward."

Q12081011 shines as brightly as 500 galaxies yet is a fraction of the diameter; a mere light month across. The quasar is the most powerful known, capable in one hour of generating as much energy as the sun does in its entire lifetime. Distance is seventy-three billion trillion miles from earth. Moving at a speed of 36,000 miles per second away from us this makes the quasar a front runner at the edge of the expanding universe. If God wears a jewel in his forehead, this is it. I have felt myself waiting for a discovery of this power. If I could see it, see any part of its light…

David's sister knocked at his door. "What?"

"Open up."

"Why?"

"Please!"

David unlocked the door. Tina stood there in her school clothes—parrot green pants and an orange T-shirt hanging down one shoulder. She had just gotten home from the mall where she went with her friends every afternoon to see boys and play Whirlyball. "Mom won't come out of her room."

"What are you talking about?"

"She won't come out. I tried calling to her that I was home and she didn't answer."

"Maybe she's asleep."

"She isn't asleep. She never sleeps in the afternoon. You go and see if you can get her to come out."

"Not me," David said. He backed away. The thought of entering his mother's room unbidden scared him. He hardly spoke to her as it was. They saw each other at dinner and in the hallway only when he found it unavoidable. She was a ghost or he was a ghost. Either way, the idea of knocking on her locked bedroom door was out of the question.

"Leave her alone. She's just resting," David said, making himself believe it.

"Will you please do something?"

David shook his head.

"You make me so mad! You're so snotty about everything because you can't even do a somersault in gym you're so spastic!" They were back to this again. She was liable to say anything now. He sat with his arm around the barrel of his telescope and waited. "I hate you! I hate everyone in this family!"

David heard her running up and down the hallway, to no apparent purpose. If anything was to get his mother out of her room, this was sure to do it—noise.

But she didn't come out. And his sister returned and pleaded with him to do something, please do something. Now, too, Wayne came jiggling into his room and looked up at David with bloodshot eyes.

David went down the hallway and took a few deep breaths before knocking lightly on his mother's door. There was no answer.

"What should we do?" his sister said. Her purple eye shadow, smeared from crying, was the color of eggplant.

He rested his hand on the doorknob; it turned. "Didn't you try the door before?"

She shook her head. "I thought it was locked," she said, as surprised as he was. They spoke in whispers to each other.

He opened the door. His mother was sitting at the table where she had coffee every morning by the window. She was wearing her bathrobe. She must have been there since morning, David realized. "Mom?" he said. His sister looked over his shoulder. Wayne's uncut claws clicked across the wood floor, but even he stayed back. "Mom, are you okay?"

He walked closer and then touched her shoulder and looked at her face. It was empty, chalky pale in the light from the window. Her hair was flat against her right cheek as though she'd slept on it all night. Her bathrobe was open, and he turned away from her flaccid breasts. She said something, but too faintly to hear.

"What?" David said.

"I'm going to make dinner."

"Mom," his sister said. "What's *wrong* with you?"

"We'll have green beans tonight. Both of you children. Don't you? You both like green beans?"

Her voice was barely audible, the words at the tail end of a breath in a monotone that made him shiver.

"Watch her," he whispered to Tina, who stood against the wall, her eyes huge; she held on to Wayne and stared at their mother, who didn't move. "I'm going downstairs to call Dad."

In the kitchen, he dialed his father's office. The new secretary—Fran had left five months ago—asked if she could take a message. His father was in conference.

"This is his son."

"Oh, hi, David."

"Could you interrupt him? It's important." He added "urgent," but she had already put him on hold.

"What's the matter, David?" His father's voice was quick, annoyed. It was his busiest time of the year. Two weeks before tax day, April 15.

"Something's wrong with Mom. She won't come out of the bedroom."

"What do you mean she won't come out of the bedroom? Is she lying down?"

"She's just sitting at the window. She's still in her bathrobe."

"Put her on."

"She can't talk."

"What's going on, David? Stop playing games and put your mother on the phone."

"I'm not playing games. Don't talk to me about playing games!" He was shouting. He cradled the phone under his chin and calmed himself. His temples pounded with blood and he could hear all the noise inside his head that his mother made in the mornings when she went on her drawer-slamming rampage. "If you're not home in a half-hour I'll tell everyone— everybody you ever met! I swear I will. You know what I'm talking about."

"David?"

"You better come home. That's all I got to say. If you don't come home…I swear if you don't come home…"

He hung up, then took the receiver off the hook so his father couldn't call back. He went upstairs. His mother and sister were as he had left them. "Is Dad coming?" Tina asked quickly.

"He'd better," David said. He sat down beside his mother.

"Can I get you anything?" She didn't answer him. She started to move her lips, there was some spittle between her bottom teeth and lip, then she closed her mouth. She thought she had spoken.

David touched her palm, open flat in her lap. She let his finger lie there, then closed her hand around it. Tina was swallowing her tears. "Come here," he told her. She came over immediately. "Sit down next to us and hold onto Mom's other hand." She did so obediently, glad to be following orders. "Tell her what you did at school today."

"What?"

"Tell her anything."

His sister talked about a math quiz and planning her class's project for Ecology Day and the spicy burritos for lunch. He listened to her voice…how hard she was trying. Their mother began to cry silently. He thought about the new quasar, to know he might one day see it! But its light was 12.4 billion years old, just now reaching the earth—who could know if the quasar itself still existed? He felt his throat tighten in pain. His sister rushed on about choral practice and a fire drill at school and her friend Joan's spiked hair, and he held tight to his mother's hand and looked out the window with her and down at their world.

Stranger

AFTER PACKING UP THE apartment and helping her sister deal with their father's estate, Elaine was flying back to Denver. Her father had died peacefully in his sleep at the age of seventy-nine. He had been strong and healthy right up until the end. He walked a mile a day at a brisk pace. He drank celery and carrot juice, watched his weight, and kept his mind active with everything from crossword puzzles to practicing piano to the occasional nine holes of golf. And he played a sharp game of poker with the other "youngsters" at the Jewish Community Center in Philadelphia. His blood pressure and cholesterol count had been those of a teenager, and his doctor expected him to live another decade or two. On the dark side, as her father put it, he liked his cigars and his martinis. But he hadn't died of smoking or drinking; he'd gone out just as he said he would: "They'll take me when I'm not looking, without a fight." And they had; he'd died right in the middle of the seven hours he slept a night.

Elaine's Aunt Winnie, her father's sister and a spry seventy-seven herself, had walked across the hall from her condo and found him lying in bed on his back, one hand across his stomach. "He looked like he'd just eaten a good meal," Aunt Winnie said. Elaine thought that everyone was trying to make his death appear so serene because her mother's had been so violent. She'd died at forty-eight in an automobile accident when Elaine was in her senior year of high school.

Sitting now in the waiting area for her flight home, she glanced at the Philadelphia newspaper and then heard the ticket agent's voice on the intercom. The news was not good. The flight coming from Chicago had been delayed by bad weather and would be at least an hour late. She slumped in her seat. She just wanted to get back to Denver. Richard and Katy—or "Caidee," as she spelled it now—their thirteen-year-old, had already flown home a week ago. As it was, Elaine would be coming in late at night. She'd made a reservation on the last possible flight of the day because she wanted to pack up as much of Dad's stuff as possible and not leave her sister, Rachel, with the entire mess. She'd decided she would need to make another trip back anyway. There was too much to sort through, including all the clippings from the local theater productions he'd been in. She read each of them, going back to the forties, when her mother had been in *Oklahoma!* with him. Elaine's expectation had been that she'd race through all the old photographs, accounts, bills, medical and insurance records and pave the way for Rachel to finish. But she'd been painfully slow, and frankly, at the end of two weeks, she felt as if she'd failed to make meaning of the details that profaned death into tabulations and schedules, receipts and scribbled notes, worn shoes and dusty suits.

Her father had never remarried. Plenty of widows and divorcées had been after him, but he rejected their interest. "Marriage is for life," he told Elaine once, "and in my case, death." The gloomy sentiment drove Elaine crazy. He could have remarried and had a full life, even perhaps another family. Instead, for the past thirty-one years, he'd kept a shrine to his dead wife. Her pictures were everywhere in the condo. In his later years he became even worse, referring to "we" all the time, as though Elaine's mother were still alive. When Elaine and the family visited from Colorado and he had his only grandchild in front of him—Rachel and her husband had never had children—he told stories not about when Elaine and Rachel were young but about his life with Elaine's mother: the ballroom dancing they did so suavely (Foxtrot champions), the husband-wife golf tournaments, the charity balls they organized. "We were quite the team," he boasted to Elaine in a phone call, just before he died. She held the phone through his reverie hoping for him to ask about Caidee, let alone her and Richard. But he didn't, and she could see now that he'd been bowing his head at death's door all this time, waiting to knock.

She awoke to the announcement that her flight would be delayed another hour. She'd fallen sound asleep; her head had lolled back on her left shoulder, her arm flung out as if she'd died in battle.

Reflexively, she touched her collar for any sign of drool; it had been that kind of sleep—deep and insular, from which you returned as if kidnapped. She sat up and started off to the bathroom. An older woman with white hair and thick tinted lenses in square frames stopped her.

"Your husband," the woman began, and gave Elaine's hand a friendly squeeze, "will be back in a moment."

"Pardon?"

The woman wore pink slacks and white sneakers and had a large straw bag that said "Grand Cayman." Fragile, slight, about the same age her mother would have been if she'd lived, she squeezed Elaine's hand again. "He's coming right back. He had to take your wallet for a minute to buy some travel items."

Elaine immediately plunged her hand into her bag, then dumped the contents of the purse out on the floor, combing frantically through the items—keys, lipstick, sales slips—her checkbook!—but no wallet. "Who?" Elaine said. "Who took it?"

"I don't...I thought—"

"What did he look like?"

"He was tall, blond—"

"What was he wearing?"

"A dark suit and a blue tie, I think. My goodness, I thought—"

Elaine quickly scraped everything back into her bag. A suit and blue tie. Every businessman in the world fit the description. "What else?" she said, her voice shrill. But she couldn't control her impatience, directed now at this woman who shrank from her. How could she have just watched someone take her wallet?

"He was carrying an overcoat on his arm. I'm so sorry. I didn't even look which way he went. He was so nicely dressed, and he...I thought he must be your husband," the woman said, obviously distraught now. "He kissed you, after all."

"What?" Elaine asked. "*What* did you say?"

"He kissed you. Right there," and she pointed to Elaine's right cheek, close to her lips. She touched her cheek and felt incredulous that this had been done while she slept, a violation disguised as sweetness.

The elderly woman said she was going to Miami, a flight that was scheduled to board in ten minutes. There was no time to search the airport. The best thing would be to call Richard at work and have him start the process of canceling their credit cards. He was teaching today, so she'd have to leave a message for him on his phone, or with the department secretary, and how could she succinctly explain that a stranger had kissed her while stealing her wallet? She felt the burn on her cheek, his lips creeping toward the moist corner of her mouth.

A ticket agent came up to her. The elderly lady from Miami had brought him over while Elaine had been trying to remember her calling card number—that card gone too.

"I understand your wallet is lost, ma'am."

"Stolen."

The agent nodded noncommittally.

"I saw him take it," the older woman spoke up. Elaine felt grateful for the witnessed support.

"We can have security look into it."

"I have to make my flight. I know it's delayed but I don't want to miss it just to have…" She was about to say just to have nothing happen, because she knew nothing would. The airport police or whoever was in charge would get information from her about something she'd not even observed. The woman who had seen it all, who had been an unwitting participant, searched nervously in her own handbag for something to write her name and address on, as directed by the ticket agent, so she could make the last boarding call of her flight. She gave Elaine a hug—it felt awkwardly inappropriate—and looked back over her shoulder once before she disappeared into the jetway. Elaine summoned enough generosity to smile back at her, then sat down with her purse, gutted of its wallet, her license, pictures of Caidee, credit cards from too many stores—she'd been meaning to consolidate—emergency phone numbers, her AAA, library, and insurance cards, a picture of her mother and her taken at a photo booth in Atlantic City when Elaine was eight years old and that she'd kept in her wallet all her life.

She looked for a tall man carrying an overcoat over his arm, dressed in a blue tie and a dark suit. Hundreds of them, of course. A crowd of travelers safely on their way. That's all, nothing else.

The airline gave her fifteen dollars in food vouchers and ten dollars in cash. "We're not required to do this," the woman at the customer service desk told her. "But we certainly understand and sympathize with your predicament." Her plane, coming through Chicago and held up by weather, was now two hours delayed. Elaine had made her way to customer service, then to security, filled out papers, and said what she knew. Which was nothing. A man had taken her wallet from her purse. She'd been sleeping.

The purse had been wedged next to her in the seat. He'd apparently kissed her—though she left this part out, because she didn't want to undermine her claim. She had talked to a round-shouldered man with an airport badge and she didn't want to see anything cross his face that would indicate he thought she was imagining or fantasizing the incident. The kiss was both the least relevant part of the robbery and of course the most. Long after today, she would remember it beyond any money gone or other inconvenience. For now, it was her own private piece of news, not quite a secret—that bestowed on it too much intrigue and hinted of pleasure— just a lone fact only she would know.

"We'll contact you as soon as we hear anything," the security officer had told her, then sent her back to customer service for further assistance— the vouchers. She thought the choice of "as soon as we hear anything" instead of "if we hear something" sounded much more positive, even if she didn't believe a word of it. It was all public relations at this point. She herself worked in the marketing department for a large software company in Denver, so she knew all about making a concept appealing. You sold the idea, not the thing.

Now she sat in a bar, using part of her courtesy money not for food but to have a glass of wine. She should buy some food to fill her stomach— her appetite had been off anyway ever since the funeral—but she was not hungry. The airline meal for sale would be expectantly horrible, and she would pass and perhaps order another drink. The thought of doing so, of having another glass or two of wine with the chintzy little bag of pretzels made her happy for a moment. Something to look forward to. She should also get off her stool, find a quiet place, and call Richard. Who knew how many charges had been made to her credit cards? But she was feeling lazy, knowing she would not be responsible for unauthorized purchases and dreading having to explain the whole annoying mishap to Richard. She continued to sip her wine.

A tall man sat down next to her.

He had an overcoat over his arm. But he had brown curly hair, not blond, and he wore a herringbone sports coat, not a dark suit and blue tie. Nor was it a surprise that he'd have an overcoat; it was cold and damp outside, and this was Philadelphia where people dressed more formally than they did in Denver with parkas and ski jackets. Indeed, nothing about the man looked like the description of the thief. He was what her father would have called an ordinary Joe, and after he ordered a Scotch from the bartender he turned to her and said, "Your flight delayed too?"

Elaine placed her wine back on the cocktail napkin. "Yes," she said, and left it at that. It had been a long time since anyone had tried to pick her up. She was forty-six and although she did not feel old, she didn't think men noticed her anymore, not in that way. Her figure was still good, trim. But it was her "figure," no longer her "body," and she was trim, not hot.

"I've been here since noon," the man said. "How about you?"

"A little after three."

The man—he had a strong, slightly hooked nose and his short curly hair was speckled with silver, about fifty she guessed—checked his watch. "What I hate," he started to say, and then looked up at the TV. "Oh, Jesus, we're never going to get out of here now. Did you hear that? There's a blizzard in the Midwest." He shook his head and took a long sip of his Scotch. "So, anyway, I cut you off, what were you saying?"

Elaine laughed at this, and she did not know whether he laughed along with her because he understood that he had only cut himself off or because he had no clue. It was sometimes hard to tell with men like him. The good-natured salesman type, who rolled from one segue to another without noticing much in between. She could say anything to him, she supposed, and he would listen pleasantly and meaninglessly. "My wallet was stolen," she told him.

"Oh for Pete's sake," he said, an expression she hadn't heard for a while. "That's misery. When'd it happen?"

"About an hour ago. I fell asleep in my seat and a man took my wallet." She paused a minute, to let him finish shaking his head. "He kissed me on the cheek."

Elaine waited to see his reaction. She would explain nothing further, a test of sorts.

"The kissing thief," he said. "Herman Grace," he added, extending his hand, and she wanted to laugh again—his last name. Was it real? She certainly wouldn't give a stranger her full name, but he was a man, after all, and on much safer ground here. "So anyhow," he was saying, "it takes all kinds, doesn't it? Next thing you know we'll have apologetic murderers and counseling prostitutes. What's the world coming to? Criminals kissing you on the cheek. That must be some sort of new age mugging."

"I don't think he meant it as a sensitive gesture."

"No," Herman Grace said, shaking his head. "You're quite right. There is nothing the least bit kind or caring about what was done to you. I've taken your comment about being robbed and kissed and made it into fodder for chitchat. I stand corrected."

At least he believed her.

The bartender came over and asked if she wanted another glass of wine. Immediately, she checked the remaining cash in her hand. Always a good budgeter, Richard had said about her, and the thought of Richard made her unhappy with responsibility: she should be calling him to inform him of the theft, checking in about Caidee, too.

"I'll have another," Herman said, holding his empty glass aloft. "And for the lady too, whatever she pleases." He turned back to her, his mouth, it seemed, suddenly full of extra teeth. "You don't mind if I buy you a drink, do you?"

"I should really check on my flight."

"Me, too," he said. "Me, too," but neither of them made a move to go, and when their drinks arrived, he slipped the bartender a twenty-dollar bill and told him to keep the change—a conspicuous, even vulgar gesture meant to impress her, she decided. She checked her face in the mirror behind the bar. Her hair curled smartly at the neck. Her eyebrows were darkened, her cheeks lightly—very subtly, she thought—rouged. And her eyeliner modest, restrained compared to, for instance, the spook show of Caidee's eyes. No, she didn't look like someone waiting to be picked up, not in her black turtleneck and gray skirt, her unpolished nails and stylish if discounted camel-hair coat that she'd gotten at a factory outlet mall in Denver. She looked, she thought, like her mother did before she died, if she hadn't dyed her hair and had let the gray show through like Elaine. It would soon be all gray. "Where are you from, Herman?"

"L.A. Born and raised. And trapped there. You?"

"From Denver."

"Terrific skiing. We try to make a trip there every season."

So, he had a family. He was not wearing a wedding ring and there was no mark from where he might have slipped it off. Now she was curious. "Do you have children?"

"Grown," he said. "Two boys and a girl. My daughter, she's at Haaavaad."

"You must be very proud."

"I certainly am," he said and took a swallow of his Scotch.

"And your wife? Is she back in L.A.?"

"Divorced." He drummed his fingers on the bar, smiled—defensively chipper?

"I'm sorry," she said.

"No need to be. We waited until the kids were grown, did our duty. Ten years of love, ten of stale bread." His eyebrows twisted a bit. "I'm not trying to pick you up, you know."

"Oh?" It was all she could manage.

"Am I insulting you?"

"Of course you are. I suspect you know that, though."

"You needn't worry about me. I'm harmless."

She considered him for a moment while he lit a cigarette, offering her one, which she refused. She never smoked. "What exactly *do* you want?"

"To talk. Just to talk."

She put her drink down half finished on the napkin. It was time to go.

"In which case I don't know anything about you," he said.

"Pardon?"

"You want to be anonymous. You would have told me something about yourself if you didn't."

She should leave instantly and decisively, but the wine made her legs feel as if they were kicking lazily through water at the bottom of the barstool. "If I'm not mistaken, you didn't ask."

"Because you weren't going to tell me. If you were, you would have told me your name when I told you mine."

"I must be out of practice. I don't make a habit of talking to strangers."

"I can see. Otherwise you would at least have given me an alias."

She looked at him for a long moment, then laughed. Alarmingly, she was finding herself less afraid of him. "What line of work did you say you were in?"

"I'm a private investigator."

"No, you're not."

"That's right, I'm not. I'm in the electronics industry. Semiconductors."

"Now I believe you, Mr. Grace."

"Is it Mr. Grace, now? We were on a first name basis a minute ago, at least unilaterally."

"A minute ago you were asking if I wanted to be picked up."

"If memory serves"—he put his glass against his forehead to feign concentration—"I was saying the opposite."

"You were *thinking* it. Am I wrong?"

"I was thinking you are very attractive, sure of yourself, and guarded, as you should be. I was also thinking you wouldn't believe me if I told you I have never done this before."

"Done what?"

"Approached a woman at a bar."

"You're right. I wouldn't."

"Let me ask you a question or two," he said. "Is that permitted?"

"Yes."

"Your name?"

"Elaine."

"Elaine," he said, as though examining her name like a small, pleasing, striated rock. "What is it you do?"

"Marketing, software. But don't ask me anything too technical. I depend on R and D to give me the details and then I spin them into gold."

"I'm sure you do." He picked up a pretzel from the bowl of party mix the bartender had left them and slowly chewed, then took a long drink. "I want to tell you something, Elaine. You won't mind, will you?"

"That depends."

"That's the sensible answer. But you needn't be afraid. I won't offend you."

The bar had become noisier, almost six o'clock now, and she could see by the crowd at her gate that her plane had still not arrived. She put her palm over her empty glass of wine, her second glass, to keep herself from ordering more. That was her limit usually, two glasses when she and Richard went out for the evening, but the idea of limits had suddenly become just that, an idea. She studied his hands; he had strong smooth fingers and clean nails. She appreciated a man who gave his fingernails attention. She stared at the white half moons of his cuticles, then raised her eyes and said, "Tell me. I'd like to hear."

"I'm not here on business. My children lured me here, perhaps that is the best word. They are fed up with me and have tried an intervention of sorts, to no avail. That's what I was doing in Philadelphia and that's why I am leaving alone. The intervention failed. They are furious with me. This is my fourth Scotch and my second pack of cigarettes in as many hours. Airport delays are unstructured, unhealthy time and I am as weak as I've ever been." He stared out the window a moment at the parked planes. "What nakedness would you like to tell me, Elaine?"

Names were being called over the paging system, Mr. Simon Agler, Mrs. Alsa Hong, Ms. Susan Lewis...Elaine heard them dimly along with the announcements of flights; the electronic beeping of courtesy carts going by; cranky children screaming at being dragged another inch through the miserable terminal with its delayed passengers. Right now the dirt of her father's grave would be running muddy from the rain, while a thief somewhere was picking through her assets, discarding credit cards, throwing her wallet with the photograph of her mother and her in Atlantic City into a filthy dumpster behind a warehouse. Her mother had hated the cold and damp, and on such mornings her father would warm her sweaters over the old steam radiators in their house on Belmont Street.

If her mother had remained alive, Elaine might not have made certain mistakes—entered into a disastrous first marriage or cut off friends when she needed them most. She might have told her mother, as she never did her father, about the "struggle" with the boy in college—what would flatly be called date rape now. She might have drawn more comfort and courage for this second part of her life had her mother lived and had her father not expected her and her sister to handle everything on their own, because Mother's death was mostly his loss. And yet she had loved her father all the more desperately after her mother died, jumping to him, her only remaining oar.

"My father just died," Elaine said. She was thinking about Herman Grace's grown children surrounding him, pleading with him to save his life. The image had an exquisite pain, so much love and so much stubbornness, so much trouble and so much spilled hope.

"I'm a man who still carries a handkerchief. May I?" and she let him dab at her eyes—she had started to cry. He worked tenderly, as if his fingers themselves were gloved, touching her cheeks with the soft cotton cloth, fresh and clean as a white veil.

"Can I help you get somewhere?" Herman Grace asked, because he could see when she stood up she was slightly unsteady from her two glasses of wine.

"I'll be fine," she said, but then leaned into him anyway, and he put his arm around her shoulder. He smelled of aftershave, Scotch, and smoke, a not unpleasant combination at the moment, and she listened to his breathing—heard all the discordant sounds of his life commingling into a stand against oblivion.

They walked silently toward her plane. She held his arm for comfort more than support, and she felt safe next to him. At the gate, passengers were gathered around the ticket agent's podium.

They went over and listened. The flight had been cancelled, stuck in Chicago. People were angry, asking why they hadn't been told sooner. "We got the information to you as soon as we received it," the ticket agent said, a thin man with droopy eyes. One other flight this evening was scheduled for Denver, but that was on a different airline and presently at full capacity, the ticket agent said, studying his monitor. "Everyone will be rebooked on flights tomorrow morning," he told them. "We can't control the weather. I'm very sorry, but if you need assistance with arrangements for staying overnight we can try to help."

"*Try*," Herman Grace said. "Key word. They're not obligated to do anything because it's weather-related."

She stared in disbelief at the scrolling red letters on the board: FLIGHT CANCELLED. "I can't believe this. I can't fucking believe this." Herman Grace looked away, quieted, she wondered, by her profanity. "You'd better check on yours," she told him, though she did not want him to leave her alone.

"I did," he said. "It's still cancelled."

She stared at him. "Still? What do you mean?"

"It was cancelled hours ago. I've been—how shall I put it?—*reluctant* to leave the airport. I didn't want to face my children, and I didn't want to go to an empty hotel room. And then I met you."

She knew now he was asking her to spend the night with him, and she was thinking that she could do it and live with the guilt or not do it and live with the relief and that the two choices didn't seem that far apart in consequence. She had assumed such parallel lines would never converge—and they never had for her. But, as Richard was fond of saying, she was in a state. All the more reason to behave badly and irresponsibly, not be accountable for her actions from the shock of her father's death, her stolen wallet, her cancelled flight…

None of this equaled the clarity of knowing that what she was about to do was wrong.

She could—*should*—take a cab to Rachel's house and spend the night. Her sister would surely be glad to drive her the next morning to the airport, as she had done this afternoon. She could even sleep in her father's apartment, the bed where he died, a communion of sorts, maybe finding a macabre peace in his penultimate resting place. She certainly had resources, unlike Mr. Grace. "I need to make a phone call," she told him. "Where should I meet you?"

"Same old, same old." He pointed to the bar where they'd been. "Shall I order you anything?"

"Water, please."

"Me, too," he said. "The healthy choice."

Her cell phone was out of juice, and she didn't want to ask Herman Grace to use his. She went over to the pay phone and made a collect call to Richard, prepared to hang up if he didn't answer after three rings, long enough to fool herself into believing she tried.

"Hello?"

"Richard," Elaine said, and could feel herself saying his name as if she had just dropped all her heavy bags in front of him with utter relief.

"Where are you, Laine? What's wrong? You're calling collect."

"I'm still at the Philadelphia airport. My flight's been cancelled. Oh, Richard, what a day it's been."

"I was just about to go out the door to pick up Caidee after her swim practice and go straight from there to the airport. What happened?"

"My wallet was stolen. I'm so sorry, I should have called earlier."

"Your wallet? Are you all right? Were you hurt?"

"No, no," she said, imagining his worried face. "I'm fine. I was sleeping. It was stupid. He took it from my bag by pretending…" She looked over at the bar. Herman Grace waved to her and she back at him.

"Laine? Are you going out on a later flight?"

"There are no others tonight. I'll have to fly back tomorrow morning."

"You'll stay at Rachel's, right? Can we reach you there? I want to know you're safe. It will be good to be with your sister after such a miserable day."

"I think," she said, playing with the phone cord, "I think I'm going to stay near the airport. The flight leaves early."

There was a pause, and she thought that Richard didn't believe her, but he said, "That's a good idea perhaps." She nodded, as if she'd gotten a forged permission slip. "But what will you do for money?"

"What?" she asked, understanding clearly what he had said.

"Money for a hotel."

"Maybe," she said, placing a hand on her stomach, "I can get the airline to help."

"Are you sure? I hate to think of you there without a cent. You really should call Rach—"

"I'll be fine. Give Caidee a kiss for me. I miss you both."

"I love you, too. And, Laine, be good to yourself. Your father and all."
She touched her cheek where the thief's lips had been and felt a bluish
heat, ran her finger up near her earlobe where Richard liked to kiss her and
felt Herman Grace's mouth there.

When she got off the phone, she didn't look over at Herman Grace
at the bar; she didn't want to show anything on her face. She went into the
bathroom and sat on the toilet and listened to more names being paged...
Mr. Callahan, Ms. Wilkens, Mr. Pintauro...a dull drone of missing people.
She looked at herself in the mirror for a long time after she brushed her
hair: her brown eyes, such pretty, warm eyes her mother would always say,
like little poems.

She walked out of the bathroom, joining the dwindling crowd—
people on their way home or to hotels overnight or back to where they
started. There were only two men sitting together at the bar, younger men.
She stood in the middle of the concourse and watched both ways, and then
kept her eyes on the men's bathroom for a moment. She went into the bar
and sat down to wait; he was no doubt in the bathroom himself.

The bartender, the same one who had been there before, came over
to her. "The gentleman said to give this to you." He handed her a business
card. Elaine looked at it: Herman Grace, Tritronics Electrical Systems.
She turned the card over: *Is it cowardly or honorable of me to leave? Try to
think well of me. I always will of you. Love, Herman.*

The bartender had his back to her and was washing a glass. Elaine
stared out at the terminal—the people passing through. When she'd been
young, her whole family would watch the show *To Tell the Truth.* She'd sit
with them on the couch with its rose-patterned brocade fabric, running
her finger across the delicate petals, the sturdy stems, the sharp thorns,
imagining the touch of a boy's spine. One night, while her parents held
hands and she shared a pan of popcorn with her sister, the show's host had
declared to the three contestants, *Will the real thief please stand up?*

Beside her was the bottled water Herman Grace had ordered for
her—she'd only noticed it now—poured into a glass, with a slice of lemon.
Elaine looked down and smiled to herself. Her sweet, gentle mother would
have said, you're smiling from ear to ear, darling, why?

Society of Friends

As soon as we get in his Volvo, Marty puts on a tape, Little Anthony and the Imperials. "Remember?" he says. "Remember, Loon, when we saw these guys at the Latin Casino?"

I remember I haven't been called "Loon," my high school nickname for Lewis, since I graduated thirteen years ago. Nor have I seen Marty more than twice in all that time. He was my best friend for two years, fourteen to sixteen years old. We used to argue about our record collections (whose was immortal), about everything I suppose. When we happened to see each other at a movie last night, he insisted Sidney and I join him and his wife for dinner this evening.

"I got something to show you before we pick up the sitter," he says.

Marty turns onto the dirt road of a farm where I often went with my parents to buy fresh eggs, sweet corn, and cider. The area still looks the same, a row of oak trees bordering the long driveway, and a wire fence tangled with blackberry bushes. Then I see a change where the oak trees stop abruptly. At the bottom of the valley are five high-rise buildings, three of them naked to their steel girders; the other two are finished, with only the soaped X's left to be washed from the windows. Except for a few half-moons of grass, the entire valley has been cleared and graded.

"I own three," Marty says.

"You own three of those buildings?"

"Three *condos*. Five thousand down, Loon—that's all I paid for each one. You know what I can sell them for today?" He wets his finger and writes the figure in the air, complete with comma. "*Two-hundred thousand.*"

"So you're a speculator now?"

"Come on, Loon, pull together a little cash and I'll set you up with some nice holdings. Don't play the poor man's martyr. Nobody's noticing these days."

"I'm not looking for anyone to notice." A station wagon turns up dust as it speeds by us to the apartments. "We'd better go," I say.

"Now you're mad at me, Loon. I'm trying to give you a little pep talk and you're mad at me."

"I'm not mad. I'm hungry."

"Sidney asked me to bring you out here, you know."

"Sidney? Never, Marty."

"It's the truth! You were in the john. She said you might go for something along this line."

"Come on, Marty, grow up. She was kidding you."

"Hey, buddy, ask the lady yourself," he says, opening his hand flat the same way we did in high school when we were talking tough.

The rest of our ride is in silence, except for when the sitter joins us and begins chattering, apropos of nothing, about her volleyball team. I catch myself shaking my head over Marty's remark, remembering how he was too impatient to ever listen carefully to me or anyone else.

Edna and Sidney are waiting on the front porch, evidently not hitting it off on their first meeting, Edna looking grim and Sidney not much better. I never knew Edna before. Marty met her in college. And Sidney doesn't know anyone in the East at all. We've come back for a while to visit my parents. I've learned to distinguish between her silences, and this one seems more uneasy than contemplative.

The baby begins crying as soon as she sees the sitter. Like Edna, the baby has red hair and pale blue eyes. She wears a hot-faced scowl and screams upon being turned over to the sitter. Marty tells us to hurry and nudges us toward the car.

"The restaurant has no phone," Edna says.

"Let's roll," Marty says, but he rushes inside the house and returns with two six-packs of beer under his arm. "Got to bring our own. No liquor license yet."

"What should I do about the number?" Edna asks. "How's she going to reach us if she needs to?"

"We'll call from the restaurant. Come on, get in the car, Edna."

"There *is* no phone."

"Of course there's a phone. There's got to be a phone."

"Marty, I'm telling you—"

"All right, for Christ's sake get in the car! I'll leave the address! She can call the police!" Marty searches in his wallet for something to write on, and finding nothing he can spare, he scribbles the address on a five-dollar bill and stuffs it into the babysitter's hand.

"I love this place!" Marty says. Mounted on the wall are golden dragons, the jaws of one protruding right above my head. Aggressive Chinese music (someone angrily striking a xylophone?) comes from speakers hidden in the ceiling. Marty appreciated these places in high school. "Wait till you taste the mu shu beef," he says.

Sidney and I are vegetarians, and I can tell Marty is disappointed when we order the Eggplant in Garlic Sauce and the Northern Style Vegetables.

"Veggie fanatics?" he asks.

"No," I say. "Vegematics."

He slaps his hand on the table, making Edna jump. "I love your humor, Loon!" He smiles, shakes his head, seems to grow warm toward me again. "So you're no longer a hotshot advertising exec?"

"Not anymore."

Somewhere between getting a job at an ad agency right out of college and then quitting after five years and trying to run a restaurant, I collapsed from nervous exhaustion and was hospitalized. Afterward was when I met Sidney, who brought peace and sense into my life. "Sidney and I work in a medical clinic now," I tell him.

Marty's eyes widen. "You went to med school?" I remember this was his dream. He wanted to be a surgeon and quit the football team—two hundred pounds in tenth grade—to join the biology club so he could do a cat dissection. But he got a terrible score on his college boards and barely made it into a junior college. On graduation night, he hit someone in the mouth for meowing at him in the lavatory.

"I'm not a doctor. I assist Sidney, who's a nurse. A doctor volunteers his time. The clinic is free." I pause a moment. "It's run by Quakers. Sidney and I are Quakers."

Sidney frowns at this last piece of information, confirming the hesitancy I had. A member of the Friends since she was young, she never talks about our work, never suggests that it's a noble or even valuable task. But the experience—the satisfaction—for me is so new and pleasing that I brim over with enthusiasm, promising anyone the same steadiness, the delight of working hard without worry (this most of all), the wealth in service.

Marty takes a beer from the sack. "Do Quakers indulge?" he asks.

"We'll split one," I say.

"I think I'll have my own," says Sidney, surprising me. We usually share a glass of wine, if we drink at all.

Marty places a can of beer on everyone's empty plates. "So what should we do after dinner?" he asks. "Do Quakers dance?"

Sidney leans over and touches his wrist. "Quakers have no legs," she whispers.

Her serious tone and the lack of any past kidding from her on the subject of Quakers makes me as silent as Marty for a moment, half believing it myself. Then Marty bursts out laughing, and even Edna warbles a little chuckle through her tight lips. Marty keeps erupting—emptying his lungs with great blasts of joy, his eyes squeezed shut in unbearable delight. His fervor wins me over, and when he takes out a handkerchief, wipes his neck, and calls out *Bring on the unfortunate cookies!* I laugh like a fool, until I, too, ache.

At the bar that Marty drives us to, we find a table just large enough for us all to crowd around while we watch the dancers on the floor.

"Gimps!" Marty hisses. "You call that dancing? That's a chain gang out there! Who wants to dance?" he asks.

"Cut in on someone," I recommend when no one answers. "They don't know you're here yet."

"We'd better call the sitter if you plan on staying long," Edna says.

He takes off his tie and stuffs it in his pocket. "Okay, who's going to be the lucky lady?" He stares at Sidney.

"Face it, Marty," I say, "we're chaperones now."

"I'll dance," Sidney announces and abruptly stands up, gulping down half the wine the waitress has just brought her. They weave their way onto the floor and find a spot in the corner. Marty jitterbugs with surprising speed, stretching one arm out to make room for himself and shooting Sidney back and forth with the other. Her cheeks are flooded with color. Her shoulders sweep up when Marty spins her under his arm. Sidney is laughing, out of breath, alternately patting her chest and waving her hand in imitation of Marty. "Do you see that?" I say, amazed. "She's dancing with him. Sidney never dances."

For a moment when I glance at Edna, I think I see two white carnations, one on each breast. But it's only her hands folded into tight fists across her chest. Her face couldn't be more stoney: her mouth drawn taut, her eyes the blankness of blond wood. Then the expression suddenly shatters when she drops her head to the table with such forceful sobs that her glasses fly off.

Before I'm even sure I've seen anything, she removes a tissue from her bag, blows her nose, and without looking at me takes back her glasses that I've picked up from the floor and puts them on.

I realize she's younger than I thought, probably several years younger than Marty. Her mouth tries to open several times, compresses with tension, and then strains to the side. "Don't visit us." She slides her hand forward to keep me from speaking. "Don't visit us anymore. Please."

I stare at her, waiting for an explanation. None comes. She says nothing, has nothing else to say. Any answer she might make is buried in the opaque whiteness of that hand, the skin looking as though it could be peeled back to expose another layer, one shade lighter, one lamination softer, going on like that indefinitely, whiter and more tender, never translucent, veinless. Her hand stops at the edge of mine. I nod, not sure why or for what purpose, promise we won't see them again while we're here, and she withdraws her hand, turning away to stare vacantly at the dancers.

I drive Marty's Volvo back to his house. Sidney sits up front and Marty lies in the back, his head on Edna's lap, one shoeless foot sticking out the window. He keeps patting me on the shoulder. His voice is deeply hoarse and just listening to him I can feel my own throat burning. "Could I have been a contender? Could I have been somebody, Loon?" I'm not sure what the correct response is to this question, but I vaguely remember something about answering the remark with a question in the negative. "Could you not?" I try.

"You remember!"

"Dare to be great," I add...but evidently press my luck too far, because he keeps repeating the phrase, "Dare to be great...dare to be great," trying to figure out how we used that one.

When we get to the house, Marty tells us, "You're coming in for some coffee."

Edna hurries inside to check on the baby. The rest of us stand in the driveway.

"I don't think so," I say. "It's late. We should be going."

Marty sighs heavily and walks to the front door. "Look," he says, "you had a great time, right?"

"The best."

"How about you, Sid? You like that high-stepping we did?"

"Very much."

"Terrific. Ask me if I had a good time. Go ahead."

"Did you, Marty?" Sidney says.

"Just ducky. Remember, Loon? Just ducky?"

"Gotcha Natasha. Stash it, Satchell."

"What's that mean?"

"Who knows," I say, giving up. Edna doesn't return.

"Marty, say goodbye to Edna for us."

"You call me, Loon. You call me before you leave or I'll cork your head and snap your mother!"

"*Jesus*, Marty."

"Remember?"

"Yes, yes," I swear, not remembering in the least and a little alarmed by his desperation. Marty stands inside the screen door, his face pressed against the wire mesh, flexing his two pudding thumbs goodbye at us.

"Loon!" he calls, but doesn't say anything else.

I wait until we're a respectable distance down the road before I ask, "What do you think—fun couple, huh?"

Sidney nods and pulls a yellow windbreaker over her shoulders. I loosen her short blonde hair from her collar, massaging her neck. She closes her eyes, drops her head—murmurs for me to continue.

"I was joking about them being a fun couple."

"Hmm?"

"You didn't really have a good time?"

"Yes. Didn't you?"

"Not exactly. Edna was very upset about something. She started crying while you two were out on the dance floor."

"So did he."

"Come on! Did he?"

"There were tears in his eyes after we started dancing. I don't know if it was from the exertion or what."

We drive for a few minutes in silence. "Well," I say, "we'll never see them again anyway."

Sidney slides down in her seat. "I'm tired," she says.

"Listen, this sounds crazy, but Marty said you spoke to him about wanting me to be in real estate. Isn't that a bizarre thing for him to say?"

"I did talk with him. I said you should be in a field where you can be more competitive." I slow the car down. Her voice has an unfamiliar inflection. "It's still very much in you, Lewis, all that rivalry—except now you want to be the best Quaker on the block."

I don't answer for a few minutes, weighing the criticism. I know I've changed in not leaping to my defense. "Why did you say you had fun tonight?"

"I liked dancing. I liked drinking. I liked all the noise. I even liked Marty twirling me and practically snapping off my wrist with his fandango. It felt good."

It's hard to keep my foot firmly on the gas pedal and not drift to a halt in the middle of the road. A current of pain heats the air in my lungs. I breathe with care until we pull into the driveway. We go upstairs and sit on the edge of the bed. The TV in my parents' bedroom goes off, and when it does my throat tightens, the picture tube crackling for a few seconds as I remember it always did. We move only slightly, staring into corners, fingering curtain hems. After what seems ages, Sidney says, "You're not trying to force silence, are you?"

I tell her I'm not.

My mother walks by our closed door, down the hall to click on the night light; she returns just as quietly to her room.

"So what happens tomorrow?" I ask. It's starting to sink in. "Do I put on my long black robes and you your red satin dress and we go out solemn and sassy?" She makes a face. "What exactly are you suggesting?" I say.

"Sleep. Let me sleep," she says.

I'm sitting down, but my feet clop nervously on the wooden floor. So I stand up, let them move around a little. "I'll be back," I tell her. Before I realize it, I'm two flights below, in the basement, arguing with myself, making points with my hands, my chin—the crown of my head.

Upstairs, I pace some more until Sidney comes out from the

bathroom, a pale smile on her face. I return an even weaker smile and try to make up for it by giving her a tap on the arm—just like Marty and I used to do in junior high when we passed each other in the hall. We were at the height of our friendship then.

She hits me back. I stare at her. She socks me again. I look; she punches harder. I can't believe her violence. She smacks my other arm. I knock her back. Her knuckles rake my shoulder. Mine touch bone. We keep punching each other, not making a sound, wincing, refusing to budge.

Mort à Las Vegas

"FUN" WAS THE WAY Tess phrased it. "I want to have *fun*." Gene had asked her how she wished to remember Mom this year and Tess, at fourteen, two years older than she was when Janice died, answered, "I think I've done the grief thing." Teary and clingy on the first anniversary of Janice's death, his daughter had gone through a swift transformation and was now dismissive of any adult claims that she might be suffering residual effects over her mother's death. Her favorite phrase, in regard to cooperating or pleasing anyone, was the bored, "Whatever ups you," and her favorite activity was to lock her bedroom door, blast her iPod—Gene could hear it through her door and only imagine what it was doing to her eardrums—and thrash around in stomping madness. When she came out, her face was blazing red, her hair sweaty, and her clothes rumpled as if she'd been mauled by a bear or undergone some ecstatic ritual. He heard her sobbing in there too, but she always denied this was over anything other than it just "felt good." Fortunately, she wasn't cutting or starving herself, didn't smell of liquor or pot, wasn't purging or hoarding food or sleeping constantly, all signs of depression, Gene knew.

Regardless, she was firm about skipping the mountains and not doing a memorial service again, including having Janice's large family come visit them in Colorado and be smothered by their sadness and pity. "Mom would want us to have fun," she told him. The whole idea of going to Las Vegas made him wonder if Tess, having reached adolescence and its insistent focus on the now, was in a race to bury the past and her mother for good.

But perhaps he was conjecturing too much. He was a journalist and not particularly inclined toward the speculative or philosophical; it was a liability that got in the way of the facts. And the fact was, unlike him, she was doing remarkably well for losing her mother in a freak accident. "She'd want us to live it up, not get all gloomy," Tess reiterated.

Gene didn't know about this. He couldn't say *what* Janice would have wanted. After all, she was dead, having choked on a sandwich while alone at home. He didn't believe, as his religious mother-in-law did, that Janice was watching over them and approving or disapproving of their behavior.

"That is just so insensitive," said Kate, Janice's younger sister. "She's only been dead two years and you're going to *Las Vegas*." Even his own brother, not one to miss a good time, sighed and admitted, "Well, I could think of less tacky places to be observant." Gene, ignoring the criticism, wanting only to please Tess, invited everyone to join them; he wasn't surprised when no one accepted.

He'd promised Tess that she could bring a friend. And she had, Allie, who was as tall as Tess was short. They made quite a pair strolling through the casino arm in arm, careful not to step off the carpeted track for anyone under twenty-one and into the gambling areas.

They raced off to the pool, wearing their bikinis under their cover-ups. Janice would have had a word to say about this—indeed she would have made both of them change or never let Tess buy the revealing suit in the first place. Starting as she was to develop at an astonishing and uncomfortable pace for Gene, her suit showed off to explicit proportions the same maturing curves that her mother had possessed. Allie, by comparison, was long and thin, as lacking in bust as Tess was plentiful.

He had a list of medications for Allie's allergies, a medical release for emergencies, cell phone numbers—three of them—and a roll of money that Allie's parents insisted on his taking, even though he'd said it was his treat. He was just barely getting by on his salary. Janice had worked as a doctor's receptionist, and her job offered good benefits and stable employment, unlike his position. In fact, he was fairly sure when he got back that either (a) the Denver paper would not exist or (b) he'd lose his job anyway. No matter that he'd been there for fifteen years and had won a Pulitzer for his series on the Denver Christmas blizzard of 2006 that had shut down the city, immobilized its airport, and sent him out to interview stranded, near-frozen motorists, some of whom had been in their cars for thirty-six hours. That was so then, as Tess liked to say. And (he hated to think of it in these crass terms, but such was the reality) Janice had left them with little. A minimal life-insurance policy and no survivor benefits. Who planned for such things anyway—choking on a sandwich! People didn't really die from such a cause. Somebody was always there to rescue you, perform the Heimlich maneuver. You *almost* choked to death like you almost died from being too hot. It was an exaggeration, more a figure of speech than fact. How many times had he heard people say, "I almost choked on…" Whatever. A piece of meat, a grape. But with Janice it had been the real thing, dying alone, her face as blue as a dead baby's.

A month after Janice died, Tess told him "I want you to remember that I hate spinach, and that I get headaches in April, and that I can't walk as fast as you, and that Mom and me used to put our foreheads together and stand like that without talking, and that I get the hiccups when something scares me."

Such directness of communication all seemed so long ago now, when he swore his allegiance to remember every tiny detail of his daughter's life, never forget an orthodontist appointment, make it to every school play, recital, and tennis match, and generally be the Greatest Single Parent Alive. He'd started a shared journal; they were each to record their more personal feelings in its pages. No facile texting, emailing, tweeting…just a solitary fountain pen next to a leather-bound journal.

At first Tess wrote openly: *I'm sad up to my neck and only my head is clear.* Which he'd interpreted to mean she felt all the grief in her twelve-year-old body but kept her mind busy enough to function. But the rules of the journal dictated that you couldn't question the other person about what was put down. Gene wrote, *I hope you'll forgive me if I say anything stupid over which Mom would have rolled her eyes and told me to go wait in the other room while she spoke to you.* Tess drew a smiley face beside that one. He wrote about how wonderful her birth was and how ecstatic he and Janice were when she was born ("we tried for years"), and how they used to stare at her as a baby and sigh over her gorgeous eyebrows and dark, excitable eyes.

But gradually the journal morphed into a place for Tess to note her social life. *I have two-tone nails, a blue stone toggle bracelet, black high heels, and a party dress from Indigo Rose,* she wrote about going to her first dance. *Ryan's not as short as some and has less acne than others,* she observed about the boy who was taking her. *Funny!* Gene jotted next to it. Then, shortly after Tess turned fourteen she wrote *Why can't I wear a thong?* And Gene wrote back, *Do I need to give you an entire social discourse on why you can't wear a thong?* Tess had written *NO!!!!* And underlined it three times. That was the end of their journaling. He made a few more stabs at neutral entries (*I'm cooking your favorite tonight—mac and cheese from scratch* and *I think we could watch the movie* Thirteen *together, if you would be comfortable*) but she hadn't bit on any of these and the pages remained blank over the next several months. It wasn't until they started talking about how to commemorate the second anniversary of Janice's death that Tess wrote in the journal again: *LAS VEGAS—HOT!*

It was hot all right—the temperature sign outside the hotel registering 110 at nine o'clock in the morning. The girls had been up since six, watching TV while waiting for Gene to awaken and supervise them. He'd heard them moving around in their side of the suite, but couldn't make himself get out of bed—no excitement in his joints. Surely this was a sign of depression, or a deeper depression than the anti-depressants he'd been given by his family doctor could mitigate. He had seen a therapist, but his health plan, recently updated (more like *down*dated), limited him to six sessions, and he pretty much exhausted those the first week talking about how ludicrous it was that Janice died because of choking on a sandwich when she was in perfectly good health, fantastic health, actually. Unlike Gene, she exercised faithfully, ran marathons, sweated through Bikram yoga, ate sensibly, and was super conscientious, given she worked in a doctor's office, about washing her hands. She rarely got sick. Her immune system, she used to say, came compliments of five generations of Irish stock that had survived epidemics, famines, and alcohol.

Meanwhile, Gene sometimes nursed a cold for weeks that would inevitably turn into bronchitis and twice pneumonia. He was overweight by thirty pounds, hard of hearing at forty-six, both his elbows had bursitis, and he was a negligent flosser with receding gums. His father had died of a coronary at fifty-four and his mother of cancer three years later. By the natural laws of predation, *he* should have been the one picked off like a sickly gazelle. There was no earthly reason why Janice, a perfect specimen of health and vigor, should wind up stone dead instead of him.

He suspected people were embarrassed to talk about the nature of Janice's death, as if it were slightly in that category of being the victim's fault, like drunk driving. Something for which you had to take personal responsibility. Only one person, their dotty next door neighbor, Louise, had spoken up loudly at the funeral and dared to ask, WAS THE SANDWICH STILL IN HER THROAT WHEN THEY FOUND HER? Someone hushed her up—Neil, the husband, maybe—the appropriate appalled whispers had been sounded, but old Louise had hit it on the head with her morbid curiosity. Most untimely deaths dignified themselves by their dramatic circumstances: the catastrophe of a plane crash; the ferocious consumption of a fire; the brutal decline from cancer; the swift strike of a heart attack; the sucking undertow of a drowning. You felt the hand of God in these cases, the reminder of a force snuffing out life with a destructive smack. But to choke on your lunch was to be sabotaged by an effort to nourish yourself. Death came not galloping on a winged black stallion with a sickle to do battle ... but with a peanut butter and cucumber sandwich to waste you. Just a big fucking joke.

Oh, he was bitter all right.

He sat by the side of the pool reading while the girls went down the water slides. The clientele were either bronzed and buff singles, or honeymoon couples, or screaming children on summer vacation. Meanwhile, the pool was so crowded you could walk across it on people's heads.

Tess and Allie popped up in front of him, their hair dripping wet and their faces full of girlish excitement. "We were invited to a party!"

"What!" said Gene, rising quickly from his chaise.

"*Shh*," said Tess. "You're *embarrassing* us." And it was true, several of the shimmering brown bodies on the chaises had roused themselves and shielded their eyes to see what his outburst was about.

"Okay," said Gene, lowering his voice a notch, "you understand that this is dangerous and that such men—"

"They were our age," put in Allie, who with her height could easily pass for sixteen.

"I'm sure not," said Gene.

"Really, they were," said Tess. "We carded them."

"You what?"

"We made them show us their school IDs. They're going into ninth grade like us."

"Listen," said Gene, trying to keep his voice that of a reasonable adult and not a hysterical widower with two hormonally at-risk teenagers in Sin City. He had visions of thirty-year-old pedophiles shaving to baby-faced extremes and using fake middle-school IDs to lure girls into depraved quarters. "You are *not* going to any parties, you are *not* going anywhere without me, and you are *not* going to give out any personal information about yourselves."

"Mr. Guthridge," said Allie, "Tess already explained to them that we couldn't accept their invitation. By the way, your shirt's buttoned crooked." When she came over, Allie would always look around for something to tidy at the house. She'd fold the towels properly, stack the magazines squarely, put the salad dressings in their right places in the refrigerator door. She also organized Tess's closet, fixed her sluggish computer, and cooked dinner at their house when Gene wasn't around. He'd more than once heard Tess favorably call Allie "Mom."

"Well, I'm proud of you then," said Gene. "Both of you. You're going to get a lot of attention now that you're getting older and—"

"*We know*," said Tess, raising her hand like a traffic cop for him to stop. "You haven't even gone swimming yet, have you?"

"I'm fine, thank you," said Gene. "We should go get ready for tonight."

Terrible visions of losing them and having to explain to family members why he and the FBI were presently negotiating a ransom with Eastern European gangsters disguised as ninth graders made him insist on following closely on their heels, as they took the elevator up to their room to change for the evening into more modest clothing.

Sex was not something he let himself think about. Curtailing such thoughts was less difficult than he would have imagined at one time when he was in better shape and had a willing wife. Now all he had to do to shut down his libido was look at himself in the mirror: the slack skin of his cheeks; the hair loss that had accelerated since Janice's death; the belly that had widened his navel into a small hairy mouth. Ugh. And the anti-depressants did their job, too, falling just short of chemical castration. Oh, God, he could be so tough on himself. If Janice could only see him now. Of course, according to his mother-in-law, she was watching all the time, disapproving of his being in Las Vegas with his fourteen-year-old daughter and his prurient thoughts about contacting an escort service. "Hello, I'm Gene," he said to his reflection. "Please send a companion up to the fat man's room."

"Can we go now?" Tess called from the door of their adjoining room.

"In a minute," he said. He deliberated what shoes to wear. The thought of walking on the hot pavement in hard shoes made his feet ache. But they were going to a magic show later at the Monte Carlo, and he imagined they had to dress up a little nicer for that than being the slob he was around this fading discount hotel.

He put on his loafers and khakis and cinched his belt painfully tight so he'd remember not to gorge himself. He knocked on the girls' connecting door. They appeared in full makeup, including eyeliner so dark that they looked only a generation removed from the Pharaohs. Thankfully their dresses were of reasonable length—Tess's white and strapless, and Allie's peach-colored with a ruffled neckline and hanging loosely from her narrow shoulders. They had on platform sandals that he knew would kill their feet. The phrase "sensible shoes" belonged to a distant galaxy, far, far away. Their nails were polished to a lacquered shimmering pink—the whiff of acetone had hit him as soon as he opened the connecting door—and they'd washed their hair and blown it dry, despite the instant microwaving heat outside, to a blossoming silky sheen across their shoulders. And here they stood, framed in the doorway, awaiting his approval, as if any male attention, even his, might satisfy their budding sense of power and allure about their approaching womanhood.

"Well, I wish your mothers could see you now," said Gene. Their faces fell. Tess especially looked alarmed. "I mean that as a compliment," he added.

"Oh," said Tess. "I get it." Her voice broke a little.

By now Gene was so prepared for the disappearing car on stage, along with the child volunteer inside it, that its vanishing (and inevitable reappearance) had little impact. But he'd ooh'd and ahh'd along with the crowd and to make the girls think he was enjoying the show. They themselves found it "just okay." Tess, a militant animal lover who would have been comfortable throwing blood on fur coats, worried that the doves and bunnies had been abused.

"Actually," Allie explained, "the animals enjoy working with the magicians and look forward to the snacks and special treatment they receive."

Where she got this very reasonable-sounding information Gene had no idea. But he was used to her knowledgeable observations by now and attributed it to her genius father, a physicist, who at barbeques would smile modestly and brush aside the mention of the *New York Times* article that had quoted his expertise on a breakthrough in particle physics.

"I just wish we'd gone to see Cirque du Soleil," Tess lamented. "They don't use animals in any of their shows."

Gene was feeling pretty annoyed that he'd spent a small fortune for this almost equally expensive magic show and just when he was about to tell Tess to stop her complaining and as a result possibly blow the entire good will of the vacation and the idea that they were here to have *fun* on the occasion of her mother's death, Allie the Wise One draped her arm over her friend's shoulder and suggested, "Let's go look at the fancy stores and pretend."

"Is that all right, Daddy?" Tess said.

He was so taken aback by her calling him "Daddy" and by Allie's deft move at distracting her, that he said, "Sure," and let them run off by themselves to roam the shopping halls of the Monte Carlo.

He half-sat, half-reclined in a plush chair under a tonnage of crystal chandelier in the hotel's all-marble lobby. Getting to the show early, they'd checked out the four swimming pools and the upscale casino that wafted European flair and put their own long-in-the-tooth hotel with its worn carpeting, paint-thirsty walls, and smoky (despite the prohibition) hallways to shame. He could almost be seduced by the city's faux classicism—the steroid-size Roman statues at Caesars Palace—or its opposite, the campy, sexy siren-and-pirate show at Treasure Island. Sure, why not. The girls? They enjoyed the place for what it was, and that's why he had brought them here, to distract Tess, to associate the occasion of her mother's death with fun. Oh, that word! Would it ever mean anything to him again? Had it meant much to him before? That was a question Janice used to ask him. "Do you ever think of just having fun?" Sweetly, of course. But it got the point across. His personality "set point" was fairly low, pessimistic and moody, whereas hers was buoyant, untroubled, and conversant with other human beings. At parties, he affected the reporter's cynical reserve, smiling pleasantly but one-step removed, he knew, from morose. Janice truly was his better half, and her mere presence doused him in a sort of irascible lovableness. She was always taking his arm, or smoothing her hands against the front of his wrinkled shirt, or making peppery if affectionate remarks about his slovenly ways. Oddly, he had never doubted why she cared for him when she was alive and now he questioned it every day: she haunted him with ghostly expectations. He could not shake the idea that he was a complete and utter failure in her dead eyes.

"I found this incredibly cute bag," Tess said, running up to him. "And it goes *really* well with the dress Aunt Kate sent me. Please?"

"How much?" Gene asked.

"Not much," said Tess. "For Las Vegas."

He glanced at Allie who kept the neutral expression of a high-end real estate broker on her face.

"Allie said she'd loan me half the money."

Gene made a bird nest of his fingers. "Allie is not loaning you half the money. It's very generous of her, but if she has to make you a loan beyond your spending money, then this item is ridiculously overpriced to begin with." To him, this sounded like a reasonable approximation of what Janice would have said. Except it wasn't. Janice would have said, *Let's go see*, and then told Tess no. She would have participated fully in the event until its need, not its goal, had been exhausted.

"Why don't you just stab me in the heart," Tess said, and turned on her heels to go.

After Gene offered—and they accepted—ice cream as a consolation, they went back to their rooms. He let the girls watch a pay-per-view movie for an exorbitant sum. He'd blocked himself from doing the same, particularly the pornography that only made him bemoan his loneliness. Lust had been replaced for the most part by the less stirring involvement of overeating, as he'd done tonight. Ordering three scoops of cookie dough ice cream with chocolate jimmies, he tried not to look at Allie who, sensibly, had gotten a single scoop of orange sorbet. That girl was in control of her destiny, and anyone else's, and he seriously considered revising his will to make her Tess's legal guardian instead of Janice's sister.

A light tapping came from the door between the rooms. He opened his side and saw Tess standing there in her pajamas, the blue haze of the television flickering in the darkness. "Can I come in?" she asked.

"Of course."

"Allie fell asleep. Can I lie down in the extra bed?" Gone was the white strapless dress highlighting her smooth and too-tanned shoulders. She'd turned back into a little girl in pajamas with hems that draped over her feet.

He pulled back the covers for her and she crawled under. He wasn't going to dissuade her. Allie would wake up in the morning and guess Tess was in here. She would understand.

Gene sat on the edge of the bed and held his daughter's hand; her eyes fought off the full assault of sleep. He knew that she kept herself so busy that it was only in this quiet space before she drifted off that she was vulnerable to the stomach-churning misery of being motherless. "You okay?"

Tess shook her head. "I'm having a bad night."

"Do you want to talk about it?"

"I'm too tired."

"Would you like to say a prayer?" It was the only other thing he could think to do, unreligious as he was.

She shook her head back and forth. "Something else," she said. "It's something Mom used to say when I was little and scared." She buried her face in the pillow and indeed she looked like his six-year-old daughter Tessy again. "I'm embarrassed."

"Don't be. What is it?"

"You have to tell me, 'Goodnight, lovely.'"

"Goodnight, lovely."

"You have to say it over and over until I fall asleep, and your voice has to get softer as you do it."

He did as she instructed him, and in no time her breathing surrendered to the stiller rhythms of sleep. He kept it up for quite a while, softly as his dry throat would allow, until he could only hear the words in his own head.

In the morning, Tess was still sleeping and Gene peeked in on Allie who was sitting up in bed reading *The Iliad*. They were to leave that afternoon.

"Tess is still in bed," Gene said.

"That's okay. I've already packed for the both of us. But it would be fun to hang out a little longer, too."

"I'll see if we can get a late checkout."

"Good thinking," said Allie, as if rewarding him for his ingenuity while allowing him to believe he'd come to the idea on his own.

"A classic," said Gene, nodding at *The Iliad*.

"You sissy, curly-haired pimp of a bowman!"

"Pardon me?"

"That's what Diomedes says to Paris. At least in my translation. I have some problems with, let's say, the choice of idiom, but it's supposed to be the best translation on the market. You have to go with what's available."

"I suppose so."

"Don't vex me, bitch!"

"Huh?"

"That's Aphrodite. She can be rather intemperate."

"Oh," said Gene, and stood uncertainly a moment. "Thank you for being such a good friend to Tess."

"I think Tess and I will be friends forever."

"I hope so," said Gene.

"Hope is the thing with shards," Allie said brightly.

"I think it's 'feathers.'"

Allie smiled patiently and a bit sadly at him.

"Right," said Gene. "I guess you already know that."

"I'll wait for Tess to wake up if you'd like to go eat in the meantime, Mr. Guthridge."

How did she know? "I'd appreciate that."

"No problem," she said and picked up her book.

He took the elevator down and waited in the buffet line, willing himself to select only two items plus coffee. Still, he couldn't resist the temptation and piled his plate with eggs, Maine lobster, oysters, and a smaller plate with melon, assorted cheeses, and peach cobbler. He wanted to throw a napkin over it as he made his way through the line. Decency dictated that he should have restrained himself on a first-run and come back again if he wanted more, but he couldn't stop and added the Dover lox and Dungeness crab legs. A middle-aged woman in front of him turned around and looked with disgust at the tower of food on his plate, the duck with green peppercorn he was trying to make room for, the eggs Benedict leaking its yellow river of Hollandaise over the Canadian bacon. At least that's what he thought her face expressed until he realized she was choking. Fierce guttural noises emanated from her throat. She was bending toward him, unable to do anything other than grab her throat and stare with boggled-eyed panic at him.

And then suddenly anonymous hands were being wrapped around her from behind and Gene watched as a piece of jumbo shrimp flew like a dart directly into his breast bone. The woman, who had started to sink to her knees, was caught by her savior, a man Gene would later learn was an EMT and visiting Las Vegas with his family and who had rushed across the room recognizing the sounds of distress. Through it all, Gene stood with his mountainous plate of food to be consumed as proxy for his lost insides.

"Thank you," the woman whispered to the EMT. "Thank God you were here," she said. Her family joined her now. They'd gotten up from their table and hurried over to see why a burly stranger had grabbed her and with one powerful yank beneath her rib cage expelled the perfidious giant shrimp that left a bloody orange stain on Gene's white shirt.

"I'm sorry," the woman told Gene. Speechless in front of her, he set his plate down to cast it out of his sight. "I'm so embarrassed. I should know better than to eat in line. It's bad manners and now I understand why. My God, I couldn't breathe at all! Can I get your shirt cleaned for you?" Her voice strained and raw, she was offering him—*him*—contrition.

"It's fine," said Gene. He actually didn't know if he wanted to preserve it or burn it.

At his feet lay the offending obstruction. Esophageal juices had already denuded the shrimp into a wan lump. No one dared pick it up. He almost felt sorry for it but stealthily tapped it like a hockey puck into oblivion under the buffet table.

"Come sit down, Marla," her husband said, visibly shaken too. The woman's two daughters—dark-haired twins about ten, wide-eyed at the scare—took each of her hands and led her gently away to a far corner of the restaurant. Her husband stayed behind, clasping the EMT's hand between his and thanking him profusely. "No problem," said the EMT. "It's just another day for me."

Surely, Gene thought, this entire scene had been played out for his benefit, if only he believed in such coincidence, if only he could make himself see its lesson and redemptive meaning and all else that such an occurrence might bespeak to his damaged soul. But the reporter in him was already debunking the significance of the event and its relevance. Rather, despite her supreme competency, Janice was just plain unlucky. Some things, no matter how much you're used to being in charge, you just can't do. She simply could not wrap her arms around herself to save her life. One's own embrace had its limits. And he had not been there to help. At the very moment that he was in a restaurant stuffing his own face with a Reuben sandwich following a tedious interview with a city councilman,

Tess was walking into the house after school to find her mother dead and bent over the high back of a dining room chair, trying, the police had conjectured, to thrust its hard edge into her chest.

Such were the facts, as they were: one soul was lucky, one was not, and he, presently being in the most infamous capital of luck—or not—had no choice but to stop pitying himself about that chilling fact. You could not figure out who was a winner from luck alone. If he had lost anything, it was his belief in his own insignificance. He had started to imagine that he should make some difference in the world and that Janice would have wanted him to. When, in fact, he had no other purpose than to dwell on the ineffable question as to why he, an overeating, ill-equipped and damaged man, should be the surviving parent to a daughter who so loved and adored her mother that Gene had once overheard her say, "I couldn't live without you, Mommy." Implying, if made to choose, she could do so without him.

Las Vegas, with its fake history, fake pyramids, fake Venetian canals, fake Eiffel Tower, with its artificial waterfalls and buxom Greek sirens from a Homeric fantasy land, all of which he'd schlepped the girls to, was the most platonic *un*ideal—a shadow more vivid than its referent, and he couldn't wait to leave its artifice. Even death was a facsimile of itself out here, a conceit that would amuse, say, the French with their trenchant irony and condescension about everything American that fell short of their puffed-up standard of seriousness. Yet more than anywhere Las Vegas offered a strange commiseration for his loss: the garish surroundings; the acquisitive, maddening search for luck; the left-behind hopes; the loneliness of an empty wallet. Here he was smack at home among his fellow brethren—all of them bearing up under life at its most desperate. He too had come seeking that great wave of release, hoping to be tossed upon its forgiving shore.

Tess came into the restaurant, her arm linked in abiding kinship with Allie. So lightened was his daughter by her friend's presence! The two of them were in shorts and sleeveless tops, their bare shoulders squared toward the task of finding him. Each had a yellow rose in her hair. Where had they gotten them? He could only guess—a flower cart? Their putative ninth-grade admirers? Freshly rested, their burgeoning youth had been renewed, their faces effulgent in the morning light.

They looked a bit mischievous. Eager, yes, for more fun.

He waved to them from across the room. Tess spotted him and whispered something to Allie. And then they both waved back in unison—big, circling waves hello, as if they were making the great world whole right in front of him.

Bless Everybody

THEY'D BEEN LED TO our land. The woman, Meredith, was far along in her pregnancy, and the coincidence of her name being close to "Mary" struck me, no place to lay their heads as they awaited the birth of their child. We—I—owned two hundred acres, cut out of the red rock along the Wyoming-Colorado border. Indians had long ago run stolen horses into the box canyon at the end of our property, and after them, rustlers had done the same thing with cattle. I'd poked around in the red dirt and once dug out the shoulder bone of a bison as big as my thigh. Arrowheads, spear points, and shards of clay pottery I'd turned over to the local museum; rumor had it that this was as sacred ground as any that ran along the Front Range from Colorado to Wyoming.

Peck Foster, my neighbor of the adjacent two hundred acres, had given the couple my name and number and told them to call me about the one-room cabin on our property. The young couple had parked outside the gate and took it upon themselves to walk the land and see if they could find the person who presided over this "magical" place. It seemed like a good story, this being led to the land. I didn't believe in providence, but I was retired and had time on my hands to be amused by such notions and told them I'd meet up at the gate to our property.

That "our" is misspoken. I'm divorced and Rosalyn took her share of the property in a cash settlement. I used a chunk of my retirement money to buy her out—I'm sixty-eight years old, and I'd worked as an inspector for the highway department thirty-nine of those years. I'd always wanted a piece of property as fiercely beautiful as this one. Every time I passed it on the road at sunset the red rock glowed like hot coals in an evening fire—a view of the openhearted earth. When it went up for sale, I talked Rosalyn into putting our money down. I was land proud, no doubt about it. A little stream called Watson Creek ran through the valley and turned the cottonwoods leafy with shade in the spring, as they were now.

They were waiting for me by the gate. When I'd spoken to the husband on the phone, he described their lifestyle as "migratory," but he certainly didn't sound like a dangerous drifter. I'd have put the man in his mid-twenties and the woman a few years younger and their Volkswagen bus older than the both of them combined, rusted on its fenders and painted a robin's-egg blue with a bumper sticker on the back that said BLESS EVERYBODY. NO EXCEPTIONS. The van's tires were bald and its grill had picked up a couple of tumbleweeds and was chewing on them like too much spaghetti in a child's mouth.

"Thank you, sir, for meeting us," Calvert said, sticking out his hand. He was a thin man with a big toothy grin, and blond hair down to his collar, his eyes all afire at hello. He tipped his hat to me, a brown felt fedora with a white feather tucked in the band.

They showed me their wares: ceramic leaf earrings and beaded hemp necklaces; tiny "sweetheart" notebooks no bigger than the palm of my hand with paper that still looked like the wood it came from; sassafras and strawberry scented drip candles in Day-Glo colors. They went to craft fairs and sold what they could, and took temporary jobs. "We're realistic people," Calvert said. "You can't live off today what you did in the sixties."

Sixties or not, they didn't look like they had a practical bone in their bodies, not with that baby in their future.

"Sir, we'd just like to stay here a few nights," Calvert said. "We want our child to absorb some of this"—he spread his skinny arms in a panorama over the expanse of my land—"*holiness*, before we move on." I thought: people really talk like this?

He patted Meredith's swollen stomach. She looked as if she were due any day.

"Where you going to have the baby?"

Calvert clasped his hands together. "Wherever we may be."

I looked at Meredith, hoping I wasn't hearing what I just did. But she had that dreamy come-what-may look. "There's a good hospital in town," I said. "You should check in with them."

"No need," Calvert said. "We'll be taken care of."

"Uh-huh."

"We just followed our hearts here. We came over the pass and looked down and just knew. Isn't that right, Mer?"

Meredith nodded, still with that dreamy look.

"I'd feel much better if you saw a doctor or midwife while you were here. We got a clinic in town that helps those in need."

"You *are* a kind man," Calvert said, as if my reputation preceded me. "Your hospitality will not go unnoticed."

Meredith's stomach made a shelf of the long dress she was wearing, a thin faded shift of yellow daisies, not suited for pregnancy, just oversized. Her ankles and toes had a film of dirt, and I wondered how long it had been since they'd had hot showers.

Before she retired a year after me, Rosalyn had worked in the public school system, first as a teacher, then a district administrator. She appreciated the threat of liability. I did too, working as an inspector for the highway department. She'd moved out to Eagle Estates (I still had our old place in town) and her backyard sloped down thirty yards to an artificial lake with her own dock.

"You haven't heard the best part," I said.

"I can't wait."

"The wife is pregnant." I suddenly realized I'd been calling her "the wife" with no good reason. They'd never said they were married. "I tried pushing them to see a doctor while they're here."

"Wait…did you say *pregnant*? As in living-out-of-a-van *pregnant*? How many months?"

"I'd say seven. Not being the best judge of such matters. She's pretty ripe, though."

"Oh, Charlie. What have you gotten yourself into?"

"Maybe nothing. They just want a couple days to rest their bones. I'd be more worried if there was anything there to *get* into. It's still the same empty one-room place with a bed and stove and a hard tile floor. Nothing to lose, nothing to break, and nothing to disturb. They want to walk the land, that's fine with me. Soak up the vibes or whatever they believe. Anybody breaks a leg, blame it on nature. I'm not running an amusement park up there."

"Anything happens they could sue you."

"I'll take my chances."

I'd come over to pick up Martin, our golden retriever. Rosalyn was going to Atlanta for a week. We shared custody of Martin, going on twelve years now. Before that we'd had Betsy, a springer spaniel, and when we first married, Reginald and Cora, a couple of dachshunds who fought like the brother and sister they were. It wasn't lost on us that we always gave our dogs dignified people names, no Bandit, Snuggles, or Doodles for us. These were our children with hopes for their futures, limited as they might be. Rosalyn traveled every month or two working part-time now as an educational consultant. Last month she'd gone to Hawaii. She didn't travel alone either; she had met a man when she was in Cleveland. He was a VP at a large educational testing company, and all I knew about him was that he was divorced with three grown children. She had put up a picture of him on her dresser. Her new man was a square-faced gent with blue eyes, a tennis tan, and hair graying around the temples—mine had gone almost all white. He was closer in age to Rosalyn, who was thirteen years younger than me at fifty-five, the new thirty I heard. Nobody said that about sixty-eight. Not yet anyway.

Rosalyn put down her iced tea on the marble patio table. She'd fixed up the place with abstract paintings that reminded me of geometry problems (we'd had pictures of those grinning dogs of ours hanging in the old place—I still did), plush white sofas (she was always chasing Martin off of them), and long drapes.

"I'd better be going. I got some painting to do on the basement."

"Almost finished?"

"I'm getting there."

Rosalyn hadn't been inside our old house for months. I was fixing it up to sell. We still owned it together, free and clear, our one common possession if you didn't count the dog. Just to keep it fair, I paid her a little rent every month until I could get it sold and move out. I was going to live up on the land. I'd priced running electricity from the utility poles at the road, and it would cost me three thousand dollars. Right now all I had was a well that pumped out rusty water. I'd warned the couple not to drink from it. Nothing would happen to them, just the poorest tasting water around from all the iron in it. They said that wouldn't bother them, the water was still purer than any that came from a faucet.

Rosalyn had spit out that water when we first went to look at the land. "Ugh," she'd said. She'd spoken with such vehemence that we got into an argument.

"Well, you don't have to make such a sour face," I said.

"It's terrible. It tastes terrible."

"You coming or not?" I had asked her.

"I'll wait here," she had said, standing by the locked cabin. She had looked in the windows and shaken her head. It was clear she didn't appreciate the place. She wanted some mark of human existence up there, or maybe she just couldn't imagine endless days with me and my thoughts and nothing between us but open space and sky above. And those thirteen years that separated us in age.

When I got back from walking the property, I asked her, "Are you going to complain every time we come up here if we buy the place?"

"Maybe," she said.

"Then maybe you shouldn't come up here," I told her.

"Maybe I won't," she said.

I looked at her. "What's that mean?"

"It means I'm not going to sit around and warm my feet by the fire and watch golden eagles nest and pretend to be happy." A dust devil had come up and was spitting dirt in our faces. Rosalyn shouted through it. "I'm going to continue working part time, I'm going to volunteer more, I'm going to the health club, the malls, the museums, I'm seeing friends, eating out, traveling. I want a life, not an *afterlife*. I don't want to close up shop. It's all right if you want privacy, Charlie, but that's not what I want. This fucking dirt!" she said and swatted at the dust, then ran for the car. I went after her, walking slowly.

"And does this busy life of yours have any room for me?" I asked.

"We should get back," she said. Which was answer enough.

It's a terrible thing to get to the end of a marriage and run out of good will about the future. Once you stop talking about what's ahead—or start talking about it separately, as we had done—it makes you feel as if you're on a train platform waving goodbye to the departing life you used to have. I always wondered if she agreed to sign the papers for the land just to have a reason to divorce me—two years ago now—and if I'd made her sign them because I honestly believed the place would bring us closer, like people do in a last-ditch try to stay happy by having a child.

"I'd be a little more concerned about letting those people stay up there if I were you," Rosalyn said now. We were sitting on her dock. She didn't own a boat and didn't want one. But she liked to come down here and read a good mystery and have me come over and join her for a drink. "It's your pride and joy," she told me. "I'm surprised you don't make them produce a passport to step on it." We could joke about what it meant to me now. And she was right, I could have planted my own flag up there. She wore white slacks and a low-cut pink sweater that I wanted to believe she'd put on for me. She'd never looked better. It all agreed with her, retirement, this big house, the traveling, the new man, the freedom—even me being here to always depend on. I would come over as long as she needed me, and not a moment longer than she wanted me to. That she knew this should have made me an object of concern if not outright pity in her eyes, but all I saw was gratitude when she put her hand on my stubbled cheek and said, "I don't know what I'd do without you, Charlie."

Over the next few days, I finished painting the house, replaced a couple leaky windows, and pulled up some soiled carpet beyond cleaning in the dining room where we never could get Cora's and Reginald's markings out—always fighting for dominance, those two. Martin followed me around, seeming to enjoy the liberty of jumping up on the old familiar couch without getting shooed off, and made a few half-hearted attempts to chase rabbits around our backyard. He was good company, and I would have liked more of it, but we were pretty fair about sharing him, and Rosalyn said he still liked to stretch out his front paws for a dive into the lake when she threw a stick, like the excitable puppy he used to be. So it was good to shuttle him between us. Just like a kid, he had his own bag packed and ready to go with his special food, blanket, and medicine for his arthritis.

I was pulling some unidentified boxes from the crawlspace in the basement when the phone rang. I ignored it at first, let the voice mail pick it up. But it rang insistently again, and I went upstairs and answered.

"Charlie?" It was Peck, my neighbor up at the land. "You better get up here," he said without any preliminaries.

"What's going on, Peck?"

"Those people, the ones you let stay…" Peck was slow to rile, but he sounded mad as I'd ever heard him. "That fella shot a deer. With a *pistol!*"

"I'm coming." I got my rifle and was in the truck in seconds. Martin jumped in the back. I still had paint on my hands.

You would have thought a wounded mule deer shot in the leg couldn't get far. That would be a misconception. A deer on three legs can outrun any man on two. This wasn't the point, of course. The point was that this crazy fool had tried to shoot one out of season with a pistol and without a hunting license and with No Hunting signs posted on both our properties. That made him a poacher in the eyes of the law, even if I lied and said I'd given him permission. His van could be impounded, his gun taken away (a good thing, in my view), and the both of them fined more than they were worth.

"What the hell got into you?" I said when I drove up. I was jumping out of the truck before the engine had stopped coughing. "Are you nuts?"

"Sir," said Calvert, "I...we needed food." Where was Meredith? Down by the creek I suspected, maybe washing clothes in the stream.

"Food?" Peck was standing there red-faced. His family had owned a thousand acres of this land going back a hundred years until they divided it up. Peck and I had worked out a lease to let his horses graze on my property, and between our parcels the animals found plenty of room to roam. I'd gotten a better offer for cattle from the sprawling McDonald ranch to the east, but cattle tore up the place worse than horses, and frankly horses were just prettier. I'm sure Peck was thinking the same thing as me: this fool could have shot one of his horses. "What gave you the idea you could hunt up here?"

Calvert, all twenty-something years of him, let out an exasperated sigh. "I was just trying to feed my family."

"You ever heard of a grocery store?"

"I thanked the land for its bountiful offering," said Calvert. I looked at Peck, who screwed up his face in disgust. "I thought you'd understand."

"Here's what I understand. You leave that deer out there to die and it's wanton waste, not to mention cruelty. I'm obligated to report this to Wildlife, and if I don't, I'm up my own damn creek. Any way you look at it, you've done something mighty illegal."

Calvert mumbled something. He had the fedora pushed down over his forehead, his eyes darting around under the brim. I asked him what he said.

"Nobody has to know."

"*I* know."

"We're wasting time," Peck said. "Let's go. We'll argue about what to do later."

•

We went in three different directions. I told Calvert that if he found the deer first to stay with it and we'd be by eventually. I mapped it out so we'd circle the perimeter and move toward the center, gradually tightening our radius. We'd meet in the upper canyon where I suspected the deer had gone to bed down, if it were still alive. The shot could have hit more bone than blood depending on where it went in the leg. I won't lie and say I didn't enjoy getting off a double lung shot. You could drop a bull moose in its tracks with a clean shot like that and I'd always been taught that was the fair shot you took—and you didn't take it until you were sure.

Martin started barking when we came to a pile of brush with some wooden boards from a collapsed outbuilding. The deer, a big one, close to three hundred pounds, I figured, had his black-tipped tail drooped between his legs and had risen up from the thicket. His antlers were budding out and his coat had started to turn reddish brown from its winter gray; those big ears were twitching independently of each other just like a mule's, trying to hear our movements upwind from him. He was considering whether it was worth bounding out of there, his flanks moving in and out like a bellows, exhausted, pained, and I saw too when he did bound up that his back leg was barely attached to the bone. Calvert had shot him in the hip and about severed the leg. It was a horrible sight. The leg was swinging around as if it were a piece of the poor creature's intestine hanging out.

I squared my shoulders, calmed my shaking hands and squeezed my left eye shut to line up a shot I prayed would go straight into his heart. It did, or close enough to drop him after a good two hundred feet before he flopped over. Martin ran up, sniffed warily and then backed off and lay down with his face on his front haunches, whining and waiting for me. The buck's eyes bulged with hard pain in them. A mule deer ran different than a white tail, starting up from go and bounding eight feet and then coming down on all four feet at once like a landing craft, and I thought it was terrible to lose one of your legs when you got around like that, and that this buck had died without his due dignity.

I blew my whistle in short bursts. Before long Peck showed up. He'd already heard the shot, and we stood there silently looking over this big fellow and trying to decide what to do with him now. We could try to get one of our trucks up here and move him back to Peck's place and gut him there, but I didn't think that would be easy given the steep incline and loose shale down to this spot. If we were going to eat this meat, and I sure as hell wasn't going to let it go to waste, we needed to cut him up now and let him cool and then pack him out. The worst thing was to let him stay warm. He'd spoil for sure.

"Where's the kid?" Peck said to me.

"I don't know. Did you see him shoot it?"

Peck shook his head. "All I know is he's carrying around a pistol and shooting up things like he's in a saloon. I gave them your number, Charlie. I should have checked with you first. We got no business letting strangers stay up here. This ain't no Woodstock."

"Can I have your knife?" I said.

Peck's knife was good and sharp and I cut around the diaphragm and reached all the way up and felt for the trachea. If you did it right, cut from stem to stern, and you had the strength and a steady hand, you could pull the whole business down from the windpipe and avoid the mess of cutting out the gut sack by itself. I sliced the trachea across its diameter and started pulling. We each had a foot braced on one side of the buck and were yanking. I told Peck to hold up a moment while I sawed more through the center of the pelvis channel and then we started pulling again. It was the easiest way. I didn't want to cut out the organs one by one and risk piercing the gut sack and transferring the digestive juices to the meat and spoiling it. Somebody was going to eat this creature and do him the honor of a good death. It was ugly to think of his last hour or two with his leg twirling around like that. I stuck my hand back up past the lungs and grabbed inside the throat and Peck pulled with me and we gave it one good heave and tore everything out. It was about then, just when I'd started to skin it and fold back the cape, that Calvert came up, panting. He took a good look at the buck's insides and bloody cavity and fainted.

Peck said, "This fella's one lame excuse for a human being." We stared at his sprawled out body and shook our heads. "If he don't come to in five, you'd better take him over to the hospital." I said I would and asked him what he thought I should do about the deer.

"Might as well enjoy it," he said.

"But should I report it?" Peck gave me a puzzled look. He'd bred horses all his life and he knew them as well as anybody, but an animal was still an animal to him. "Nobody's going to know any different if you don't."

"I'm not worried about somebody finding out. I just want to do what's right."

Peck opened his hands; he'd lost two of his left fingers in Vietnam. He was quiet about it except once to tell me he woke up every day and looked straight through that hole and saw the war. "If it was me? I'd get those people on their way and fill up your freezer with that meat. Case closed."

This made sense to me. You could say that an ignorant individual had made the mistake of thinking he could shoot his dinner and that it was more an accident than a crime. You could say, too, that they were young and naïve. But what you couldn't say is that any of it was right, the way a crooked line down a highway wasn't right, and you had to fix it. I'd had a perfect record over the years of inspecting roads. I saw plenty of bulges and rough spots in the concrete and places where the excavation had cut corners, and I had offers, some lucrative, if never put in so many words, to look the other way. Rosalyn once told me that cheating was so pervasive in the schools these days it was almost an anachronism to be honest, maybe even quaint. But I'd never been tempted.

When we got back to the cabin, Meredith was there staring dumbfounded at her groggy man coming through the door. She'd set up a little housekeeping in the cabin, a box of teabags and some water boiling in a pot on the stove, a couple toothbrushes and toothpaste on the one windowsill, and two sleeping bags rolled out on the bed next to a flashlight. This was no kind of place to be expecting a baby. I'd always planned to build on and shore up the foundation to get the drainage working right so there wasn't mold growing up the walls. The last owner had used the place for storage and that was about all it was good for now.

"What happened?" she asked, her eyes wide.

"I'll see you," Peck said—wisely making his exit. Up to our elbows in blood, we'd washed our hands and arms in the stream, but you really never got out the stains unless you scrubbed at them with a brush. We had the deer and all its dismembered parts in the back of my truck after dragging up the whole mess—and Calvert too—on a tarp.

"He just needs to sit down," I said. "He fainted." I helped Calvert over to the bed and he lay down and held his head and moaned. He put his arms across his eyes and stayed that way. Meredith sat down next to him. "You have one?" she said to him. He made a clenching sound with his teeth and nodded. She turned to me. "He gets these terrible migraines. They make him vomit and faint." She got up and went over to a plastic jug of water. A towel and washcloth were laid out neatly on a corner of the bed and she picked up the washcloth and got it damp and then came back and folded it over Calvert's forehead. He was still gritting his teeth and his toes were pointed out the door, his fingers clenching the bare mattress.

"I'm going to report this in the morning."

Meredith turned her head toward me. "Report what?"

"The deer. You can't shoot a deer without a license. Even on private property." I repeated what I'd told Calvert, it was illegal and despite having the animal all carved up in the back of my truck and no one to know any more about it, we'd broken the law of the land.

"I'm sorry," Meredith said. "We should have asked permission first." She had changed from this morning and put on some stretchy sweat pants and washed her feet and combed her brown hair, her eyes a soft shade of jade. "Calvert didn't want to. He said we'd sell some of our stuff in town. But I can't wait. I need some meat now. My baby needs it. Calvert doesn't think so, but I know different. I'm hungry all the time."

"Where'd you shoot him?"

She pointed down by the stream.

"I was *hungry*," she said again.

"You should have just asked. I could have brought you something."

"We're not beggars," she said.

Calvert moaned, "Your voices!"

"He can't stand noise when he gets like this," Meredith said. "Let's go outside and talk."

We stood there in the dark with the stars pulsing above and not an artificial light in sight. I had mixed feelings about running electricity over here and plundering the darkness. Peck's house was on the other side of the ridge and hidden from view. You could hear coyotes howling, and I'd seen the remnants of a mountain lion's kill, and what did it matter if another deer died on the property one way or another? I could hide the evidence, ignore the deed, and the taint to the land—the purest thing I had in my life at the moment—would disappear. But there's a thinner line between rigidity and tolerance than most people think. I'd always tried to stay on the latter side of that line, but I knew my position as of late had been corrupted by a foolish kind of anger that wanted everyone held accountable.

I went to my truck and got out my jacket and put it around her shoulders. She was standing there with her thin arms shivering and nowhere to go but back into that dark cabin with her partner sprawled out and his head exploding.

"I think about getting away." She looked back at the cabin.

"Are you afraid of him?"

"No." She pulled her arms tight around her chest. "Sometimes."

I wasn't surprised that Calvert who snapped his "Sir!" out at me might be the same fellow who could slap around this young woman not long out of her girlhood with her pretty pale face. For all that traveling she didn't have much color to her. She was more pallid than Rosalyn ever looked when she was pregnant and had three miscarriages, before we stopped trying. We had that river of disappointment under our feet, too.

"Come with me now," I said, and Martin trotted up behind me, as if to make his appeal too. He'd been guarding the tailgate of my pickup with its deer payload.

She shook her head. "He'll find me. He'll—"

"You need to see a doctor. You need care. Nobody's going to harm you. I'll see to that. I know a lot of people here in town, folks who can help you legally." She winced at "legally."

"I don't want anything to happen to him," she said.

I had the idea that Calvert was no stranger to outstanding warrants, and that this had made my place more attractive to him than any so-called holiness of my land. "I'll take you somewhere safe," I promised. I had in mind the extra bedroom of my house, and if she wasn't comfortable with that—I had no untoward motives—I'd put her up in a motel and talk to the safe house people in Fort Collins where Rosalyn volunteered.

"I've got to go back in," she said.

"You need to eat," I said. "You need to take care of your baby."

"When he gets a migraine, he'll sleep forever afterward. I can meet you at the gate in the morning. I have to get my things out of the van and I want to make sure he's asleep because he has the keys in his pocket."

"I'll be here at dawn. Bring whatever you can carry and don't worry about the rest. We can fix you up later." The sleeves of my coat hung over her hands like sleepy puppets. I had all these thoughts I shouldn't have had, not the obvious ones that pertained to the wants of an older man in the presence of a young, comely woman and how she might save his flesh and soul and that he might be so delirious he wouldn't know the difference between the two, but ideas about how the unexpected descended and snapped its fingers in your face and said "Awake!"

"You'll really come?"

I said I would. I'd be there at 5:45 when the sun cast its first light over the place.

I told her she could keep my coat, but she was already stripping it off saying no, Calvert would get suspicious. Before she ducked inside, she called back to me, "Bless you."

I woke with a start. I had left my wallet in my jacket pocket when I gave the coat to Meredith to put around her. I'd slept fitfully, if I did at all, on the surface of a plan that was simple in its execution and complicated in its reasons. Why was I getting involved? Peck had advised I chase them out of there as soon as I could. Rosalyn would have seconded that or told me to call social services and get the police involved if I suspected abuse. She would have told me I had some kind of hero complex to want to do this all myself, and maybe she'd be right.

I got up to check my jacket that I'd hung over the chair. My wallet was still there, all the money and credit cards inside, and I felt ashamed of myself for suspecting that Meredith had filched it while she was wearing the coat. I sat there a moment on the edge of the bed, flipping the wallet open and closed in my hands like a jackknife. I lay back down and must have fallen asleep because when the phone rang I jumped up again and didn't know where I was for a moment. The numbers on the clock said 4:50 a.m. and my first thought was that it was either Meredith or Calvert.

But it was Rosalyn. "I'm sorry," she said. "I...I feel terrible calling you."

"What's wrong?" I could hear her sniffling, then blowing her nose. "Where are you?"

"Home."

"From Atlanta?"

"I came home early."

I looked at the clock; it would take me twenty minutes to get from town to my land. Rosalyn never called at this hour. She was nothing if not independent and whatever motivated her to phone me up at five in the morning must have come at a price. "Speak to me, Rosalyn."

"I didn't know who else to call."

"Uh-huh," I said.

"I'm sitting here on the floor, it's dark, the house is cold, and I've got mascara running down my face. I didn't sleep on the plane—I took the red-eye back."

"What do you need, Roz?"

"Would you...would you bring Martin back today? I know it's earlier than I said, but I could really use his company. Is that all right, Charlie? Would you be okay with his coming here early?"

"I'll bring him over," I said. "I got to do something first, but I'll bring him back after."

"Thank you, I really appreciate it. I'm so sorry I woke you up. I didn't know who else to call."

"You said that."

"You're mad at me."

"I'm not mad." I glanced at the clock again. Ten minutes had gone by, and I still had to throw on my clothes and scrub my face and teeth. I thought about that old saying, why buy the cow when you can get the milk for free? As far as I went with Rosalyn, she got the cow free and to hell with the milk.

"Why do men lie, Charlie?" She was slurring her words and I could picture the bottle next to her; Rosalyn always held the neck of a wine bottle like she was shaking your hand with a firm grip. "You never lied to me."

"I never lied to you," I agreed. I felt pain compress across my chest, as if someone were cinching a leather strap as hard as he could; if I hadn't been talking to Rosalyn, if I hadn't been witnessing her anguish over this man she loved the way she used to me, if I hadn't been thinking I could make it all better if she'd just give me another chance, I would have thought I was having a heart attack.

"Forgive me for waking you?"

"I was getting up anyway. I have an appointment." I heard her take a long gulp of whatever she was drinking.

"An appointment?"

"Somewhere I have to be."

"Oh," she said quietly.

"I'll bring Martin by afterward. Later this morning. I promise."

I went out the door, leaving Martin snoozing on the rug with his blanket smelling of me and Rosalyn both and drove up with one thought in mind, to get Meredith out of there. I should have had the sheriff come with me. I knew him a bit, and he was a calm, reasonable fellow, but I knew too Meredith would change her story out of guilt or fear if we both showed up.

She was waiting for me, just like she said, and she had a backpack with her when I pulled up outside the gate. She looked just as forlorn as she had last night, but I shouldn't have been surprised when I got out of the truck and she gave me that faint, helpless smile, like she had no choice in the matter. Calvert stepped out from the clump of scrub oak where he'd been crouched down and pointed his pistol at my heart. The only thing I didn't know was whether or not they'd planned it from the beginning, whether Meredith had had any hesitation at all or just thought me another sad fool.

"You promised her money—if she'd fuck you." He jabbed the pistol toward me. "Right?" I looked at Meredith, that droopy mouth and pale hungered face and tried to find the truth in it.

"You told him that?"

"Shut up," said Calvert.

"What happened to 'sir'?"

"Fuck you. You were going to turn us in for shooting that deer."

"I still can."

He grinned at me, waving the gun around like he intended to lasso me with it. His fedora, with its dirty white feather, was pushed back on his head, and I saw he had a pretty good receding hairline. I should have been more afraid than I was; I don't know why I wasn't.

"You're a stupid old man, just like I thought."

"You going along with this?" I asked Meredith, who had her lips pressed tightly together.

"Hey, *you*," said Calvert. "Don't talk to *her*."

"You're not going to shoot me."

The dust splattered up at my feet. Nobody had ever shot at me before, and I stared at my feet. "Maybe I won't miss next time, old man. Maybe I'll get my deer."

"Let's just go," said Meredith. "Please."

"Throw your wallet over here!" Calvert commanded. "Get it," he told Meredith. And even this, the tone, I wondered if it was for my benefit alone. Would they have a good laugh down the road? Would she cry over what she'd done? Would they count my money and go for...whatever made them happy? Did he treat her so badly he owned her soul?

Calvert took out the cash and threw the wallet back at my feet. "Give me your keys," he said. I threw them to him. "Turn around and put your hands on that gate." He told Meredith to come over and tie my hands to the gate. She wouldn't look at me while she did. She smelled of wood smoke and oranges, and I told her so, and then I felt a whack on my head that turned my land dark.

"What happened to those people?" Rosalyn asked me later that day when I brought Martin over and she kneeled down for him to come running into her arms.

"They just left."

"Just like that?"

I snapped my fingers. "Just like it." She'd taken a shower and put on a black slip dress that had a scoop neck that showed off her freckled chest. Black for mourning or black for seduction; both were probably true. She wanted to see my eyes light up, to be appreciated by a man, even one fooled by thieves, a man who had decided he would stop punishing himself in all the obvious ways.

"Charlie," she said, "you look so tired. That's *my* fault." She seemed to have come out of her sorrow. I had a mean bump on my head and my vision wasn't back to normal, but I could see well enough to drive. The one thing Meredith had done for me was tie a slipknot, making it easy to get out.

"I've got to leave," I said.

"Another appointment?" Rosalyn said this teasingly. Then her face went soft as a bruised peach. "You want to come back tonight?" She never asked me over at night.

"I think I can do that," I told her.

Maybe fortune came with getting your head clonked.

She walked with me outside. "Whose is *that*?" she said when she saw the couple's blue van parked in the driveway. For whatever reason, either carelessness or (I'd like to think) Meredith's doing, the key had been left behind, too.

"I'm borrowing it for a few days. From some acquaintances."

She stared at the bus with its bald tires and cracked windshield. "What's wrong with your truck?"

"Nothing. That I know of." I nodded at the van. "Makes me feel young again."

Rosalyn lifted her well-shaped eyebrows. "Oh yeah? You'll have to give me a ride in it sometime."

I smiled. "That I'll do."

I had one more job before I quit for the day. I drove the van. The seats smelled of cigarettes and the engine whined and lost what little power it had going up a small rise, but I had my arm out the window on a beautiful spring afternoon, and I felt fitter than I should have when I pulled into the Division of Wildlife parking lot. You were supposed to leave the animal intact for state identification so the game warden could make the count, but I couldn't really bring the whole carcass in here and throw it across this gentleman's desk, could I?

"What you got there, mister?"

I untied the rose silk scarf that Meredith had left behind in the cabin, an awfully nice scarf for someone who had lived out of a robin's-egg blue van and had picked a bad seed of a man to father her child. "I take full responsibility," I said.

"What the hell…" The wildlife officer got one look at the buck's putty-colored testicles and about gagged. But I was all about rules and doing right by them and making the best of what time I had left on this merciful earth.

Madagascar

THIS IS A STORY I know so well.

My father, who is twenty-one, is on his way home from finding food for his family. He has traded a gold brooch for a bottle of milk, some vegetables, and a little meat. With his blue eyes and blond hair, my father is the only one in the family who has any chance to pass for Gentile on the streets. He makes sure to sit on a public bench, to pick out a paper from the trash and look comfortable, then go on. Among the many edicts against Jews—no traveling in motor cars, no leaning out windows, no using balconies open to the street, no going outside after dark—is one that forbids them to sit on park benches.

On the way home he takes another chance meeting his fiancée in South Amsterdam. Before the deportations started they were to be married; now they must wait until the war ends, each of them hidden in different areas of the city. After dark when he returns to the apartment cellar where his father, mother, and sister hide, he sees the Gestapo drive up. It is May 26, 1943. Tomorrow he will learn the Great Raid has taken away all the remaining Jews, those in rest homes, in mental institutions, in orphanages, those too sick to walk, those who have cooperated with the Germans thinking it would spare them. Even the entire Jewish Council will be shipped to the labor camps. Now he knows nothing, only that he must avoid the house, that if he is caught out after curfew he will be imprisoned or shot. He steps into a bakery where the baker—a Gentile though trusted friend of the family—offers to hide my father. If someone has informed on the family and the Gestapo do not find all the members, the baker knows they will search the whole block; they have been through here before. They will check the back room, the bins of flour, the attic above. They will tap the floor and walls for any hollow spaces. But, ironically, they will not check the ovens.

The baker tells my father to climb into an oven no longer in use. At first my father resists. He is afraid. Afraid he will die in there. But there is no other way. The Gestapo will not think to look in such an obvious yet unlikely place. My father crawls in. The sirens stop. His family is taken away to Majdanek, never to return. He lives in the oven until the end of the war, coming out every two hours when business has slowed sufficiently so that he may stretch. Some days the baker stays so busy that my father must be inside for three, four, and once even six hours. Without room to turn over or extend his legs, he remains curled up in a ball. On one occasion, much to his humiliation, he must go to the bathroom in his pants. The baker and his wife kindly provide him with a long apron while his trousers are washed in back. In the oven, he makes up waltzes in his head and has long, complex discussions with himself, marshaling arguments for each side, as to which of the two Strausses, father or son, is the true Waltz King, despite the son being known by the title. He recreates each note of their compositions and discusses the works with a panel of experts, but always delays the final vote another day so he may weigh the evidence more carefully and reconsider the merits of "Joy and Greetings," "Loreley-Rheinklänge," "Shooting Stars," and a hundred others.

After the war my father will listen to music in a high-backed chair. The record player during my childhood, a hi-fi, will be near a whisper in volume, perhaps the loudness at which he originally heard the melodies in his head. When I come into the room, he does not mind being disturbed, but asks me to sit and listen with him. I am ten. "Ah, now," he says, raising his hand when the French horns begin to play. "Our favorite part." I do not know if "our" includes me or someone else or if he just speaks of himself in the plural. Soon he closes his eyes, smiles, and extends his hand for mine. Although we are sitting down, me at his feet, our arms sway together, my father waltzing with me from this position. Softly he releases my hand, tells me I have good timing and to remember practice practice practice. Mastering the clarinet is no easy task—even for a bright ten-year-old. He rises from his chair, pulls down the sides of his coat—on Sunday afternoons he wears a jacket and tie at home—returns the record to its sleeve, closes the lid of the hi-fi, and stands with his hands behind his back for a few seconds as though making a silent prayer. Then he says, "Ephram, would you like to accompany me on a walk in the park?" I have my coat on within five seconds.

In ninth grade, I am caught shoplifting. I steal a silver pen from a drugstore. I am taken to the police station in Haverford, the small town where we live outside Philadelphia and where my father teaches European history at Haverford College. My mother is in New York visiting her sisters, so I must call my father. The department secretary informs me that he should return from class within the hour.

"Are you at home, Ephram?"

"I'm at the police station," I say, shocked by my own admission. Perhaps I want to confess right away and get it over with, not hide the shame I feel, or perhaps I want to boast.

Without comment, she makes a note of my situation and promises she will get the message to my father immediately. While I wait for my father in front of the sergeant's desk, on a plastic chair a faded aqua color, I think how I've wanted to succeed at something, most recently sports. The basketball game I made sure my father attended, positive I would be put in since we were playing a much weaker team, we wound up only narrowly winning, coming from behind. I sat on the bench the whole time. "Very stirring match," my father said afterward, walking me to the car, his arm around me. He knew I felt bad, of course, but there was nothing he could do, nothing I could do.

I lack the speed and agility to be first string; and by this season I have lost interest in sports, don't even try out for the team, and instead have fallen in with a group of kids who hang out at the edge of the parking lot, wear pointed shoes with four-inch Cuban heels, pitch quarters during lunch, comb their hair in duck tails (a style that requires me to sleep with my hair parted the opposite way so that the curls will straighten out by morning), and who generally get in trouble for everything from smoking cigarettes to belching "The Star-Spangled Banner" in the back of Spanish class. It is 1964. School has become intolerable.

My father soon comes to the police station. I am released into his custody and we leave the old armory building of massive, buff sandstone, me in a blue corduroy coat that says Haverford Panthers, my father with his walking stick and tweed overcoat, a cream-colored scarf tucked under his chin. He puts his hand lightly behind me and I reflexively sink back against his open palm, no easy feat going down a flight of steps. I keep expecting him to ask me what happened. Though I know he won't raise his voice, he never does, let alone physically punish me, I anticipate a lecture, as is his custom when I've misbehaved, which to be honest has not happened all that often. An only child, I have learned how to fulfill my parents' wishes better than my own. They have little reason to find fault with me, so trained am I in the subtlest of ways—a raised eyebrow from my father, a frown from my mother—to find fault with myself first.

"Why don't we walk a little bit, Ephram." We stop at the post office. My father buys a roll of stamps and some airmail envelopes for letters to Holland. We have no relatives over there anymore but he keeps a regular correspondence with friends and some members of the Amsterdam Symphony. Before the war he, too, had studied the clarinet and planned to become a professional musician, a source of conflict with his father who wanted my father to have a career in business like himself. When I was younger I always eagerly awaited the letters from Holland so I could steam off the stamps for my collection.

We sit down on a bench in front of the post office. It is December but the sun is bright enough for us to rest a moment outdoors.

I am prepared to apologize, no longer able to stand my father's silence. At the same time I want to explain that school offers me nothing but hypocrisy, lies, false values and mush-headed teachers who haven't read a book themselves in years, and that I know this frustration has something to do with what I've done. But before I have the chance, he says he wants to tell me something about the war, one subject about which I am intensely interested because I always hope he will speak, as he rarely does, of his own experience.

"You may not know," he says, "that Hitler had several plans for the Jews. The camps came much later, after he had ruled out other possibilities, such as selling Jews to different countries. He also considered sending the Jews to the island of Madagascar. He wanted to permanently exile them there. Not destroy them, just isolate them on a remote island. This was to be his answer to the Jewish question. I have imagined many times what this situation may have been. I see the beaches, I see the shops, I see the clothes my mother and father wear there—light fabrics, colorful, soft cotton, a little lace on holidays. The sea is blue, the houses white. My mother does not like the heat, but my father welcomes it every morning by doing calisthenics on the balcony. They have settled here, done well, as Jews will do most anywhere, even in Nazi Madagascar. But you see how childish this is of me, don't you? That I want there to be a refuge in the midst of such undeniable evil. Perhaps it is why I decided to study history after the war. I have the liberty to make sense of the many possible pasts historians can always imagine—but the duty to choose only one. Sometimes I fail to honor my task because it is too unbearable. I do not think you are in a very happy period of your life now, Ephram. We are perhaps letting you down, your mother and I. I hope, though, that you will see I am far from perfect and struggle to make meaning of things as much as you do. It is my wish only that you will not harm others in the process, nor assault your own dignity. Leave yourself a small measure of respect in reserve. Always. You see, even in my worst memories—and I know nothing that can be worse for a man than to remember his mother and father and sister while he walks free in the world—even here I have left myself an escape to Madagascar. So allow yourself the same opportunity and do not think so poorly of your own promise that you must succumb to the disgrace of crime. You are bright, imaginative, resourceful. Surely there is a way out of whatever hell it is you too experience. I do not doubt that you can do better than this."

Chastened, I sit in silence with my father while we drive home. After his intercession, charges will be dropped by the drugstore. My mother learns nothing of the incident, and I soon separate from the group of misfits I've joined earlier. I also give up the clarinet when I discover—as my teacher agrees—that I feel nothing for the instrument.

My college roommate freshman year is named Marshall Tiernan. I have chosen to go to a small liberal arts college in Ohio that is not too far from Haverford but far enough so I feel I'm leaving home. Every Tuesday afternoon he asks if I can vacate the room for three hours and fifteen minutes (exactly) so he can listen to music.

"I don't mind if you listen while I'm here," I tell him.

He shakes his head. He must have privacy. Marshall Tiernan, reedy and tall as elephant grass but not nearly so uncultivated, has an enormous collection of classical records that takes up one quarter of our room. He is studying to be an engineer. Unlike the rest of the men in my dorm, who in the fall of 1968 have grown their hair long and wear patched jeans and army surplus coats, Marshall dresses in Arrow shirts with button-down collars and keeps a well-inked pen protector in his pocket. He has an unfortunate stutter and does not socialize beyond a fellow engineering student he knows from home. We have a respectful relationship, but I can't say that Marshall is a friend.

I agree to leave him alone on Tuesday afternoons, but one time I come back early. I have forgotten some notes that I need to take with me to the library. Expecting to hear music outside the door, I hear nothing and decide to go in. On the bed, with large padded earphones, is Marshall, his thin body rigid as slate. He sees me but does not acknowledge that I am here. His clothes, the sheets, everything is drenched with sweat. His legs tremble, a kind of seizure starts. When the record ends, a composition by Satie, Marshall sits up, quickly strips the bed, throws the sheets in the closet (Tuesday the maids bring new linen), changes his clothes and returns to his desk to study.

We do not discuss the incident.

Shortly afterward he drops out of school and moves home. I have the privacy of my own room, a lucky situation that enables me to spend time alone with Iris, whom I've met at an antiwar meeting. One night while I am telling her, with some amusement, I am sorry to say, about Marshall Tiernan, I suddenly stop. Iris says later the look on my face is as if I've seen a ghost, for that is what happens. I suddenly see—no, *feel*—a twenty-one-year-old man curled painfully in a baker's oven, his body kept alive by music.

Thanksgiving vacation my sophomore year I bring Iris home with me. Several years older than I and a senior in anthropology, she helps my mother with Thanksgiving dinner, talks at length with my father, who retains a lifelong interest in Margaret Mead, and makes such a positive impression on them both that my mother whispers to me as we are about to leave for the airport, "*She's a jewel.*"

But at school I sink into a profound depression. My grades plummet and although Iris tries to stand by me, I manage to chase even her away. She finds her own apartment yet continues to call every day to check up on me. I become more withdrawn, however, and after a while I ask her to stop phoning. I watch television and eat chocolate donuts, drink milk from the carton and stare at the dark smudge marks my lips leave on the spout.

My father appears one afternoon, a surprise visit, he says. I know by the look on his face, though, that he has come because of Iris. I burst into tears when I see him.

"What has happened, Ephram?" he says.

But I don't know what has happened, only that I can no longer study, I don't care about school and have no chance of passing finals; I don't care if I flunk out.

"Your mother is very worried. She wanted to come with me but I thought it best if I came alone. Is there anything I can do to help you? Is there something wrong in school, you don't like your courses, the pressure perhaps of too many hours..."

"I haven't been to class in weeks," I say. "I can't go. Even a trip to the store is overwhelming." I start to cry again. "I want to go home. I want to go back with you."

"But what will you do back there?" my father says. "There is nothing at home for you now. You have your studies here, your friends."

I look at my father. As always, he is dressed neatly, and warmly, a blue blazer and gray slacks, a wool vest under his coat. Meanwhile, my apartment remains a mess, dishes in the sink, clothes everywhere, my hair unwashed.

"I'll find a job, I'll work and make money."

"And live at home?"

"Yes, what's wrong with that?"

My father pauses. "I don't know. I would think that you'd enjoy the freedom of living on your own."

"I have freedom and privacy at home. You've never told me what to do or when to come in. I'm not happy here."

"But Ephram, changing the place you live will not solve your problems. You need to get to the bottom of this."

"I don't care, I just want to go home! Can't you understand that?" I am almost screaming. "I have to go back. I can't make it here!"

For the rest of the winter I work in a bubble gum factory near Philadelphia. It is miserable, but the more miserable the better because I feel as if I deserve the punishment of tedious, demeaning work for failing in school. I am paid minimum wage, $1.85 an hour. So much sugar hangs in the air—we throw bags of it into a mixing contraption resembling the gigantic maw of a steam shovel—that the people who have worked for years at the factory have lost many of their teeth. The gum itself comes out on long (and unsanitary) splintered boards that I carry to racks, which are taken to another station where these long tubular strips of bubble gum—more like waxy pink sausages than gum at this stage—are cut into bite-size pieces with a tool akin to a large pizza wheel.

One day at the beginning of spring I receive a letter from the draft board. According to their records my student deferment has expired; I am now eligible to be considered for military service.

My father comes home early from his office hour at school. He himself hates the war, the senseless bombing and killing. He has marched with his college's students and protested the presence on campus of recruiters from a chemical company that makes napalm. He has, in fact, been more active than myself who has withdrawn into the routine and oblivion of factory labor, for which there are no deferments.

"What are your plans?" my father asks.

"I don't know. Canada, I suppose, if all else fails."

"And what is 'all else'?"

"A medical deferment."

"On what basis?"

"My mental condition."

"But you have never been to a psychiatrist. You have no history."

"I don't know then." I shrug. I feel numb, resigned. Why not basic training and then the jungles of Southeast Asia? Could it be much worse than the bubble gum factory?

"You will not go. That is all there is to it. We will make sure of that."

"And how will you do that?"

"We'll hide you, if necessary."

I look at my father and almost laugh. But I can see he is serious, alarmed.

"What are you talking about—hide me? Where?"

He picks up his newspaper and folds it back, once, twice, three times until he has a long strip of news in front of him. It is the idiosyncratic way he likes to read the paper—folding it up like a map until it is down to a small, tight square of information the size of a wallet or obituary. I think that it must make him feel some control over the world's chaotic events to read about them in such miniature, compressed spaces.

My mother brings in a stuck jar for one of us to loosen, and my father puts down his newspaper, which pops open on his lap like an accordion. I am still thinking about his wanting to hide me, aware that the draft has touched off buried fears for him, a flashback to the war, some instinctive response to the personal terror of his family being taken away from him. "I'll get out of it, Dad," I say. "Don't worry. I won't go."

"Don't worry, don't worry, is that what you think is the problem here? You have put yourself in this position, though I begged you not to. What is there to do now but worry!" He stands up. "I am *sick* with worry, if you must know. This is my fault. I should have demanded you stay in school, not let you come here!"

I have never heard him raise his voice like this. His body begins to tremble, and from the kitchen my mother hurries in with her hand over her heart. "What is going on here?" she says. "What are you arguing about?"

"Nothing," my father answers. "The argument is finished," and he goes into his study and closes the door—a sight I am used to from childhood. I hear him weep, but rather than sadness I feel a great relief; finally, something I've done has touched him.

I do not get drafted but receive a high number in the first lottery. The long and tiresome depression, the deadness I have felt, is replaced with the exhilaration of a survivor, a life reclaimed. I make plans to visit Europe, use the money I've saved from the bubble gum factory to travel for three months. Guide books about England, France, Spain, and Italy cover my bed.

I pore over them and come up with a tentative itinerary. But when I actually get to Europe, I find I make a detour from England to Holland. I locate the Jewish quarter where my father hid during the war, find his school—the Vossius Gymnasium—and then what I've come for: the bakery. It is still there, although the original owners who saved my father have long ago died. I explain to the current owners who I am; they tell me in broken English that yes, they have heard what happened here during the war, they know about my father and the Koops who saved him; the story is legend. "Does the oven still exist by any chance?" I ask.

They take me to the back, outside to a shed. It is here, covered with a tablecloth. I ask them if I can be by myself for a few moments and they say certainly, no one will disturb me.

A squat and solid object, the oven stands only chest high. I pull open the door and look inside. The opening is deeper than it is wide, the height a little less than two feet. I hoist myself up to sit on the edge. Then I swing my legs around and push my body in feet first. My neck is back against the left edge. I cannot go any farther. My shoulder sticks out too much even when I bend my knees into my chest. I do not understand how he did this, but I am determined to fit inside, so I slide out again and try to enter without my shoes and without my jacket. I tuck my legs under and pull my head inside, my back curved tight as an archer's bow. I hook my finger through the match hole and close the door. The stove smells of mildew and carbon; the scaled roughness of the iron ceiling grates against my cheek. It is pitch black except for the match hole through which I can see. I put my eye up to it and watch. Soon I hear footsteps and I feel frightened, but the footsteps recede into the distance and the bakery becomes silent.

Many years later my parents come out to celebrate the occasion of our son's fifth birthday. My father helps Philip build the space station they have brought him. I watch them play together, my father with no awareness of the world around him other than this mission to be his grandson's assistant.

While my mother and Judith, my wife, put Philip to bed, my father and I have coffee on the porch. It is a cool summer night and we are in Boulder, Colorado, where the shimmering night sky looks, to my parents, like a planetarium. Judith works in the university's office of communications, while I teach literature. Like my father, I have become a professor.

"What are you going to do now?" I ask him. He is on transitional retirement, halftime teaching, and is scheduled to leave the college next year. "Will you finally go to Europe?"

"Perhaps," he says, "but your mother's back may not permit it."

I nod. The trip out here has cost her a great deal of pain that she has accepted stoically. If she walks for more than half an hour or sits for that long, the result is the same, inflammation.

"Have you thought of going yourself?" I ask.

"I could not leave your mother for that long. She would not be well enough."

My father sits with the hiking boots he has bought for this trip out west laced tight on his feet. They are spanking new and he has already cleaned them of mud from our climb this afternoon. I take pleasure in seeing him so fond of the mountains, so open to the world out here. "You and I could go," I say. "Together. A nurse could help mother if we went next summer."

"I will give it some thought," my father says, but I can see that the veil has already dropped—the complex configuration of blank terror that can still scare me with its suddenness, the yearning on his face vanished. He has gone to Madagascar.

He empties the coffee he has spilled in the saucer back into his cup. "I have made a mess here," he says, replacing the dry saucer underneath. He stands up. Pulls down the sides of his jacket. Despite the hiking boots, he has dressed for dinner. "Would you like to go for a walk with me, Ephram?"

"Yes," I say, and get my coat, eager as always.

Last summer Judith and I took Philip to Europe because I wanted to show him where his grandfather grew up. Though the bakery was no longer there—an insurance office now—I described everything about the original building, and the oven. I held him in my arms while he listened with intelligence and care, and I kissed his long lashes and felt his soft cheek against mine. I wondered what he knew that I would never know about him, what pleased him that could not be spoken. When would he grow past me, leave his fatherland, hack and hew whole forests until he could find one piece of hallowed ground on which to plant the seed of his own self?

One night in our hotel I could not sleep and began to write: "Every son's story about his father is, in a sense, written to save himself from his father. It is told so that he may go free and in the telling the son wants to speak so well that he can give his father the power to save himself from his own father." I wrote this on a note card, put it in an airmail envelope, and planned to send it with its Amsterdam postmark to my father.

The following morning a call from my mother let us know that my father had suffered a stroke. We flew home immediately, and I rushed to see him in the hospital while Judith waited with Philip at the house. My mother was there by his bed. An IV bottle was connected to his wrist. His other arm I saw had purplish bruises from all the injections and from the blood samples taken. The effects of the stroke made him confuse the simplest of objects, or draw on archaic uses—a pen became a plume. A part of his brain had lost the necessary signals for referencing things and faces with words, and now dealt in wild compensatory searches to communicate. When he spoke of Judith he referred to her as my husband, called me "ram" trying to pronounce Ephram, and, saddest of all, could not understand why I had so much trouble understanding him. He had once spoken three languages fluently, and to see him in this state was more of a shock than I could bear. When he fell asleep, I left his room to speak with the doctor, a neurologist who explained to me that a ruptured blood vessel was causing the illogical and distorted speech. Bleeding in the brain. The image for me was vivid, his brain leaking, his skull swelling from the fluid's pressure inside and all one could do was wait.

One day while I sat and read by his bed, he said my name clearly and asked if I could help him get dressed. He had a white shirt and tie in the closet. He spoke with difficulty from the stroke, although his condition had improved and we all believed he would be released soon. I dressed him and because he was cold I put my sweater over his shoulders and tied the arms in front so he looked like a college man again. While he sat up in bed I held onto his hand to steady him, reminded of how we used to waltz together when I was ten. I said something to him that I had carried around with me for a long while, something that had no basis in fact, only in the private burden of a son traversing the globe for a father's loss. "I'm sorry if I've disappointed you," I told him and he answered me in speech slowed by his stroke, "I forget everything, Ephram." I nodded, but then cried later at his funeral because I thought and hoped he had meant to say forgive.

Acknowledgments

I'm grateful to the presses that first published many of these stories: Autumn House Press; University of Illinois Press; University of Missouri Press. And to the publications in which the stories originally appeared: *Ploughshares, Kenyon Review, North American Review, Epoch, Crazyhorse, Tikkun, Florida Review, Mid-American Review, Puerto del Sol,* and the *Chicago Tribune.*

I'd also like to thank the following individuals for their help with this collection and their valuable support: Victoria Barrett, Andrew Scott, Stephanie G'Schwind, John Calderazzo, Deanna and Gary Ludwin, Jenny Wortman, Toni Nelson, Robert Boswell, Charles Baxter, Rob Cohen, Grant Tracey, and especially Emily Hammond.

About the Author

Steven Schwartz is the author of two novels and three previous collections of short stories. A two-time recipient of the Colorado Book Award for Literary Fiction, he has also received the Nelson Algren Award from the *Chicago Tribune*, the Cohen Award from *Ploughshares*, the Sherwood Anderson Prize, two O. Henry Prize Story Awards, and a National Endowment for the Arts Fellowship. He teaches in the Warren Wilson MFA Program for Writers and is Professor Emeritus of English at Colorado State University.

CPSIA information can be obtained at www.ICGtesting.com
Printed in the USA
LVOW07s0308050816

498893LV00001B/1/P